I'm an award-winning novelist of strong contemporary romance and characters you'll fall in love with. I am also a full member of the Romantic Novelists' Association and a contributor for Loveahappyending Lifestyle.

As well as being a self-confessed Twitter addict, I also like to show off my singing talents on YouTube! I've auditioned for X Factor, appeared on ITV1s Who Dares Sings and I long to duet with Bryan Adams. I love white wine, mashed potato, country music, Corfu and World's Strongest Man.

I live very close to Sting in Wiltshire with my husband, two daughters and two cats called Kravitz and Springsteen!

Follow me on Twitter @mandybaggot.

Made in Nashville

MANDY BAGGOT

A division of HarperCollins*Publishers*
www.harpercollins.co.uk

Harper*Impulse* an imprint of
HarperCollins*Publishers* Ltd
77–85 Fulham Palace Road
Hammersmith, London W6 8JB

www.harpercollins.co.uk

A Paperback Original 2014

First published in Great Britain in ebook format by HarperImpulse 2013

Copyright © Mandy Baggot 2014

Cover Images © Shutterstock.com

Mandy Baggot asserts the moral right to
be identified as the author of this work

A catalogue record for this book
is available from the British Library

ISBN: 9780007591916

This novel is entirely a work of fiction.
The names, characters and incidents portrayed in it are
the work of the author's imagination. Any resemblance to
actual persons, living or dead, events or localities is
entirely coincidental.

Automatically produced by Atomik ePublisher from Easypress

All rights reserved. No part of this publication may be
reproduced, stored in a retrieval system, or transmitted,
in any form or by any means, electronic, mechanical,
photocopying, recording or otherwise, without the prior
permission of the publishers.

This one's for everybody with a little bit of redneck going on inside. Be proud of who you are - live, love and line dance if you want to! Be unashamed of Gingham, bandanas, Stetsons and Cuban heel boots! Thank you once again to all my wonderful readers and supporters - I couldn't do this without you! Much love to the Bagg Ladies and the Loveahappyending Lifestyle crew - you are amazing!

Playlist for Made in Nashville

Songs to complement Honor and Jared's story

'Kick it in the Sticks' – Brantley Gilbert
'Your Side of the Bed' – Little Big Town
'Love Like Mine' – Hayden Panettière
'Stars Tonight' – Lady Antebellum
'Highway Don't Care' – Tim McGraw (featuring Taylor Swift)
'Pickin' Wildflowers' – Keith Anderson
'Homegrown' – Lynyrd Skynyrd
'Goodbye Joe' – Mandy Baggot
'Done' – The Band Perry
'Runnin' Out of Moonlight' – Randy Houser
'Outta My Head' – Craig Campbell
'No Easy Way' – Logan Mize
'Sin Wagon' – The Dixie Chicks
'Bonfire' – Craig Morgan
'Beat This Summer' – Brad Paisley
'Fall Into Me' – Emerson Drive
'It's Five O'Clock Somewhere' – Alan Jackson
'American Beautiful' – The Henningsens
'Leave the Pieces' – The Wreckers
'Who I am' – Jessica Andrews

'Guitar Slinger' – Vince Gill
'Every Storm (runs out of rain)' – Gary Allan
'Crash My Party' – Luke Bryan
'Since You Left' – Millers Daughter
'Trapped by Love' – Mandy Baggot
'Redneck Crazy' – Tyler Farr
'Can't Shake You' – Gloriana
'Carolina' – Parmalee
'Used Up' – Logan Mize
'What Matters Most' – Raintown
'Hard to Love' – Lee Bryce
'Somewhere With You' – Kenny Chesney
'A.M.' – Chris Young
'Gasoline & Matches' – Leann Rimes
'Days of Gold' – Jake Owen
'What Hurts the Most' – Rascal Flatts
'Goodbye in Her Eyes' – Zac Brown Band

Prologue

2004

The lights were so bright, brighter than the strongest spotlight Honor had ever stood under. They were coming from all directions. Right. Left. Overhead. The crowd was roaring, clapping, stamping their feet, dancing. They moved like a sea, swaying, bobbing, rising up and falling back in time to the music. This was what she'd dreamed of since she was a little girl. Her place was here. She was born to perform, granted a gift from God in the form of a voice that seemed to know no boundaries. There wasn't a note she couldn't reach and in six months she had gone from supporting artist to headliner. At just eighteen she had everything she'd ever wanted.

She felt every note, every punch of the drumbeat, every chord of the guitar, every thump of the bass. When she sang she was lost. Caught up in that one moment of time where her vocals could reach people, where her lyrics could teach people, preach, about love and loss, the family she'd never had and everything she'd experienced at such a tender age.

She held that top C with every ounce of hurt, rejection and determination. It came from her gut. It was a statement. She was almost out of breath when she heard the sound of breaking glass. There wasn't time to move. There wasn't even time to scream.

Chapter One

'Taylor Swift?'

'I'm looking for a supporting artist not a girlfriend.'

'You're too old for her.'

'Are you saying my life's over at twenty-seven? Man!'

'Mark Warren?'

'Are you kiddin' me?'

'Jared, if we discounted every artist you'd ever had a bar brawl with we'd be down to two hands.'

'*Two* hands? You do remember there are ten fingers on each hand, right? Anyway he deserved it. He was hustlin' a waitress and you know how I stand with that. You don't put your hands on a woman unless she asks you to.'

'How about Leann Rimes?'

'Now she's cute.'

'Thought you're looking for a supporting artist not a girlfriend,' Buzz mimicked. 'And anyway, she's married.'

'That's too bad.'

Buzz let out a sigh and folded his arms across his chest.

Jared hated it when Buzz did that. The pose reminded him of a school teacher he'd had. All the teachers had thought he'd amount to nothing but Franklin Barratt had worn his opinion of him all over his face. He'd shown him. He'd keyed his brand-new car and framed the school geek.

'Jared, you employ me to do two things. To advise you on what's right and to try and stop you making a first-class ass of yourself,' Buzz said, holding his stance.

'I take offence at that.'

'Which part?'

'All of it. I only employed you because I was jealous of your 'fro, man,' Jared said, laughing.

Buzz put his hands to his hair and Jared laughed louder.

'Well, I tell you what. You don't want to work with any of these great artists, then *you* go out and find someone. The tour organizers want faces and names on posters and they want them yesterday.'

'Hey, man, I wasn't meanin' to be disrespectful...' Jared began.

'I have to be somewhere other than here. I'll call you tomorrow.' Buzz got up from the diner table, collating his papers and iPad.

'Buzz, come on, let's say we have another coffee and look through the list again. I might be able to do somethin' with Vince Gill. I mean everybody loves Vince Gill. Hell, *I* even love Vince Gill,' Jared said. He stood, pulled his baseball cap down a little lower over his head.

'I'll see you tomorrow. Try and stay out of trouble for twenty-four hours will you?' Buzz gave him one of his stern looks before buttoning his suit jacket and making for the door. Jared opened his mouth to speak but his advisor was already through the exit and heading for his car.

'More coffee?' the waitress asked, waving the pot she was holding.

'Hell, why not? Thank you, ma'am,' Jared answered. He smiled at her and sat back down.

'I love your music,' she began in a coy voice.

'Really? Lookin' so fine like that I was thinkin' you might be a Carrie Underwood kind of a girl.' He studied her face and waited for the blush. And there it was. Those pinked-up, heated-up cheeks he seemed to be able to magic up in women just by being polite.

'Well, I...like things a little bit edgy now and then,' she flirted.
'Is that right? What's your name, darlin'?'
'Angie.' She tapped the name badge pinned to her chest.
'Well, Angie, it sure is a pleasure to meet you. I'm Jed Marshall and if you tell me you can sing you're gonna get me out of a whole heap of trouble.'

Looking in the mirror, Honor traced her fingers along the Z-shaped scar that ran from the corner of her right eye to halfway down her cheek. Ten years and twice as many operations. It was no longer red, bumpy and angry but it was there, a silver, rutted streak that made her feel ugly every minute of every day.

Why in hell did she bother with moisturizing cream when only one side of her face saw the benefit? Now, if they sold cream that made zigzag-shaped scars disappear overnight she would sell her house for it. Actually she'd probably sell her house *and* a kidney.

'Are you OK in there, darlin'?'

Larry knew she was hiding. He'd put on his J. R. Ewing voice when he'd arrived. That meant he was going to try and sweet-talk her into doing something she didn't want to do. She wasn't really surprised. It had been the same for the last ten years. Him always trying to drive her back to the place she'd left and her backing up.

'Give me a minute, Larry. Ladies don't just zip up and go,' she called back.

Damn him for turning up. He hadn't even had the courtesy to call her first. He'd just turned up at the door and expected her to be in. She did have a life. She'd become quite the regular at Target. She even had a loyalty card. And there was her job at the music shop. That job had saved her in so many ways.

She smiled into the mirror, widened her cheeks, trying to make them do the same thing. Symmetry was such a pain in the ass. She ran her fingers through her long, dark curls and settled her hair on her shoulders, pulling the right section forward to hide the scar.

'No, Larry. I don't want to.' She sighed. 'We've talked about this before, Larry, and the answer is no.' Was that determined enough?

Taking a deep breath she fixed a smile on her face, put her hand on the door and opened it.

'Shall I make us some tea?' she greeted, striding into the kitchen.

'Sure, darlin'. I have to say you're looking really wonderful today. Better,' Larry announced.

He'd taken his Stetson off and was perched up on one of the stools at the central island. She knew when the hat came off he was disarming himself. It was like putting a pistol back in the holster. It was supposed to subliminally say 'there's nothing to be afraid of.' Except she knew him. Knew how he worked. If the hat was off he meant business.

'Whatever it is, I'm not doing it,' she stated, turning to face him.

Where had that authority come from? Usually she had a hard time doing anything but mumbling when Larry put another job proposition to her. It was often an hour of politely trying to say no in ten different kinds of way.

'Now, Honor, you don't even know what I'm going to say,' he responded. He reached for his hat and put it back on his head. Hat back on. Gloves were off.

'I do know what you're going to say. You're going to say the same thing you've been saying to me for ten years, only you're going to try and word it differently. *Honor, this isn't about you, this is about your fans. Honor, you can't let what that man did ruin your life.* I've heard it all before and more. I've had ten years of hearing it and the answer's still no. I'm not getting up on stage again…ever.'

She'd fired the words out of her mouth with no consideration for breathing. It left her gasping for air and feeling faint. She clung on to the worktop, trying to maintain the impression she was in control. Epic fail.

'The record company wants to bring out a greatest hits album,' Larry stated flatly.

What? What had he said? A greatest hits album?

'Now, it doesn't have to be one of these twenty-track,

super-deluxe albums with a free poster or a link to a secret fan message. We have your two great albums plus the best of the live recordings. But I thought we'd take the opportunity to pitch them something new. Get you back in the studio; get you back in the saddle. The fans will love the new stuff, they'll beg for more and before you know it you're out promoting a brand-new record,' Larry informed her.

A greatest hits album. The words sent shockwaves right through her. She was twenty-eight. She stopped performing ten years ago and had done nothing since. Her life in country music spanned two short years and Micro wanted to release a greatest hits album. It was official. She was done.

'I don't think so,' she answered, no conviction in her tone.

'Honor, I'm going to give it to you straight. Micro are even *talking* about releasing something of yours is little short of a miracle. A greatest hits album is one hell of a compliment when you've not sung for ten years.'

The serious voice. The voice that contained his true feelings. The tone that said *Honor, we all feel sorry for what you've been through but it's gone on too long.* Understanding had started to wear thin a good while ago.

'I don't have to live in this big house. Only this morning I was thinking about selling it. Downsizing,' she replied, nodding.

'Honor, no one is asking you to go on stage right now. I'm just asking you to get back in the studio. Make your beautiful music again, just a couple of tracks. You don't even have to write them. I could see what's out there,' Larry said, his brown eyes pleading with her.

'I don't need the money.'

'You think that's what this is about?'

'I don't know what this is about. If Micro wants to release a greatest hits album I say we let them. They don't need new material and I have nothing to offer them,' she said.

The sentence pulled at her heart. She did have new songs. There were scores of them. She wrote alone, sang to the walls and locked the paper up in a drawer. How had this happened? Country music had been her life. At one time it had been the only thing she had. Because of one brutal act on one night, her life course had been altered entirely. There was no going back and there was no going forward either. Here she was. This was it. A retired country music star who would never make it into another karaoke bar let alone the Hall of Fame.

'Honey, will you think about it? Just a couple of tracks?' Larry asked.

'Are you still on that weird sugar-free diet? Because I don't think I have any sweeteners,' she answered.

Chapter Two

'...and that was Vince Gill with *Guitar Slinger*. So, right now on Countrified 103 I'm truly excited to welcome into the studio, CMA award-nominated country rock sensation...Mr Jed Marshall.'

'Hey,' he spoke into the microphone. His host, Davey Duncan had stuffed a foot-long Sub into his mouth seconds before they went on air and there was chili sauce still drizzling down his chin. Jared hated interviews and was easily distracted. Cue a wave from Buzz, who was sat the other side of the glass.

'CMA award nominee last year. How did that feel? Was it a realization of a dream?'

'It felt awesome, man. I mean I just feel so blessed to have people supportin' me and my style of music. And I know it ain't for everybody, but I just feel lucky that right now it seems to be for the majority. There's strength in them numbers.'

'There sure is. Now we hear here at Countrified 103 that you're soon going to head out on the road. It's your first headlining tour. Tell us all about it, Jed.'

'Yes, sir. Well, we're at the plannin' stages right now but I can tell you that I'm gonna be all over the country. We're aimin' to visit over forty states so watch out for some rebel country comin' to you real soon.'

'I know our listeners love that rebel country. So, tell me, how much of that is the real Jed Marshall?'

Jared adjusted his baseball cap and saw Buzz rise out of his chair. He felt it stir inside him before Davey had finished the end of the sentence. His belly had become a pit of molten lava, heating up from zero to boiling point in seconds. The hairs on the back of his neck prickled.

'I'm not sure I understand the question.' He said the words through gritted teeth. He understood alright. He just wanted clarification. He needed to know Davey Duncan was committed to the route he'd gone down. This was his last chance to back out. His only chance.

'Well, you're giving country music fans something different, something harder and rockier – an edgy sound. Some people have questioned the authenticity of that so, tell us, how much of that is the real you?' Davey asked him.

He made fists with his hands, the silver rings tightening below his knuckles. Bad move.

'Now, I love your show and all, Davey, but I take exception to you insinuatin' that my performance might be fabricated in some way.' His tone was brutal but that was him. He said what he thought. He made no allowances. He didn't pretend to be anything else. For a presenter to suggest as much on live radio was a punch below the belt he wasn't willing to take.

'I...' Davey started to back-track.

'I write all my own songs. I write about what I know and who I am. The only thing fabricated in this studio is you. Ladies and gentlemen, if you've checked out his photo on the station website just imagine him fifty pounds heavier and twenty years older and you'll be gettin' closer to it.'

He stood up, grabbed a nearby staple gun and fired it down onto the desk, missing Davey's hand by millimeters. The presenter let out a yelp.

'We're done with this interview. Thank you so much for the opportunity,' Jared snarled.

He snatched open the door and almost bowled into Buzz.

'You can't leave,' Buzz said, blocking his path.

'Get out of my way, Buzz.'

He was hot and heaving with rage. He couldn't stand still. He made to move past his advisor.

'You need to go back,' Buzz repeated, risking a hand on his arm.

'I'm not doing anything with that jerk-off. You put me in that room with him again and I'm gonna use his body parts to redecorate!'

'Calm down. Take a few deep breaths.'

'Get fucked.' He leveled a boot at the wall and the plaster cracked.

'Jared! You can't do that! We're meant to be building your reputation here. You know what a lot of the industry professionals think of you. A maverick. Someone who doesn't play by the rules. Someone who doesn't fit in with the all-American country scene.'

'I don't fit in. I never asked to fit in. I just make music, Buzz, you know that. My music, my way,' he appealed.

'I know. But there are times that require a little diplomacy. This was one of them.'

Jared kicked the wall again and put his hands to his baseball cap. He rested his eyes on Buzz and swallowed.

'I appreciate what you're sayin'. I'm not gonna take any of it on board but I appreciate it. Thank you kindly.'

Honor wasn't due to work at the music store but she just needed to get out of the house. Ever since Larry's visit earlier in the week she'd been unsettled. What was she going to do? She'd been so sure when she'd told him *no*, that she meant it, but now she didn't know. Perhaps this *was* a golden chance to get back something of what she'd had. She could record a couple of her new songs, slip them onto the greatest hits disc like Larry suggested and see what happened. If it earned the record company money maybe she would get a new contract. Making music again. The idea gave her goose bumps.

'Don't tell me, Target is all out of cut-price DVDs,' Mia greeted, bashing the cymbal of the drum kit she was sat behind.

'You got me.' She smiled.

Tawny-haired Mia had been a good friend for the past five years. Honor hadn't known her when she was at the peak of her career and in some ways that really mattered. Mia knew Honor the way she was now. She didn't know her any different. She kept her opinion on Honor's music career to herself and was only ever supportive. She listened. She understood. She did everything a true friend should.

'Come on, doll. What are you doing here? Aren't there some great bands playing downtown today?' Mia asked, getting up and putting the drumsticks down.

'I have no idea. That's your thing not mine. In fact, why don't you go? I can take care of the store and you can go get drunk and rowdy with the roadies,' Honor suggested. She took an acoustic guitar off the rack and put the strap over her head.

'Doll, I can't afford you more than two days.'

'Who said I wanted paying?'

'Hold up there. Who's gonna keep you in Target goods if you're giving yourself for free? What's going on? Spill it.' Mia backed herself up to the counter and leapt up onto it, crossing her legs and focusing on her friend.

'Micro Records want to release a greatest hits album,' she blurted.

'That's nice. Anyone in particular? My grandma loves Vince Gill.'

'*My* greatest hits album.' She finished the sentence with a sigh and dropped her eyes to the floor.

'Is this a good thing or a bad thing? Because I don't want to get my reaction wrong. I can feel it might be critical,' Mia responded, chewing her middle finger.

'I don't know. When Larry walked through my door and said it, the vibration of the "no" I gave him ricocheted off the kitchen walls. I don't have a say about it coming out but I do have a choice about putting some new tracks onto it,' Honor explained.

'Uh huh,' Mia said, nodding her head up and down.

'So what do I do?'

'What do you *want* to do? In your heart.'

In her heart. Deep down in her heart there would always be a musician. But because of what had happened to her, that musician was composing secret melodies. But was that how she wanted it to stay?

'You don't have to answer that. I can see it written all over your face. What are you waiting for? Make the call. Get back in the recording studio!' Mia exclaimed, sliding down off the counter.

'It isn't that easy.' No matter what her heart told her, her head and the memories were fighting hard to tell her something else.

'It's as easy as you make it. What are you scared of? It isn't like someone's going to break into a recording studio and jump you, is it?'

The bluntness of the statement hit her hard. Honor was familiar with Mia's straight-talking and shock tactics but that didn't mean it didn't hurt. It was still a fragile area she barely spoke about. Everyone knew what happened and sometimes that made it harder. It was like a barrier between her and the world. People didn't want to speak about it but it was the first thing on their mind whenever they looked at her. The scar on her face did all the talking.

'That was a really stupid thing to say. I didn't mean it like it sounded. I just know when I heard your first album all those years ago...well you have such a talent, doll. But it has to be what you want. The way that Larry talks sometimes, he could almost get *me* to do anything,' Mia said. She put an arm around Honor's shoulders.

'He does have a way about him. And this time I know he's right. It *has* been too long and...if I don't do something now I may never do something again,' Honor said. She played a chord on the guitar.

'Listen, you want me to come to the studio with you, I'm there.

I'll get Rocky to cover the store and we'll do it together. But only if I get to play something on the album. I don't care if it's only the tambourine,' Mia said, squeezing her into a hug.

'That sounds good,' Honor agreed.

'Then you've got a deal. So, were you serious about covering here? There's this great new bluegrass band I'd love to check out. The lead singer has a tattoo of Johnny Cash on his shoulder and the cutest butt,' Mia said, grinning.

Honor laughed and played another chord on the guitar. 'What are you waiting for? Go!'

Chapter Three

'Hit me with another one.' Jared slammed the beer bottle onto the bar and wiped his mouth with the sleeve of his black t-shirt. He'd left Buzz an hour ago in the radio station parking lot. He couldn't listen to any more of it. What had he expected him to do? Let Davey fucking Duncan diss who he was live on air? No way. He couldn't sit there and listen to it and let it run off of him. If someone was saying something wrong you put them right. That's just how it was.

'Hey, Jed. I just heard you on the radio.'

Jared turned on the bar stool to greet Byron Starks, a guitarist he knew well.

'Man, where've you been hidin'? I've not seen you in weeks,' Jared said, slapping his arms around him in a tough hug.

'I've been on the road with Lindy Mason.' The tall, dark-haired man took off his Stetson and put it down on the bar.

'Lindy Mason...now that's what I call a gig. Is she at a loose end? Because I need a supportin' artist for my tour,' Jared responded.

'She doesn't support for anyone...unless you're country royalty like Vince Gill,' Byron answered.

'The whole of Nashville's in love with him,' Jared said with a laugh. 'Say, you want a beer?'

'That depends. Are you going to let me drink it this time or throw it over me?'

'I did that?'

'Yes you did. Right before you leapt up on that stage over there and hi-jacked someone else's gig,' Byron informed him.

'Hell. Get this man a beer,' he called to the bartender.

'So, what happened with Davey Duncan?' Byron asked, getting up on the adjacent stool.

'The dude is a tool, man. You heard what he said?'

'Yeah but that's what he's like. He asks the controversial questions. You gave him exactly what he wanted.'

'Is that right? Because when I hammered the staple gun into his desk that wasn't the feelin' I got.'

'The phone lines were jammed up after you left the studio,' Byron continued.

'Hell, Buzz is gonna drop me on my ass the first chance he gets.'

'Your fans were outraged. They had to filter out all the F-bombs directed at Duncan. There was nothing but support for you,' Byron ended.

'There was?'

'Absolutely.

'Man, that's made me feel better. Hey...' Jared turned his head away, listening to the music playing over the speakers. 'What's that?'

'What's what?'

'That music? That voice? Sshh. Hey, man, could you please turn this track up?' Jared called to the bartender.

'Another beer. The music louder. Want some nuts?' the barman grumbled, twisting the dial on the sound system.

'Oh my God, man. I've never heard anybody sing that way before.'

The woman's voice was soulful and sensual and as she made her way up a run to a high C, Jared felt a shiver run over his entire body. He clutched at his beer bottle and closed his eyes.

'Have you not heard this before?' Byron asked, taking his drink from the bartender.

'Sshh, man.'

Neither of them spoke again until the song came to an end.

'Man, who was that?'

'You don't know?'

'No, I don't know. If I knew I wouldn't be askin',' Jared snapped.

'Her name was Honor Blackwood.'

'*Was*? Man, are you telling me she's dead?' His heart leapt at that thought.

'No, not dead, just not singing any more. She got attacked on stage, something like eight or nine years ago. She's never performed since,' Byron explained.

'Hell, are you kiddin'? You're tellin' me some asshole got onto the stage and attacked her? While she was singin'? Singin' like *that*? Like an angel?' Jared exclaimed. His hands were already clenching into fists. He balled them together.

'Yeah, it was terrible. They caught the guy, some crazy stalker and he got serious jail time. But she never recovered from it.'

'Is she still around? Here?' Jared asked him.

'I don't know. As I said, she doesn't sing anymore. Not anywhere. Not even somewhere like here,' Byron said, indicating the small stage in the bar.

'Well, Byron, I think I'm gonna have to change that.' He took a slug of his beer, then wiped his mouth. 'Because I think I want Miss Honor Blackwood to support me on my tour.'

She picked up the same guitar every time Mia left her in charge of the store. It was a Takamine limited-edition, glossy, dark-blue electric acoustic. It had ornate Japanese fish entwined with gold detailing printed on the neck and body and it cost over a thousand dollars. Every time she played it she thought about buying it before someone else did. But what would she do with it? She had her battered-up first acoustic at home she knew she'd never part with. It had always been the guitar she wrote with and the rest of her collection she had auctioned off for charity. She'd had no use for them and they'd taunted her just by being in the same space.

She looked around the store, eyes alert, checking. Only when she was sure there was no one around did she start to play. It was a song she'd been working on the previous day at home. The lyrics were about a broken woman finding the strength to end a bad relationship. She'd had all the experience she needed to write it.

He came home on Friday, a little worse for wear
Wrapped his arms around me, like he didn't have a care
Sometimes sweet and loving, other times keen to bruise
It was time for us to say goodbye, nothing left to lose

Goodbye Joe, it's been so nice to know you
Goodbye Joe, give me back my heart
Goodbye Joe, you let me down now I'm picking me back up
Goodbye Joe, this girl has had enough

You cried out when I told you, begging me to stay
Held me back from leaving, blocked out the way
Told me I'd be nothing, a loser without you
I'd rather be a loser than have you tell me what to do

Goodbye Joe, it's been so nice to know you
Goodbye Joe, give me back my heart
Goodbye Joe, you let me down now I'm picking me back up
Goodbye Joe, this girl has had enough

Where next? She was really struggling with the bridge on this song. Nothing sounded quite right. She grabbed a notepad and pen from behind the counter and took it from the top.

Google had provided Jared with the answer he was looking for. After one more beer and a bucket of fries, he'd got on his Harley and rode across town to Instrumadness Music. He parked the bike

and took off his helmet. He put on his baseball cap and walked toward the door. When he reached it he stopped. Through the glass he could see her. She had her back to him, but he knew it was her from the head of raven curls. She had a guitar slung around her neck and she was playing. Then, within seconds, the strongest, most sugar-coated voice was floating into the air.
He nodded in time to the song. It was good. Soft. Not his style. But strong and emotional. She strummed an angry chord and stamped her feet. He smiled at her display of frustration and put his hand on the door.

Chapter Four

The bell rang and she whipped around to face him, cheeks flaming, hands shooting down by her sides.

'Good afternoon, ma'am. I didn't mean to interrupt,' he started, stepping into the store.

'You didn't... you didn't interrupt. What can I do for you?' she asked, taking the guitar off her.

She didn't recognize him. Or if she did there was no showing it on her face. What he did see, though, was her scar. A Z-shaped mark about four inches long on her right cheek. He chewed the inside of his mouth. How had someone done that to her? A man had thought he had the right to hurt her. Behavior like that made him sick.

'I'm looking for a new guitar, ma'am. I play a little and, well, I just want something new. Any suggestions?' he began.

Where had that come from? He didn't need a new guitar. He had twenty of his own and hundreds at his disposal. Why didn't he just ask her what he wanted to ask her?

'What do you play?' He watched her look him up and down. 'What style?' she asked.

'Kind of a rocked-up country, ma'am. A little dirty Southern style, I guess you'd call it,' he said, grinning.

'Dirty Southern, huh?' She looked at him, her blue eyes seeming to evaluate.

'Yes, ma'am,' he answered.

Her eyes left him and went to the racks of guitars on the wall of the store. She strode confidently toward a walnut-colored instrument. She took it down and held it out to him.

'A Gretsch?' he queried, a laugh escaping.

'If you can't play dirty Southern music with a Gretsch, then you're no player at all. Haven't you heard Vince Gill?' she asked. Her dead-pan expression was challenging him to disagree. He took hold of the instrument and put the strap around him.

'The amp is on just there.' She indicated a Marshall stack to his left.

'This one?' he said, pointing.

'Well, you can plug it into any amp you want, sir. But if you break it you're gonna have to pay for it,' she warned.

She'd smelt the alcohol on him when he'd taken the guitar from her hands. Biker boots on his feet, torn-up jeans with chains hanging from his belt and a black long-sleeved top under a leather jacket. He was at least a week unshaven and wore a baseball cap low down over his face. He didn't look like he could afford a place to sleep let alone an expensive guitar.

She watched him take a pick out of his pocket and then without any hesitation he began to play. Straight away, the other guitars hanging on their hooks began to vibrate as Jared let fly. She knew her mouth was hanging open but she couldn't help it. She'd never heard anyone play like that before. Not on stage and certainly never in the store. He had something special, something unique. It was grungy. It was bluesy. It was some sort of amalgamation of country and metal.

He took the volume down and smiled at her.

'I couldn't help hearin' you singin' there earlier. And it seemed to me that you were kinda fightin' with the bridge,' he started.

The mouth came up and her shutters went down. A cold, icy

feeling spread from her boots, up through her body and ended in her shoulders. She flinched. He'd heard her sing. No one heard her sing now unless Countrified 103 played a track on their old-school morning country show. Not that she ever heard it. She hadn't turned on the radio in ten years. The only country music she listened to was piped through the store sound system and now it was as good as white noise.

'Don't get me wrong or nothin'. It sounded like a great song. It's just you stopped right before the bridge and...you stamped your feet a little.'

'It was nothing.' She stuttered her words, giving away her apprehension.

'Well, if it were *my* song I'd probably go for a long ripped-up guitar solo. But, bein' as it's not my song and you sound a little more traditional.' He took off the electric guitar. 'How about this?'

He grabbed an acoustic from the rack, put the strap over his body and started to play. Within a few seconds he paused, played again and this time added a line of lyrics.

And we couldn't break through, no we couldn't break through together

His voice had a gruff rock edge to it but the tone was tender. Something in her stirred. He'd just broken into song, in front of her, as if it was the most natural thing in the world. No hesitation, no awkwardness, just a line of music that fitted perfectly. She just looked at him, standing there in his shabby clothes, and waited.

I wasn't enough, you were just too much for ever. So I'm leaving right now and I'm never coming back not ever

He was writing her song right in front of her eyes.

You need to let me go. It's time to close the door

He strummed out the final chord and grinned.

'I guess you had other plans for it. But, you know, if you like it you can use it. I won't ask for any credit on the album.'

She stared at him, not knowing how to react. Who was he? How had he just written such a fantastic middle eight in two minutes? There was only one thing she could say.

'Do you want the Gretsch?'

'I think I'll pass. Actually, Miss Blackwood...may I call you Honor?' He didn't wait for a reply. 'I wanted to ask for your help.'

This was Larry. Whoever this guy was it was something to do with Larry. She just knew it. He'd be a reporter – wait, perhaps not, given the clothes. Maybe he was someone from a TV music show or someone new from the record company. He'd been sent here to persuade her to cut new material. That's why he'd been so keen to help her finish her song. Well, she hadn't decided yet and the more pushing that went on the more she'd back away.

'I'm sorry. I can't,' she said, taking a step away from him.

'You don't know what I'm gonna ask you yet,' he responded.

'I know who sent you. And I haven't made a decision yet. You can tell Larry that when I make up my mind I'll tell him directly. He doesn't need to send some...someone like you,' Honor snapped, her eyes flashing with defiance.

'No one sent me here. Well, that isn't quite the truth...*you* sent me here. You and that voice you have.' He lifted his head, set his eyes on her and she swallowed. Underneath the brim of the baseball cap was a pair of gray eyes. But instead of being cold or harsh there was a density and intensity about them. A sexy heat.

'My name's Jared Marshall... Jed Marshall and I'm lookin' for a supportin' artist for my upcomin' tour. I was kinda hopin' it would be you,' he continued.

Jed Marshall. She'd heard that name. She'd heard that name a lot. She'd sold a large quantity of CDs with his name on the front. The cover had a Confederate flag on it. This was him. He was a successful recording artist. Not a down-and-out who was going to rob the store. And then what he'd asked her hit her like a train.

'I think you've got me confused with someone else.' She hurried the words out and turned away from him, picking up some leaflets about an upcoming rock festival from the counter.

'You were a platinum-sellin' artist not so long ago. I know what happened but…' Jared started.

'Everyone knows what happened. It's written all over the right side of my face!'

She'd lost control. Rage was bubbling under her skin, waiting to pop out. Instinctively she pulled at her hair, tried to hide the mark behind a section of dark curls. She wanted him to leave. Just go away and leave her on her own. She didn't want what seemed to be daily reminders lately of the person she used to be.

He took the guitar from across his body and leant it up against a snare drum. Her breathing still rapid, she watched as he un-tucked his t-shirt from his jeans and began to pull it upwards. A ripped six-pack was revealed, along with the edge of two large tattoos at each side of his torso, but his fingers went to the middle of his abdomen.

'It's faded a little now, but it runs from my breastbone down to my navel. I came off my bike and I swear they used half a cow to put me back together.' She tried to hold it in but it was no good, a smile was at her lips.

'But me and the cow parts, we get on with things. Because now is all we have. Can't go back and change the then,' Jared said, covering himself back up.

She didn't know what to say. Her cheeks had pinked and the room was suddenly like a sauna. She didn't feel comfortable.

'I'm…I'm really flattered by the offer Mr Marshall but I haven't been on a stage in ten years and that's the way it's going to stay,' she responded.

He sucked in a breath then nodded his head. 'I'm sorry to hear that, Honor, truly I am. Because, just so you know, I don't give up easy.'

She furrowed her brow as she looked at him. He slipped his jacket back on, adjusting the sleeves until it was in place.

'What does that mean? There must be hundreds of country artists out there who would fall over themselves to support someone as high-profile as you on a tour. Use one of them.'

'I don't want one of them. I want the girl with the voice of an angel.'

His eyes were on her again and she felt the need to take a stance. She put her hands on her hips and tried to appear in control.

'This is my cell number. *My* number, not my advisor. You ring this any time, night or day when you're ready to say yes.' He wrote on one of the concert leaflets on the counter and pushed the paper along to her.

'I'm not going to say yes,' she told him.

'I'm not gonna stop askin' 'til you do.'

'I can't.' Her voice came out thin and wavered with emotion. What must he think of her? He was a country chart-topper offering her the chance of a lifetime and here she was turning him down like he was a telephone salesman offering her free S'mores for life if she took up a broadband contract.

'I want you to know that I would never let anyone hurt you. I would personally make sure my security detail is the best there is. I would personally vet the entire guest list for the backstage areas. I'd do anything you needed me to do to make you feel safe,' he told her.

Those eyes were promising the truth, she was sure of it. But she'd had cast-iron guarantees before and nothing could take away the fear. She shook her head.

'I appreciate the compliments, really I do, but my answer's still no,' she said.

He nodded his head, pushed the paper with his number on a little closer to her.

'I respect your decision but I don't accept it. It was a real pleasure to meet you, Honor. You take care.' He held his hand out to her.

Thick rings adorned fingers on both hands. She took hold of it and gave a business-like shake. The heat that hit her from their connection jolted her like a bolt from the sky. He let her hand go and turned, heading for the door.

'I'll be at Black Monkey Studios, Friday, if you wanna finish that song,' he called.

She watched him push open the door and head across the parking lot to his bike. Creeping closer to the door in stealth mode, as though she shouldn't be looking, she watched him climb aboard the bike. He quickly swapped his hat for his helmet, then brought the machine to life, revving up the engine. He wheel-spun out and roared away up the road.

She clutched at her stomach. She needed to vomit.

Chapter Five

The alarm clock on his nightstand roared like the engine of his Harley. He couldn't open his eyes. They felt raw and gritty like someone had snuck in overnight and poured salt in them. As he moved, a sharp pain hit his neck and he put a hand to it. Falling asleep with a guitar underneath you wasn't to be recommended. The strap had chafed the skin on his collarbone. He was lucky it hadn't strangled him. He untangled himself and lay the acoustic down on the bed. Pulling himself up into a sitting position, he rubbed his hands over his face, then his head. This was what not drinking did for you. He'd felt better after half a dozen beers.

It was almost nine. The alarm must have been going off for an hour. Instinctively, like he'd done every half hour since he'd met Honor Blackwood, he checked his iPhone. Nothing. No messages. No missed calls. Three emails. How would she have emailed? He checked them anyway. There was one about sponsorship Buzz had copied him in on; another from Vistaprint and the third was full of coupon offers. He tossed the phone back down and got off the bed. It was Friday. He was heading to the studios with his band. They were recording new material for the next album. Trouble was, the only song going around in his head was a ballad called *Goodbye Joe*.

'Good morning! Whoa! Hold up! Where did *you* go last night? You look like you did twelve rounds at Tequila Cowboy, doll,' Mia greeted as Honor entered the music store.

Honor managed a smile but her head was spinning. Last night, she'd drunk a bottle of wine alone and summoned up the courage to call Larry to tell him she'd get back into the studio. Then, after he'd whooped with delight, she'd needed a couple of tumblers of bourbon to convince herself she was doing the right thing.

'Please don't put me on Dolly Parton fan duty today. The high notes will make my brain explode.' Honor came behind the counter and put her bag in the bottom drawer of the cabinet.

'Sounds like a great night. Where did you go?' Mia questioned.

'Nowhere. I drank at home, alone.' She paused. 'But I called Larry. I told him I'd get back into the studio.'

Mia let out an excited yelp and clapped her in a hug she could have done without.

'I'm so excited for you! I'm so excited for *me*! I'm going to be selling your new album right here. We must have a signing, get a BBQ in here. Could we tie it in with the Fourth of July do you think?'

'Hold up. I haven't even done anything yet. It's up to the record company when or if it's released. There's no guarantee.' That was the trouble. Nothing was guaranteed in this business. She might have decided to give things one more shot but that didn't mean the industry was going to show any interest. It was more than likely most people would have forgotten who she was. *She'd* almost forgotten who she was.

'Oh sucks, they'll be falling over themselves to sign you up to everything. You wait, before you know it, they'll be making Koozies with your name on them and selling them in Target,' Mia told her.

'Is that meant to sound like a good thing?' Honor said, sighing.

'Sure it's a good thing, doll. And so is *this*. Want to tell me about it?'

Mia fluttered a leaflet about the rock festival in the air. Honor could see clearly, written in Sharpie marker, the phone number Jared Marshall had written down. Her stomach rotated. He hadn't been off her mind all week. She'd used the bridge he'd written to finish off her song. She was thinking of recording *Goodbye Joe* when she visited the studios next week.

'It's a phone number. A customer left it,' Honor said. She twirled a strand of hair around her finger.

'Uh huh. So, what did they want? Did you order something for them to pick up? There's nothing on the system I don't know about,' Mia prodded.

'No.' She was going to have to say something. But what?

Mia shrugged her shoulders, then opened her arms, palms raised to the ceiling, waiting for an explanation. It was useless thinking of something more sensible to say.

'It's Jed Marshall's number. He came in the other day when you went to see the bluegrass band.'

Mia's eyes very nearly came out of her head. 'Say what? Did you say Jed Marshall? *The* Jed Marshall…came here…to my store! Did he freaking touch anything?'

'A couple of guitars,' she replied. *My hand.* The memory of the handshake that had sent a heavy current down her spine caused a moth-like sensation in her belly.

'Jeez, Honor and this is the first I hear of it? What was he doing here? You know he doesn't exactly need to buy guitars. Fender practically throw them at people like him,' Mia exclaimed.

Honor's eyes went to the wall where the walnut Gretsch was hanging. She'd almost wept when a pensioner who was into Waylon Jennings had played it so badly earlier in the week. It was like the passionate rock-fusion sound Jared had made with it was being wiped away with every finger-picking note.

'He asked me to support him on his tour.' She hadn't meant to say the words out loud but out they'd flowed. Mia fell into the chair, scattering copies of the latest edition of *Rolling Stone* all over the floor.

'Holy crap! Are you playing with me?'

'I said no. I actually had no idea who he was until he said his name,' Honor admitted. A woman waved at her from over by the sheet music.

'You had the hottest piece of country ass in the store and you didn't know who he was? He offered you a supporting artist role and you said no! Had you been drinking then too?'

'I need to serve this lady,' Honor said, heading out from behind the counter.

'You need to visit your shrink! And we need to talk!' Mia called after her.

By the time the band arrived Buzz had told him about seven companies that wanted to sponsor him and get him wearing/eating/drinking/playing with their brands. Of course he wanted to be successful but the money and the free stuff didn't mean anything to him. He was in it for the music. Spreading his sound to as many people as he could. The world was actually on the cards and he'd never really believed that was possible.

'Pure Nectar is sending over a crate of their juice today. That should keep you in fruit smoothies for some time,' Buzz spoke, poking at his iPad.

'Because I drink those all the damn time,' he commented.

'Don't knock it, Jared. There are people out there who would appreciate a month's supply of Pure Nectar.'

'Then let's give it to 'em. Hell, Buzz, I don't mind being sponsored by them and I'll drink the occasional carton but man, a month's supply! Get it sent to one of the homeless shelters,' he said, lifting his head. He'd been scribbling down lyrics while Buzz was talking. When inspiration struck you couldn't ignore it. And Miss Honor Blackwood had inspired him. He knew her story, the facts of what had happened to her. But what was behind the headlines? What was she still feeling now – ten years down the line?

'I can't do that. I …'

'Give me that iPad if it ain't glued to you and I'll do it,' Jared said, reaching to take it.

'No...no. I'll get it organized,' Buzz backtracked.

'Good. Are we done? Because the band is waitin',' Jared said. He indicated the musicians behind the glass screen with his thumb.

'We need a supporting artist for the tour. I've been talking to a UK group called Raintown, Claire and Paul. They're contemporary country, kind of like Lady Antebellum minus one and no beards,' Buzz started.

'Whoa. You told me to find someone and I've found someone,' Jared said, throwing his pen down on the table.

'Who?'

'She's got the voice of an angel,' Jared said. Involuntarily his eyes closed and the memory of the sound of Honor's voice flowed over him.

'Well, don't keep me in suspense. Who is it?'

'Honor Blackwood.'

The dark-skinned man paled and reached for his plastic cup of water, sucking it in and closing his eyes. Jared observed him with interest, gauging his reaction.

'You almost gave me a heart attack. I'm on pills for that, you know. Now, do you have someone or am I going to do a deal with Raintown?' Buzz asked.

'I want Honor Blackwood,' Jared responded. His eyes were trained on Buzz. He now knew this was going to meet with real opposition. Despite her lack of confidence, there was no disputing her talent. She had something pure, untainted by industry pressures. She just needed encouragement, a reassurance that no one would hurt her again. He had made her that promise and if he made a promise he kept it, no matter the cost.

'Do I know her? Well, let's see. She was an almost overnight sensation twelve years ago. She produced two platinum-selling albums and then some crazy guy attacked her on stage. She had eighty stitches in a facial wound and she's never released another record,' Buzz concluded.

'But she still writes. I've heard her. And it's great, Buzz. She's still great,' Jared informed him.

'She's yesterday's news. You go out there on the street and you'd have trouble finding someone who remembers who she is,' Buzz carried on.

'I can change that,' he responded. The depth of his passionate response shocked even him.

'You're not her counselor, Jared. And you don't have time for a humanitarian project right now. We're trying to organize a tour,' Buzz snapped.

'She just needs a chance.'

'Grapevine says she's still in therapy.'

'I want her on the tour.' He'd made it a statement rather than a request.

'You've asked her, haven't you?'

'Yeah I asked her and she said no. But I can change her mind. We've written a song together. Granted she wrote most of it, but I said I'd be here today and she'll be here and you can hear it,' Jared explained.

'You gave her a golden opportunity and she said no. That answers all my questions,' Buzz said. He folded his arms across his chest.

'Do people round here like writin' people off? What happened to second chances? A little help? She's got a voice…' Jared started.

'Like an angel. I know, you said and I've heard it. OK, you convince me she's going to get up on stage, every night, at every stadium and open your show I'll hold my hands up and say I was wrong. But, I'll tell you, I'm confident I'll be begging Vince Gill by the end of next week,' Buzz stated.

'I've got a week?' Jared asked him.

'Seven short days and then I'm making the call,' Buzz said in his serious voice.

Chapter Six

'Hey, doll I'm gonna make a move. You OK to lock up?'

She'd sold twenty-five copies of Jed Marshall's latest album that day. Apparently he'd bitten the head off of Davey Duncan, the notorious jock from Countrified 103 and the town had loved it. One old lady said she really wished Jared had whupped Duncan's ass.

'Honor?' Mia called.

'Sorry? What did you say?' She raised her head, putting the CD down on the counter.

'Listen, I know how you feel about the scene and everything but there's this great band playing tonight and Carly's bailed on me. Want to eat burgers and fries and drink beer with me?' Mia offered.

'A country bar?' Honor said, raising her eyebrow.

'Are there any others in this town? Come on, you know I get twitchy at the hip-hop bar.' Mia pulled a face, pouting out her lips and leaning her head to one side like she'd be emotionally harmed if the answer wasn't yes.

'I don't know.' She didn't do country bars anymore. It was too painful to listen to all the talent, knowing what she'd had in the palm of her hand. Knowing what had been taken from her. Recording again was the start but she wasn't even sure she was going to be able to go through with it. Larry had been euphoric when she'd called. If she let him down…

'I swear, if they start trying a Vince Gill cover, we're out of there,' Mia continued.

She opened her mouth to respond when Mia spoke again, her eyes on the parking lot.

'Holy crap! Your boy's here again.'

Honor followed Mia's line of vision out of the store. Jared Marshall was heading towards the door, baseball cap on his head, bike helmet swinging from one hand.

'He looks pissed…but then he looked like that on the cover of the last issue of *Maverick*. I think that's his thing.'

He'd been at Black Monkey today. She knew that. He'd told her. And she'd deliberately ignored the invitation. She might have summoned up the strength to agree to try a studio session but she couldn't commit to anything else. It was ridiculous! A collaboration with country hot property! Especially country hot property with gray eyes the depth of marble.

The door opened.

'Afternoon, ma'am,' he greeted Mia, touching the peak of his cap in acknowledgment as he entered.

Honor watched Mia liquefy before her eyes.

'I…good afternoon, Mr Jed Marshall. It's an honor to have you here. Can I get you anything? Anything at all. I've got great coffee or something strong? Bourbon?'

Honor cringed as Mia actually giggled. Mia wasn't a giggler, she was a loud, raucous snorter. But she was an outrageous flirt and she was turning the store into Flirt Room 101 right now.

'That's very kind of you an' all but I'm actually just here to see Miss Blackwood. If that's OK with you. I promise I won't keep her too long,' Jared said, his gaze settling on Honor.

She was glued to the spot by those eyes. She knew what he was going to say. He was going to ball her out for not going to the studios. Well, she was ready for him. She was going to give it a try and if she couldn't do it then she couldn't do it. No matter what, she didn't need his help. Anything she decided was going to be on her own terms. She might be terrified of some things but she hadn't lost her own mind.

'Sure thing. I'll just shuffle some stuff around over here. Not your stuff obviously. After today I've got to do another order for "Crazy Outlaw" copies,' Mia rambled.

'That's good to hear,' Jared said. He smiled at her as she backed towards the percussion section.

'Have you changed your mind about the Gretsch?' Honor started. If she led this conversation she had a chance of keeping control of it.

'Have you changed your mind about comin' on tour with me?'

Shit, he didn't pull any punches.

She'd tried to give him the serious look. But he could see her nerves sticking out a mile. That dark hair, tumbling down her back and those blue eyes, wide and so innocent looking. Nervous, but there was a fire in her. He could see that too. She might be scared as hell but she wasn't weak.

'No,' she answered.

'That's a real shame. Because I haven't changed my mind about makin' you change your mind.'

There. That should do it. He needed to make her one hundred percent certain he wasn't giving up.

She jutted her chin out a little, straightened up and met his eyes. God, she was too cute. He felt a pull inside himself and it made him reposition.

'If you must know, I'm going back to the studios next week. My record company wants to release a greatest hits and my manager, well he thinks it's a chance to tag on some new material.'

She didn't know why she'd told him that. It wasn't any of his business and she shouldn't really be talking about things that weren't signed and sealed.

'That's great news. You get out your record and you can come promote it on my tour.' He smiled, unblinking.

'What's this I hear? A tour?' Mia piped up, turning to face them.

'The answer's still no,' Honor told him.

'Hold up. Let's not be too hasty here. I mean, could I butt in and…' Mia started.

'No.' Honor slammed the response. Her voice vibrated through the snare drum and Mia put a hand on it.

'That's cool. I'm tryin' to force my band on you and you've probably got your own arrangements and all…' he started.

Now she felt plain rotten. He was at the top of his profession and for whatever reason he was offering her a chance of a lifetime. She couldn't take it. She could barely look at herself in a mirror, let alone subject thousands of people to the image. But she could at least sound grateful instead of deranged.

'It isn't that. I can't…' she began. She may as well tell him the truth. He'd probably heard it all already anyway. The town grapevine had worked overtime on her back in the day.

'She can't commit to anything right now. It's the record company, you see. Chances are she could be already signed up to support The Band Perry. No communication at all. You get me?' Mia stated at a frantic pace.

What? What had she just said?

Jared nodded at Mia. He got it. Her friend was telling him what Honor wasn't. She did want the chance but she was still too afraid to take it. She needed time. He could back off a little, but come tomorrow he'd only have six days left.

She was looking at Mia with a mix of anger and confusion. He needed to leave it. This woman could be his ally.

'Loud and clear, ma'am. I'm sorry for troublin' you. I should have realized there'd be competition.' He turned towards the door.

'What? No, it isn't like that. I have no idea what she's talking about,' Honor spoke, moving from behind the counter and toward him.

He couldn't go. He couldn't leave thinking she'd had a better offer. If she was in a position to accept, then she would. But she wasn't and she was pretty sure she never would be. She wasn't even convinced she was going to be able to stand in a studio with a band, behind closed doors yet. She had that mountain to climb next week. What Simeon Stewart did hadn't just scarred her face, it had wrecked her life. His name flickering through her mind quelled everything, gave it some perspective.

'I'll see you,' he ended, pushing at the glass door.

What should she do? He was leaving. She didn't want him to leave. Did she?

'I…if it goes OK in the studio I'll…' she began.

He stopped in the doorway, turned to face her.

'You'll think about it?' he finished for her.

Her mouth was dry. What was she thinking? Thinking about thinking about it? It was crazy. She hadn't even held a microphone in her hand since it had happened.

'Say, we're hitting One-Eyed Walt's tonight if you're in town,' Mia broke in.

'Really? Any occasion or just hangin' out?'

'Just hanging. A few beers, a few bands. Real casual,' Mia continued.

'Maybe I'll see you.' He nodded.

Her lips were stuck together now, shaped into an uncomfortable smile she didn't mean.

He pushed open the door and it swung back as he went through it.

'Holy crap, doll! I think he's into you!' Mia exclaimed.

'He is not. Anyway I acted like a freaking idiot. What's the matter with me?' She took a length of hair and tightened it to her cheek.

'Nothing's the matter with you. You just need to get back on the horse. With music *and* men. If he looked at me like that I'd have torn the shirt off his back.'

Honor watched through the glass. Jared got on his bike, fastened the helmet and started up the engine. The action mirrored what she felt. Right now her future had been kicked back into life. And if she was honest with herself, her heart was dying to join in.

Chapter Seven

'I'm still not sure about this.'

Not being sure was about the biggest understatement she'd ever made. She'd caught sight of the Nash Trash bus and practically hyperventilated. She didn't go downtown. She lived in a quiet suburb, she drove to work, she came home. That was it. Whenever Mia forced her out into the world she said no to the country bars, chose a diner on the edge of town, not on the strip, opting for pop over hillbilly. Country music was something she made in secret and something she only listened to in the store, where it didn't assault her every fiber. Until tonight.

'Relax, doll. I don't know what you're so worried about. I mean it isn't like I'm gonna pimp you out to the first karaoke bar I see. But, hold up, you do know how I get after bourbon.' Mia laughed and pushed at the door of One-Eyed Walt's.

The bar was on the corner of the main strip and was almost untouched by time. There was no carpet, the bar stools were in the shape of saddles and rustic-looking Stetsons, stirrups, and sacks hung from the walls. It played a mixture of old-style country and country rock and always had two or three bands playing every night.

Honor took a deep breath as she followed Mia into a booth. As her friend was wearing the shortest skirt Honor had ever seen, she had no concerns about being the center of anyone's attention, but she ducked her head anyway and made sure her hair fell forward over her face. Despite the heavy foundation she'd covered her scar with, she knew the bar lights would be unforgiving.

'See! How easy was that? And they must have known you were coming. Vince Gill,' Mia said, raising her hand to indicate the audio.

She'd never told Mia that Vince Gill records usually made her cry. She offered her friend a smile and turned her attention to the surroundings.

Her last date with Jack Tully had been in One-Eyed Walt's. They'd shared a plate of ribs, drank a pitcher of beer and held hands across the table to someone covering a Reba McEntire number. That was just a week before it had all fallen apart. Before the madman had ended her career. Before Jack had dumped her. Before she'd even met Mia. She looked at her best friend, who was drumming her fingers on the table in time to the music. Mia didn't know the half of what she'd been through.

'So, what we drinking? Beer? Bourbon? Or my favorite…both!'

'Just a beer,' Honor replied.

'And a chicken bucket and fries. I'm so hungry.'

Within minutes a waitress had taken their order and Mia was checking out the male talent hanging round the bar engrossed in a baseball game on the big screen.

'Nice tat on that guy. I love a phoenix. One guy I dated had a phoenix rising from the flames across his entire back,' Mia commented.

Honor's mind went straight to the last tattoos she'd seen. Jed Marshall pulling up his t-shirt in the middle of the music store. The six-pack to die for.

'So, what about him? For you? His cute friend.' Mia was looking at her with such encouragement in her eyes, swirling her thumb around the top of her beer bottle.

'Oh, Mia you promised me you wouldn't do this.' Honor sighed, putting her bottle to her mouth and drinking.

'Do what? The only thing I promised not to do was make you sing…until I'm rendered incapable by alcohol. Then all bets are off.'

'I said no pairing me up with friends of guys you want to hook up with.'

'Was I cleaning the tambourines at the time?'

Honor shook her head.

'Where's the harm, huh? He's cute. He's wearing a Stetson. You like them traditional,' Mia continued.

'Sure. He's probably got his horse tied up outside. No.' Honor ended.

'Holding out for Jed Marshall?'

The heat rose in her cheeks before she could do anything to counteract it. It was a ridiculous comment for Mia to make but there was no denying his presence did something to her. That in itself was something a man hadn't done for a very long time.

'You were the one drooling when he came into the store,' Honor shot back.

'And you were the only one he had eyes for.'

'Shit!' Honor exclaimed, turning her face to the wall.

'What?'

'Those guys are coming over!' Honor brushed her hair down across her cheek. 'This is the last time I ever come to a honky-tonk with you!

Jared adjusted the towel tied around his waist with one hand and rubbed a second one over his cropped hair as he left the bathroom. His phone jumped and flashed on the nightstand. Wiping the water from his face he glanced at the display. Another voicemail from Buzz. That was the second in three hours. The first one he'd deleted. Buzz had promised him six days but he was still going on about signing the band from the UK, Raintown. He'd felt duty-bound to check them out on You Tube and they were good. In fact they were very good. But that didn't change the fact he wanted Honor.

He picked up his watch and strapped it to his wrist. Almost ten. Where'd the evening gone? The song he'd been working on just wasn't coming together. He needed to get away from it for a while. He picked up his phone, ignoring the voicemail icon and flicked through his contacts. He pressed on a name and raised the phone to his ear.

'Hey, Byron, it's Jed. Are you doing anything, man? No? D'you wanna go downtown? Say thirty minutes. Yeah, One-Eyed Walt's.'

'I've not seen you here before. Are you new to town?'

Honor hid her eyes behind the menu so she wasn't seen rolling them. Eric and his buddy Wesley had invited themselves over to their booth and seemed to be enjoying every bit of flirtatious banter that fell from Mia's lips. The question came from Eric and was directed at Mia, but Wesley's eyes were firmly locked on Honor. Any second now she expected him to lick his lips like she was a tasty steak on the grill ready to eat.

'No, honey, we're actually part of the Nashville furniture. How about you?' Mia flirted.

'Moved here a little over a month ago,' Eric elaborated. 'Do you mind?'

He indicated the seat next to Mia and she nodded and patted the fabric. Honor looked up at Wesley who had a desperate look in his eyes and was already starting to lower himself to scoot in next to her. She stood, grabbed her bottle up from the table and moved out.

'I'll get us some more drinks. Another round of beers?' Honor offered. Unanimous noises of approval allowed her to leave for the bar.

What was she doing here? Mia never went anywhere without chatting up guys. She should have known hooking up would be on the agenda.

'Can I get another four beers please?' she ordered from the barman.

'Can you turn this one up, Walt?' a guy at the bar shouted.

Honor shook her head as Billy Ray Cyrus vibrated the speakers. This had been such a bad idea. She'd almost rather be listening again to the fifteen-minute-long answer phone message Larry had left her earlier. She wouldn't forget the slot at the studios. Garth from Micro Records would be there. The lead guitarist she'd always worked with couldn't be there but they were going to find his best replacement and everything was going to be just swell.

'Say, don't I recognize you, honey?'

The guy who'd asked for Billy Ray to be turned up flashed her a smile.

'I don't think so,' Honor responded. She smoothed her hair down over her cheek and turned her head a little.

'Sure I do. You've been on the TV. You're a singer,' he continued, leaning in closer and adjusting his hat to get a better look.

'No, sir. I think you must be mistaken.'

All of a sudden she was terrified. She didn't want to be recognized. She never got recognized anymore. It just didn't happen. But it would happen. It would happen more and more if she released a new record. There wouldn't be one guy in a bar. There would be hundreds of guys, thousands of guys. Women, children, t-shirts with her face on them. The memory of that night flashed in vivid color.

'Can I give you a hand?'

Honor jolted back into the room, looking to her left. It was Wesley, still smiling as though she was on the menu. She needed to think of a great excuse to get gone or it was going to be a long night.

Chapter Eight

'You know Dan Steele's playing here tonight, right? Is that why we're here?'

He hadn't known. Not until he'd seen the name on the board outside One Eyed-Walt's. Dan fucking Steele. That guy was a complete asshole. He'd almost cost him his contract with Gear Records, trying to take the deal from under him. But the label had stuck with Jared and he'd put Steele in hospital for taking liberties. Jared had heard he'd moved out of town, tried his luck in Canada, but now he was back and the word was he was proving popular in the bars. It was just a matter of time before a major player got interested. And when that happened, he would probably have to share a stage with him and refrain from throwing the dick off it.

'Fuck.' He took a kick at a lamppost.

'We could go someplace else,' Byron suggested.

'No, man, we're goin' here. I'm not gonna let that tool take over the town.' He pushed the door and stepped in.

The place was buzzing. There was a band up on stage receiving applause from the crowd as they came to the end of their set. Jared scanned the room as Byron headed for the bar. There was Honor, with the chick from the music store and two guys. Something in his gut turned. He didn't like how close the dude was sitting.

'What you drinking?' Byron called.

'Whatever,' he responded. He was mad. He was mad because he was in the same room as Dan Steele. That worm just got under his skin. He was one of those people who skewed every situation for his own gain. He hated people like that. They were users. They screwed things up. They didn't know what hard work was. He ground his teeth together.

'Listen, Jed. I don't really want any trouble tonight. I might have a gig lined up with Vince Gill next summer and…' Byron began as Jared joined him at the bar.

'Who said anything about trouble? What, you think it follows me around or somethin'?' He grinned, picking up the bottle from the bar.

'I was there the night you dropped him in the parking lot,' Byron reminded.

'History,' Jared said.

'You guys! You're hysterical! I can't believe you thought the Cowboys played hockey. You should have had your asses kicked for that!' Mia clapped her hands together and swiped up her glass of bourbon.

Mia was losing it. She was on her third scotch of the night and was almost sitting in Eric's lap. Meanwhile, on Honor's side of the table, Wesley's thigh was pressed against hers so tightly it was making her sweat.

'So, the band was OK,' Honor offered into the conversation. Actually they hadn't been great but she'd paid them quite a lot of attention to avoid the back and forth mating ritual that was going on around her.

'Jeez, doll, they were bad. But I like the next guy. He's the one I told you about. I saw him at another bar last week,' Mia informed the group.

'More drinks?' Eric offered.

'I'll get them.' Honor leapt up.

'Hey, you got the last two rounds. What have we got the guys for?

Guys buy pretty girls drinks. Ain't that right, Eric?' Mia stretched her body, parting her shirt a little, giving Eric a glimpse of a red lace bra.

Wesley was removing a twenty from his wallet and Honor snatched it up, smiling.

'Same again?' she asked, urging Wesley to get up so she could get out. She'd sit on the outside of the booth when she came back and swing her legs sideways. She ignored Wesley's sleazy grin and made for the bar. Maybe she should join Mia in getting drunk, that might just make the evening bearable. She edged past a table then came to a stop.

Her heart dropped from her chest and she screwed the twenty up in her hand. Right in front of her, blocking her path was Jack Tully. Jack 'her ex-boyfriend' Tully. She needed to turn, go the other way. She couldn't see him. What the hell was he doing here? She could feel her cheeks heating up and then it happened. He took a step forward and their eyes locked. *Shit*. Now running away wasn't an option. She pulled her shoulders back and took a step closer. She could deal with this. He couldn't hurt her anymore.

'Honor Blackwood,' he stated, a lazy grin curling his lips. 'Look at you.'

Look at you. What did that mean? Her hand was at her hair before she could even take a breath. Her fingers brushed her scar.

'Look at *you*. Here…in Nashville.' It was all she could think to say.

'Yeah. I couldn't stay away forever. It's where I belong.'

Arrogant. Self-obsessed. What had she ever seen in him?

'So, are you still making music?' she asked.

He let out a laugh then. A full-on, gut-shaking roll of a laugh that had diners turning from their chicken baskets to look at them. Had she made a joke?

'Am I still making music. I'm sorry. I shouldn't laugh.' He smoothed his fingers across the back of his neck. 'I'm headlining here tonight. Dan Steele…that's me.' There was a smug edge to his tone.

This night was just getting better and better. The first time she'd been in a country bar for years and her ex-boyfriend, the guy who'd dumped her a week after the madman had slashed her face, was back in town.

'It's going well. Universal's sniffing around and Rock It were here last week,' Dan continued.

He was living her dream. He'd always been ambitious. Even at the beginning she'd had a feeling he'd been more interested in her fame than her personality. It had turned out her gut had been right.

'That's great.' She didn't mean it.

'And how about you?' Dan asked. The brown eyes settled on hers.

'I'm good. I'm really good. Actually I'm headed back to the studio next week.' She jutted out her chin a little. She was damned if she was going to give him any indication she was scared as hell.

'Still with Micro?'

She nodded. 'They've been really supportive.'

'Good.' He smiled. 'You're looking…better.'

Better! He was the second person to say that recently and Larry had barely got away with it. This man had no right to comment. She felt the hairs on the back of her neck respond. She straightaway recalled the look on his face when he'd met her at the hospital that fateful night.

He reached forward, brushing her carefully placed section of hair with his fingers, revealing the right side of her face. At the contact she snapped her head back.

'Don't touch me!' she hissed.

He'd seen everything from his position at the bar. That fucking asshole had touched her. He was seething with a rage bigger than anything he'd experienced in a long time. He slipped down from the stool and adjusted the sleeves of his jacket.

'Excuse me a minute, Byron. There's somethin' I've gotta take care of.' He started to walk.

'Hey, where you going?' Byron looked across the room. 'Hey man, come on, leave it alone.'

'Come on, Honor I was just…' Dan started.

'You were just what? Checking out whether or not it still makes you sick?' she blasted.

She didn't register Jared's appearance until he grabbed two fistfuls of Dan's shirt and pulled him off his feet.

'What the hell?' Dan exclaimed regaining his footing.

'Honor.' He paused. 'Did you ask him to put his hands on you?'

She saw the heat of fury in his eyes, hatred crumpling his features. She knew his next actions were dependent on whatever she said or did next. What was he doing here? Had he come here because of Mia's invitation?

'Honor.' He stopped again to take a breath and make things clear. 'Did this jerk put his hands on you?' He grabbed a handful of Dan's shirt, rolling it tighter in his hands.

She nodded.

Jared shook his head, tightening his lips. 'Outside,' he snarled.

'Oh what the hell, Jed! Are you crazy? This is bullshit. Honor, tell him,' Dan yelled, trying to move out of Jared's hold.

'You do not put your hands on a woman unless she asks you to. Outside!' Jared ordered.

'Man, I'm on in fifteen minutes. I don't need the heat here. I've got a reputation and…' Dan began.

Honor was losing her resolve. She just wanted Dan gone, but did she want him unconscious in the street? That was what Jared Marshall was proposing. A dust-up, an ass-kicking, dueling on the strip because she'd freaked out.

'*You've* got a reputation? Yeah, man, well so have I. I guess you don't remember,' Jared spat.

'Jed, man, come on,' Byron said, arriving at the scene.

'Stay out of it, Byron,' Jared warned.

Byron looked to Honor. All she had to do was tell Jared to

let Dan go. Why wasn't her mouth moving? Why was she letting this play out?

'Call security,' Dan said, directing the question at Byron.

'You either get your ass outside or I'm gonna drop you right here, right now, in front of the whole fucking bar,' Jared threatened.

'Man, come on,' Dan said. 'Please.'

He looked genuinely terrified. She hadn't ever seen him look that way before. Jared's hand was still at his throat and Dan was sweating.

'Let him go,' Honor stated.

He was so pumped up he wanted to thrash the life out of the asshole right there. Dan fucking Steele. Thinking he could put his hands on a woman like that. Touching *her*. He wanted to rip his throat out and put it on the menu as a special. He had to be taught a lesson.

'He isn't worth the trouble and…it isn't your fight. It's mine,' Honor spoke.

'Hey, I wasn't fighting with you I just…' Dan started.

'Shut the fuck up, man!' Jared yelled.

'Let him go.' She took a breath. 'Just let him go.'

Her tone affected him. She meant what she said. But he wasn't defending her, was he? He was standing up for everything he believed in. He would be reacting the same way if it was any girl. He had strong principles, values deeply ingrained inside him. When he saw someone disrespecting the rules he lived his life by, he saw red.

'Jared, please.'

She'd called him by his full name. The name he'd introduced himself with the first time they'd met. He didn't know why that'd made his back contract with a shot of something, but it had.

He pushed Dan away, sending him sprawling onto the floor. He leant over his flailing body, pointing a finger.

'You ever touch a woman again before she asks and I'm gonna

be there. I'm gonna be there to drag your sorry ass outside and put you back in the emergency room.'

He stepped back, pulled at the sleeves of his jacket and turned to Honor.

'Are you OK?'

She nodded. 'I appreciate you stepping in and everything but I had it covered.'

'I know that. It's just…well me and him, we have history and…' Jared started. She looked so small stood there, in faded blue jeans and a white v-neck tee. Her beautiful, innocent face coupled with that raven hair. It moved him. It moved him in a way he'd never felt before.

'I know it might be an imposition.' She stopped, wet her lips. 'But I spent all my cash on buying drinks to escape Wesley over there and…' She met his eyes. 'Could you please take me home?'

Those eyes were pleading with him. She'd had enough of something and whatever Dan Steele had been hassling her about had hurt her. He should have wiped the floor with him.

'Sure.' He smiled at her. 'I'd be honored.'

Chapter Nine

When she'd told Mia she was leaving it had hardly registered. Her friend had been in a lip-lock with Eric and Wesley had moved on to chatting to a pretty brunette who looked half-wasted.

She didn't know why she'd asked Jared Marshall to take her home. Maybe because he'd defended her honor. Or maybe just because he'd been in front of her when she realized she had to get out of there before she was forced to sit through Dan's set on stage.

She knew just how much she'd drunk when she got on the back of his Harley. He didn't have a spare helmet so he'd given her his. When the bike pulled away she'd clung on to him before the motion sent her sprawling to the sidewalk.

Leather underneath her fingers, the heat from his body radiating through her hands, warming her to the core. She'd leaned into him, enjoying the sensation of the ride as they flew through town and out into the suburbs she called home.

They'd stopped outside her house but she hadn't moved yet. She just sat on the pillion, her hands still on his hips, her eyes closed. She just wanted the world to stop turning, her life to slow down and her memories to stop creeping up on her when she wasn't expecting it.

He'd turned the engine off but she hadn't let go. He didn't

move. He just sat on the bike, watching the trees shift in the breeze, listening to the faint hum of the traffic from the freeway. For whatever reason she needed him to be here for her. His deadline of six days couldn't matter less right now. *She* was all that mattered.

He felt her fingers release and his body tensed, as if something had gone missing. He felt her leave the bike and he turned. He watched her take off the helmet and shake her hair loose. It fell onto her shoulders and he had to swallow. She was beautiful. Not just pretty, but heaven-sent beautiful.

She was looking at him, standing there on the sidewalk, her eyes fixed on his, unmoving, unspeaking. He didn't know what to say. Right now he was concerned if he said anything she would run. He didn't want her to go. As that realization hit he shifted on the bike and she took a step back.

'Do you drink coffee?'

She knew she needed one, but the words that had fallen from her lips had caught her by surprise. What was she doing inviting him inside? Larry was the only guy who'd set foot in the house since Jack…Dan…whatever he was calling himself. She was pulling at a curl of hair and looking back at him, waiting for an answer. He wasn't saying anything.

'Sorry, you've probably got somewhere else to be. Thanks for the ride and…' she started.

'I drink coffee. Sometimes. You know, if I've run out of beer and the twenty-four-hour liquor store isn't open,' he interrupted. 'And especially when I'm ridin'. Wouldn't be smart to get a DUI right before my tour.'

She smiled and clapped her hands against her thighs, backing up towards her gate. She watched him swing himself off the bike and position it against the curb. Her stomach was swirling with beer and fries she hadn't wanted and nervous energy brought on by Dan's reappearance.

Jared let out a low whistle as he joined her and observed the house in front of them.

'Is this really where you live or have we stopped by a concert hall or something?'

'It's ostentatious isn't it?' She sighed.

'Hell, I'm not even sure I know what that really means.'

'It's showy and pretentious. I had so much money back then it seemed the right thing to do. Get rid of it by hiding it in a luxury building.'

'I bought a monster truck for me and a horse for my sister. Does that count?'

She let out a laugh, looking up at him. He laughed too and any unease she'd felt just melted away. Those eyes seemed to have that effect on her. When he looked at her every barrier she put up against life just tumbled down.

'I stink at making coffee but I might have some beer. Just the one, mind. I don't want to be responsible for tainting your reputation.'

'What's with everybody concernin' themselves with my reputation tonight? Don'tcha'll think I can look after myself?' He lowered his gaze, raised his eyebrow up into his cap.

'There's no right answer to that one. I'm not even going to attempt a response. Come on.' She led the way. 'Come meet my pretentious palace.'

She hadn't flicked a light switch on when they'd entered the house. Instead she'd clapped her hands together and commanded the electricity to come on like she was summoning a wish from a genie. She'd ordered music on the sound system and got the air conditioning down to a subtle breath of cool.

He followed her into the kitchen.

'So what d'you do if you want food? You got a pop-out chef or somethin'?'

'That would be cool. Or maybe not. He'd probably make all that stuff with seeds.' She produced two beer bottles from the fridge and popped the tops off them before handing one to him.

'Oh man, I know all about seeds and that green stuff…is it wheatgrass? Buzz keeps orderin' them for me and I keep feedin' them to the plants down at Farley's Diner. I tell you, those window boxes could win prizes.'

She let out a laugh and he felt the wide smile that grew across her face. She was different tonight. She was less tense. Probably because he wasn't forcing her to think about all the things she'd been avoiding thinking about for ten years.

'Come through and sit on my genuine leather cow hide,' she invited. How could he refuse an invitation like that?

There he was. The latest superstar of country music, sat on her sofa, drinking a beer. He had one leg crossed over the other, strips of naked flesh visible under his ripped jeans. He was still wearing his leather jacket and his cap. She'd never seen him without either. She flushed as he turned his eyes away from her décor and directed them at her.

'So, why are we listenin' to some dance/rap combination here?' He raised a hand to indicate the music playing.

'Don't you like it?'

'Do you?'

'Were you expecting Vince Gill?'

'If you clap your hands does he appear?'

She looked away from him then, focused on her sheepskin rug lying in front of the expensive fake flame fire. Just like everyone else, he didn't understand. Why had she expected him to? He knew nothing about her. He was just paying her attention to get her to join his tour. The publicity at having a freak show as a supporting artist would be huge.

'What are you so afraid of, Honor? D'you think if you listen to country music Tammy Wynette's gonna leap out of that iPod and hit you with a six-string?'

'Listen, me inviting you in for a drink doesn't give you a right to ask me questions like that,' she snapped back.

'How can you fight what's in your soul like that? Listenin' to stuff like this - manufactured, weak, poorly-constructed bullshit – when you feel nothin' for it?' he continued.

She shook her head. She shouldn't have invited him in. It was a step too far. Going to the studios again was one thing, inviting a man into her home, one who wanted her performing to thousands of people every night…it was madness.

'I'm sick and tired of people thinking they know what's best for me! You, Larry, Mia and him! Seeing him tonight, seeing the man I used to share a life with, living my dream…' She stopped when she realized she was getting more and more worked up. Damn him! She was letting him get to her. She swallowed, then took a jagged breath. 'When we were together, after my attack… Dan Steele wanted me to spend some time in a mental-health facility out of state.'

She looked across the room and watched the light go out of his eyes.

He bit his teeth together and tried to remain in control. That asshole. She had had a relationship with that fucking piece of scum. He wanted to yell at the top of his voice. He wanted to pick something up and smash it to pieces. Instead he sat there, keeping it all inside, fighting to temper his anger.

'I'm sorry. I've had way too much to drink and you don't want to hear about this.'

He put the beer bottle to his mouth and drank down as much as he could in one gulp. He wished he'd laid Dan Steele out and left him unconscious on the floor.

'Tell me,' he urged.

'We didn't date for long…a couple of months. Then…well I had my accident and…he suggested what he suggested and we broke up.' His interest was piqued. His eyes found hers again.

'He thought after something like that you should recover quick or be locked away?' he asked.

She touched her hair, bringing it over her cheek. 'He didn't deal with it very well.'

'He had the easy role.' He hadn't meant to but the tone he'd attached to his voice was pure aggression.

She shrugged, turning her body to the side in a defensive move. 'After it happened he...he couldn't look at me.'

Before he could check himself he'd shaken his head and slammed the bottle down on the coffee table that separated them. He put a hand to his head, and clenched the other into a fist.

'I should have plastered his face across the walls of that bar.' He shifted on the seat, uneasy and mad as hell.

'I don't blame him for that. I mean, at the beginning I was on the cover of *Country Music* and after, well I'd have been lucky to make it onto *Plastic Surgeon's Monthly*.' She shrugged and let out an unconvincing laugh.

There was an ugly-looking ornament on a low table to his right. He curled his fingers into his palm and thought about throwing it against the wall. Instead he reached into the pocket of his jeans and pulled out his iPhone.

'Kill this crap,' he said, indicating the music.

She clapped her hands twice and the room was thrown into silence.

'After we met last week, I couldn't get that song outta my head. I hope you don't mind.' He touched the screen.

The second the first note played she recognized it as her song, *Goodbye Joe*. But the way he'd changed the phrasing, the way he'd altered the composition was nothing short of masterful. The more she heard, the more she realized what he'd done. He'd made the bones of her song into something that sounded like it could be a hit record.

But she didn't want that. Her songs were *her* songs. They weren't for changing and they weren't for public consumption. She shook her head. No, she couldn't think like that anymore, not if she wanted this second chance at a career. She was just about to go back to the studios and start recording new material. She'd be working with a producer, other musicians with ideas. There was also always the possibility that another artist would want to cover her music. She couldn't get protective and insular like that anymore.

The real truth was it felt uncomfortable sitting opposite someone in the country spotlight who had taken her rough start to a song and made it into something…special.

On the iPhone his voice hit a note on the bridge and goose bumps ran up her arms. The tone and edge to his vocals was so raw, so powerful. It was as if he told a story with every line he sang.

The song came to an end and she sat unmoved, holding onto the last note in her head.

'I have this principle I've stuck with since I started.' He picked up the phone. 'I never record anything but my own material and I don't intend changin' that.'

She watched him. He put the phone back in the pocket of his jeans and picked up his beer bottle.

'Work with me here, Honor. Let's try some stuff together,' he suggested.

She was already shaking her head before he'd finished the sentence. She'd barely got her mind around the fact she was going back to the industry next week. Working with another artist on new material, it wasn't something she'd done before. It wasn't even something she'd considered before.

'What happens then? We write some songs together and you force me on tour with you?' The statement had come out a lot harsher than she'd meant.

'Honor, I'd never force you to do anything.'

She swallowed as she looked at him. That comment had hit him hard. He was breathing heavy and biting his bottom lip.

'Listen, I made that track last week and I wanted you to hear it. That's all. Thank you for the drink.' He stood up, putting his hands in his pockets. She stood up too, feeling she ought to. He'd made it clear he was leaving.

He moved out of the room towards the hall, heading for the front door and Honor followed.

'Do I have to command the door to open or does it work with the handle?' he asked.

She opened it for him, letting in a draught of warm air. This felt awkward.

'I'll see you,' he said, stepping out onto the porch and touching his hand to his cap in goodbye.

'Jared.' It was a desperate sound. Almost a cry for help.

He turned to face her. Those stormy gray eyes were wide. They looked soft and honest. She was suddenly blanketed in a feeling that she could trust him, implicitly. That she could tell him how she felt about things and he wouldn't judge. It was a strong gut reaction and one which made her start talking.

'So I'm...I'm at Black Monkey on Tuesday, about eleven for a couple of hours or so,' she stated.

He didn't say anything, just carried on watching her, as if waiting for her to continue.

'I've never written a song with another artist before,' she stated.

He shook his head and his lips spread into a smile. 'Yes you have.' He tapped the pocket of his jeans and the phone within. 'We just heard it.'

Chapter Ten

'How's my little darlin'?'

She should have known Larry wouldn't let her make her own way to the studios. Mia too had already called to remind her. No one trusted her to keep an arrangement. Or maybe they all knew how terrified she was. She *was* terrified, there was no point denying it, even to herself. She had changed four times and ended up back in the first shirt she'd picked out. It was plaid. She hadn't worn it in years. It was everything she'd been and everything she wasn't now. She brushed her hand down the front of it hoping to feel inspired. She smiled at Larry and let him in.

She led the way to the kitchen, grabbing up the flask of coffee she'd been drinking from. It tasted terrible but was giving her the caffeine buzz she needed.

'A big day today, honey,' Larry said, laying his hat on the island.

'Oh, Larry, please stop with the loaded phrases and the over-the-top sentiment. I'm going to go to the studios. I said I would and I am and I don't really need an escort,' Honor responded. The coffee needed more sugar. She was sounding as bitter as it tasted.

'I know that. I'm just coming with you for moral support that's all,' Larry said.

She took another large mouthful of coffee and almost gagged. She'd had far too much.

'Everyone's making more of this than there is. I know it's been a long time but I do remember what a studio session's like.'

'Of course you do, darlin', of course you do. I just…' Larry stopped, as if unsure whether to continue.

'What?' She looked at him straight.

'Heard you met Dan Steele on Friday night.'

Her shoulders hunched at the mention of him. She hid her expression against the flask. She knew Larry had caught the body language but she didn't want him to see it in her eyes. Dan being in town had been a shock. She'd never considered their paths crossing in the future, although perhaps it had been naïve not to think about it. He was a country musician. His dream had been her dream. She remembered how badly he'd wanted the record deal, the fame and everything that went with it. He'd talked about it often enough. He'd tried to ride her career to get his own. No, that was harsh. She shook her head.

'You OK?' Larry asked.

'You might have mentioned he was here in Nashville. You could have told me he had a stage name,' she responded.

'I didn't know, honey, not 'til I saw him. He's in the Herald this morning. Been chosen as the indie act to open the Marlon Festival,' Larry informed.

'I thought you had your finger on the musical pulse.'

'He's an unsigned artist. That's the talent scout's concern not mine.'

He was right. It wasn't his job to inform her if her ex-boyfriend was back in town.

'Sorry,' she offered.

'Heard Jed Marshall almost ended up in a fight with him,' Larry continued.

She tried not to react, put her mouth to the flask. So the town grapevine was working well. She wondered if Larry knew Jared had taken her home. If he did he was sure to have an opinion on it.

'Loose cannon, Jed Marshall. Trouble follows him around.'

Honor gave him the biggest smile she could muster and replaced the flask on the counter.

'So, are you ready darlin'?' he asked.

'Can we go the long way?'

The thought of a studio session had never fazed him before but today he was something like nervous. Friday night had been weird. Dan Steele turning up. Honor asking him to take her home. He knew she was fragile, that there was nothing in it. She was still getting used to the idea of going back to music. But he'd seen the expression on her face when she'd heard what he'd done to her song. She'd come alive in that moment. She'd shown herself to him. She was country. It ran through her veins, just like it did through his. She just needed some time and some support. Maybe it wasn't his business to give it, but he was making it that way. Because of the tour. Because she was good. That was all. But, like it or not, he couldn't deny when he heard her sing something inside him folded.

He picked a khaki shirt from the wardrobe and slipped it on, leaving it unbuttoned over his black vest top. He grabbed a cap from the dresser and put it on his head. He checked his watch, then snatched up the remote for the TV.

'...and did you ever think this would happen?' It was the blonde presenter of the morning show, her microphone stuck out for someone to comment into.

'When you have a dream that's so special to you...when you feel it in your heart and soul... you're never going to give up on it.'

He felt his blood start to heat up as the interviewee came on camera. It was Dan fucking Steele on his TV. That asshole was on morning primetime! What the fuck was going on? He turned the volume up and paid attention.

'So I guess opening the Marlon Festival is a dream come true but what you'd really love is a recording contract. Am I right?'

'Sure, that's the ultimate goal. I've been working the bars, getting some great feedback. I've also got a couple meetings lined up with some labels so we'll see what happens. It's all very exciting.'

Jared gritted his teeth. That stinking ass was going to end up being signed soon and then he'd be forced to interact with him professionally. In this industry there was little rivalry. He was good buddies with most of the top stars, but Dan Steele...he wasn't sure he could put his feelings aside.

His cell phone started to ring. Buzz.

'Hey, you've reached Jed Marshall. Leave a message after the beep,' he spoke into the handset.

'I know that's you, Jed. So, tell me, are you ready to sign on with Raintown?'

'I've got five days left. Listen, I'm gonna be pretty tied up today. Can you do somethin' for me?' He listened to Buzz's aggravated breath before continuing. 'Can you call Gear? I want you to make it clear to them that if they even think of signin' Dan Steele...if they even think about thinkin' about signin' him...I'm out.'

'You heard he's opening the Marlon,' Buzz stated.

'I don't care if he's openin' for Obama. There's no way he's gettin' on my label. Make it clear, Buzz.'

He ended the call and punched the off button on the TV.

'So, this is Milo, he's your new lead guitarist and Greg and Johnny you already know.'

She was smiling so much her cheeks were hurting. Russell Johns from Black Monkey was doing the introductions and his violet-colored shirt was bringing on nausea. Greg and Johnny had been with her ten years ago. Neither of them looked changed at all. Greg's beard still needed attention and she was sure Johnny was in the same pair of jeans he'd worn that last night on stage. She shook her head, trying to make the memory dissipate. She looked to Larry who was sat on the couch at the back of the room. He stood up and was at her side within seconds.

'Are you OK darlin'?' he spoke softly.

She was being ridiculous. Why was this such a big deal? Nothing bad had happened at the studios. This was how her life had been all the time before. She'd loved it. It had been all she'd wanted. It had been her everything. She'd spent days in the studio before, pulled all-nighters to get things right.

'Could I get a glass of water?' she asked. She cleared her throat.

Everyone was staring at her. Greg, Johnny, Milo the new guitarist, Larry and Russell. Why were they staring at her? It was only when she looked at her right hand she realized. She'd been pulling at her hair so hard some of it was in her fist.

She opened her mouth to speak but was distracted.

He rapped his knuckles on the Perspex screen that separated the editing booth from the recording studio. He'd had to work his charm on the receptionist on the front desk before he could get inside the inner sanctum of Black Monkey today. Now he was being gawped at by five guys and Honor, who had a handful of hair clenched between her fingers.

He waved a hand at her and watched her cheeks pink up. He indicated the door. They were all looking at him but no one was making any move. He hit the glass with the silver ring on the middle finger of his right hand. Was there a fucking password or something?

'Honor, honey, what's Jed Marshall doing here?' Larry asked, standing in front of her. He touched her chin with his finger and made her turn to look at him. She was still holding the hair. She didn't know how it had happened. Why had she done that? *How* had she done that?

'Jed Marshall is here,' Larry repeated. 'Do you know something about it? He hasn't busted the door down but he's looking as if he might like to, darlin'.'

She looked to the other side of the room. Jed had his palm on the glass. His eyes flicked over to the door and she watched his breath steam up the panel.

'I...I can't do this, Larry.'

She unclenched her hand, dropping the hair and bolting for the door.

Chapter Eleven

She pushed open the door and didn't stop. She wasn't going to stop until she was out of Black Monkey and into some air. She was a couple of feet away from reaching the door back to reception when he grabbed her arm.

'Hey, what's goin' on? Where you goin'?'

Where was she going? Out, was all she knew. Where next, she had no idea. Not for this moment, not for the next or any time after that.

'I...' She started to engage her mouth into speech but gave up. What could she say? She had just pulled out a clump of her hair because being back at the studio was freaking her out. How lame and pathetic was she? That wasn't who she was. She didn't run away from situations. She hadn't even backed up when Simeon Stewart had pulled out the knife.

'Hey, you're shakin'. What were they makin' you do? Sing Vince Gill?'

He had taken her hand, was holding it in his. The sensation was tipping the balance. Fear was flooding out of her and being replaced by warmth, a steady stream of grounding emotion. She entwined her fingers in between the rings on his.

'You want to get out of here?' he suggested. 'I have a studio at home. No one says you have to do this here. OK, so Micro Records might *think* you need to do this here but…I actually have better equipment.'

She turned away from him, redirected her focus on the men from the room who were opening the door behind her. They would want an explanation. She didn't have one. They would say everything was cool. It wasn't. They would suggest she took five, had a coffee then tried again. She couldn't do it.

'Can we go to Target?'

She'd not said a word since they'd left the studios. She hadn't commented on his pick-up truck, just got into the passenger seat and waited for him to drive. Now she was leading the way down the aisles in Target, stopping to pick up random items. Right now she was scrutinizing a porcelain owl priced at $2.99.

'Do you collect 'em?'

She flinched as if she'd forgotten he was even there. She was still so spooked. He should have got to the studios earlier, been there when she arrived. Whatever those pressurizing jerks had said or done it had sent her internally freefalling.

'His eyes ain't straight.' He took the owl from her and pointed between its beak.

'See, here? This one's higher than the other and…'

She raised her eyes to meet his and the look there stopped him talking.

'So what, I shouldn't buy it 'cause it's not perfect? Is that what you think?'

Her voice was cold and he realized straightaway what an error he'd made.

'What should happen to it, Jared? Should we tell the cashier? Get it removed?'

He shook his head. He was in a no-win situation here. She was mad and sad and he needed to shut his mouth.

She snatched the ornament out of his hands and thumped it back down on the shelf. She moved on down the aisle and he followed a few paces behind wondering how to fix it.

Smoothing her fingers down the frame of an ornate whitewood mirror, she looked at her reflection. That was the weird thing about her 'condition'. While other people with facial scarring avoided looking at themselves, she didn't. Each time she took in the vision staring back it was affirmation. It wasn't a hopeful glance – she didn't expect to look and miraculously be cured – she just needed a reminder of how things were. Because, even now, in her mind's eye she was still the flawless eighteen-year-old she used to be.

What was she doing? She'd run away. She'd pulled out a handful of hair and fled the recording studios even before Garth from Micro Records had got there. And now she was back here, in Target. Her church, her sanctuary, the discount-store safe haven. She never really needed anything in it but the browsing calmed her, the time and the careful selection helped her process.

But this time she wasn't alone. Jed Marshall was here. Was she crazy? Why was she leaning on him for support? They barely knew one another and he had an agenda. He'd told her in no uncertain terms he wasn't going to stop asking her to be the opening act on his tour. She only hoped he'd see from each unhinged episode that she was an inappropriate choice.

'Let's buy it,' Jared stated. His voice broke her thoughts and she looked at him, not knowing what he was talking about.

He took the large mirror down off the shelf and tucked it under his arm.

'What are you doing?' she exclaimed.

'Buyin' a mirror. Can we go now? I'm kinda hungry.'

He'd removed his over shirt in the truck and the feminine chintz of the mirror looked ridiculous underneath his tattooed arm. She followed him to the cash desk and watched him hand over eighty-four dollars ninety-nine for something he didn't even want.

Without asking her what she wanted he'd got takeout from

Farley's Diner and now they were headed south. The windows of the truck were down, the music turned up and she was juggling two polystyrene cups on her lap. She assumed he was taking her to his home, to use his studio, but she hadn't checked. Since when had she lost her tongue?

He hung a right down West Washington and pulled into the drive of a modest-looking one-storey. Turning off the ignition he looked across at her. Those gray pools observed her and she swallowed. He looked so serious.

'Now, before we go on in, I just should let you know that nothin' in my place works by hand-clappin'.'

His expression was so deadpan, his tone so tight, she couldn't help herself from letting out a trickle of laughter.

He broke a smile. 'What? Are you makin' fun of the poor guy?'

'You're not poor!'

'Far-from-rich-as-you-guy then?'

'Take-out-getting-cold-guy.'

'Shoot! Man, I forgot about that. Let's go.' He flung open the door, grabbing up the takeout bags from the floor of the truck.

He wished he'd cleaned up. His momma would be kicking his ass if she could see the place. He hurried through the lounge, snatching up misplaced items as he went. Two empty bottles of Coors, a vest-top, a pair of jeans, a two-liter bottle of Pure Nectar, an empty bag of chips and a pile of back copies of *Kerrang!*. It was too much to collate at once and the Pure Nectar fell from his arms and hit the floor, splitting on impact.

'Fuck, no!'

'I'll get a cloth. Is this the way?' Honor asked, pointing to a door off the end of the room.

'Yeah.' He paused, remembering he hadn't washed up the dishes for at least a couple days. 'No. Hell, I'll get it. You have a seat and... read a magazine or somethin'.'

He thrust a copy of *Kerrang!* her way, barely hanging on to everything in his hands. The Pure Nectar carried on spurting out over the hardwood floor.

'Shit.' He dropped what he was holding to the chair and rescued the bottle. 'The place is gonna stink of watermelon and fruits I ain't never heard of for a month.'

Honor looked confused. He wiped a sticky hand down his jeans.

'It's a sponsorship thing,' he said by way of explanation.

She nodded before her eyes moved to the takeout bags lying discarded on the floor where he'd thrown them down.

'If you get some plates I could...' she began.

'Yeah, sure.' He hesitated for a moment. Did he have clean plates? 'I'll be right back.'

Having given her the first impression of a typical bachelor pad, underneath the untidiness, the room had a certain charm. There was a comfortable, easy feel to it. The wood floor that was partially covered by a Navaho-Indian style rug, was complemented by cream walls everywhere, except from a heavy stone fireplace on one wall. There were framed posters on the wall. George Jones, a Harley Davidson, a Southern flag. The wooden mantle held a selection of photographs. This was a real home.

As that thought filtered over her mind she felt a pang of envy inside of her. Her house was big and showy and filled with every gadget money could buy but it lacked the important stuff. It lacked what turned a dwelling into a place you could call your own.

Without knowing it she had folded up the jeans and the vest-top and placed them neatly on the arm of a well-worn leather chair. What was she doing?

She moved across the room, drawn to the mantle holding the photo frames. Pictures, images of friends and loved ones. That's what made a home. In her place her platinum discs were in the basement and the only photo on display was one of Tim McGraw in a cheap heart-shaped frame she'd won in a raffle at Instrumadness.

She looked at the first photo. Jared was in it, with an older woman, presumably his mother. She had an arm around Jared, her tawny-colored hair sat in waves on her shoulders and she was smiling. She was the image of how Honor imagined an everyday mom to be. She looked proud of her son, happy and content.

The next photo was of Jared with two younger people, a boy of about ten and a teenage girl. His siblings? She knew he had a sister but, in truth, she barely knew anything about him.

In a silver frame was another picture of a man in his fifties. Honor picked it up. Swarthy skin, shoulder-length brown hair that was graying at the temples and a bandana tied around the top of his arm. On first glance he was every inch a redneck. But on his face he wore the most genuine smile. It was an expression that was instantly recognizable. It was pure Jared. This man had to be his father.

'Plates.' He put them down onto the coffee table with a deliberate bang. The moment she'd picked up the photo of his father he'd stilled, not sure what to do. She'd been looking at the image so intently and his gut had turned.

She dropped the frame back down to the mantle, color rising in her cheeks.

'I'm sorry. I shouldn't have...' she started.

His heart was beating hard as he approached her.

'It's OK.' He picked up the photo, looking into the eyes of his father. 'That's my pa.'

He struggled to keep the emotion out of his voice. It had been so many years and it still felt raw. His dad had been everything to him, still was.

'You look so alike,' she remarked.

He steeled himself, took in a breath that filled his body. 'He passed away.'

Teeth gritted, he stood still as the gnawing bite of hurt started in his stomach.

'I'm so sorry. I had no idea...'

Her voice, coated with concern, hit him hard. He didn't know what to say to her.

The room was silent, except for the ticking of his grandma's clock on the back wall.

'At least you had time with him,' Honor blurted out.

'What?' He didn't know what she meant. He'd been sixteen when his father died. It wasn't long enough by anyone's reckoning.

'I don't even know who my parents are.'

Chapter Twelve

Over enchiladas she'd told him almost everything. She was Baby Blue Bonnet. Left on the porch of the Mayor of Glenville's home in the dead of night. No one had seen anything. No one had heard anything. But they all knew what to do. She would be looked after by the state. She would have a score of foster homes, share a life with hundreds of other kids and get beaten up in high school because she talked a lot like Miley Cyrus. She had no clue where she came from or who she'd belonged to. She was just Case Number 872405.

'I apologize,' she said, wiping her mouth with a napkin and looking over to him.

'What for?'

'I've completely wasted your entire day. I've ruined a recording session, I made you walk around Target... what was I thinking? And now I've told you all this and...'

'That mirror is gonna look great over the fireplace,' he interrupted.

She shook her head, smiling.

'How do you do that?'

'Do what?'

'Deal with everything like it's nothing?'

He laughed, took a sip of his Coke. 'You mean I don't analyze the crap out of everything? Well, that'd be because I'm not a girl.'

'Whoa, mister, that's low.'

'But true.'

She smiled. He did have a point. She spent quite a lot of time talking herself out of things, then talking herself back into them.

'I just take life as it comes at me. It ain't gonna change, so you need to face it head on and deal with it.'

She didn't know whether he'd intended the statement to sound as loaded as it had, but it touched a nerve.

'Like a session at a recording studio,' she said.

She was weak. She knew that. But she didn't want to be. It was the very last thing she wanted to be. She knew Simeon Stewart had ruined her career but she was also to blame because she had just sat back and let it happen.

He could see her mind working. Just from their few encounters he knew when she was thinking hard. Her brow furrowed and the corners of her mouth drooped slightly. He wondered what was riding through her thoughts. He knew how he dealt with stuff was completely alien to some people. His straight-talking, black and white attitude scared the shit out of most people. But his momma had always told him it was all down to jealousy. He said and did all the things they longed to say and do but they were too damn scared to try.

'Can't go back or stick that hair back on,' he stated.

Her eyes flashed at him then and her chin jutted out a little in challenge.

'So what freaked you out back there? Makin' music again? Or makin' music being gawped at by Stetson guy and the band?' Jared asked.

She let out a breath. 'I haven't quite worked that out yet.'

The studio in Jared's home was state-of-the-art. It had everything you needed to perform, produce and edit. It was only slightly smaller than the set-up at Black Monkey but equally impressive. There were a collection of guitars lined up on display, including a limited-edition Vince Gill original.

'What d'you think?'

She knew her expression of wonder had all but given her away the moment she'd stepped in. His pride in the area was evident.

'I guess it's OK,' she remarked.

He sucked in a breath through his teeth, shaking his head at her. 'You hurt me.'

'It's amazing.' She turned towards him. 'But you know that.'

He nodded, letting out a laugh. 'I've made over fifty songs here in the last year and Gear don't know about any of them.'

She widened her eyes, waiting for an explanation.

'D'you ever get that feelin' about something... a feelin' that it's not the right time to share something?' he asked.

'You're asking someone who hides songs in a drawer. Sure.'

He nodded, pressed a couple of buttons on the mixing desk and got up out of the chair.

'Want to help me finish one?'

He didn't wait for her response but headed out of the door towards the other section of the studio.

Her talent was incredible. Within thirty minutes she had learnt the track, suggested some alterations to the verse section and improved the song ten-fold. Now all he had to do was get her to sing.

She had hummed the track, run through short sections of it to demonstrate something to him but she hadn't let go.

As he played the last few chords and brought the number to an end he saw she'd closed her eyes. Her fingers drummed out a rhythm on her jean-covered thighs and her pure beauty jabbed at him. He faltered with the guitar and her eyes snapped open, breaking the moment.

'Sorry, I kinda messed up there. I'll take it from the top,' he stated, moving his hands up the neck of the instrument.

'Actually... I ought to go. When I dare to look at my cell I'm going to have missed calls from everybody,' she stated.

'Sure, I understand.'

He didn't. Just when he thought he was getting somewhere. He wanted to make her realize what music meant to her, let her see how much talent she had and how wrong it was to keep that in.

He knew she was running away again and he didn't like it.

He didn't sound like he understood. He sounded pissed. And she didn't blame him. He'd rescued her from Black Monkey, he'd bought a mirror he didn't need and he'd spent his afternoon making her face up to the fact that she missed country music more than she'd ever really let herself recognize. It was as much a part of her as her internal organs. She needed it as much as he kept saying it needed her.

'I wish I had half the talent you do,' he told her.

The truth was she'd spent the afternoon learning so much from him and it had affected her deeply. The way he composed was so similar to the way she worked. He was thoughtful and thorough in his composition. There weren't any missing elements. Although the music he wrote had a harder edge from what she was used to, it was nothing short of brilliant.

'You do, and you have the confidence and your own take on things and...'

Being in a tight room with him for hours, listening to the rock-edged vocals with that Southern accent – her body had been reacting to it the whole time. She knew the curve of his shoulders as he played the guitar, the way his strong fingers gripped the strings, how taut his jeans became when he sat on the stool.

'I should really go,' she repeated, taking a step towards the door.

'Yeah, why not. Run away.' It was a curt response.

'What did you say?' There was deliberate fury in her tone. She hadn't asked for this, any of it. She'd wanted to be left alone but no one could do that. They kept prodding and poking and goading.

'I'm not gonna let you do this. You have more talent in one digit than any of those other singers out there.' He threw his hands up. 'You can't live your life without music so why are you tryin' to persecute yourself?'

'I'm not ready... I'm just not ready. I thought I was but I'm not. There, I've said it.' Her voice wobbled and gave away everything she felt and feared.

'That's bullshit.'

The tears were threatening but she wasn't going to give into them. 'You know this reverse psychology has already been tried by several different medical professionals in the state.'

'I don't do psychology, reverse, up-front or any other which way.'

'I won't be bullied.' She folded her arms across her chest and attempted to look defiant.

He shook his head at her. 'Fine. I'll take you home.'

Inside she was shaking as she watched him take his guitar off his body, his vest riding up his back a little as he bent to put it down. She swallowed and closed her eyes. What was she doing? She'd been rude and stupid and he'd done so much for her. And he'd listened. He'd listened to her talk about her life as an unwanted child in care.

'Jared.'

The tone of her voice made him turn around. What he saw across the room had his stomach coiling up. Her lips were trembling and she was rubbing her palms up and down each denim-covered hip. Her curls were hanging down over her face and she just looked so lost. Had he been too harsh? He hadn't meant to be. He just wanted to help her, guide her through this... protect her.

'I want to do it but...' she began.

He kept his lips together, afraid to interrupt.

She didn't elaborate further, she just stood there, looking to him. He didn't know what to do. He was torn. He knew the obvious thing to do would be to bridge the gap, put his arms around her and tell her everything was going to be OK. But that wasn't him. Cuddling up and hand-holding wasn't his style. He had tried it once and had his heart trampled on so hard he'd learnt his lesson. Since then it had only ever been about sex. Good, wild sex with women he didn't have to make small talk with afterwards. He had no shortage on that front. But there was something so unique about Honor, something that moved him, something that left him weak. Something that made him want to behave differently.

He swallowed and made a move, spanning the distance between them in a couple of strides.

'I'm sorry,' she whispered as he reached her.

The words seemed to catch on her lips, falling into the divide and catching him unawares.

'Hey, what are you sorry for?' He cleared his throat as he gazed at her. Those clear, bright eyes were dewy with unspent tears.

She looked up at him and he saw it all written on her face. All her suffering, all the hard times she was still working through, everything she'd had to face since that maniac had attacked her. His heart was thumping so hard he could almost hear it outside of his body. He wanted to hold her. He wanted to put his hands on her and just hold her against him. But he couldn't. He couldn't do it.

Her whole body was shaking. It was like she'd swallowed a whole family of moths and they were taking flight, bumping off her insides, making her quiver and setting off a whole chain reaction of emotions.

Jared was stood so close she only had to move a centimeter towards him and they'd be touching. She could smell the heat from him, almost taste the adrenaline. His gray eyes were on fire but with what she wasn't quite sure. Was that desire she could see there? Or was it pity? A look of consolation for all that she was and all that she had been. She wanted to know as much as she *didn't* want to know.

She moved one hand from her hip and lifted it slowly, afraid if she moved too quickly the tension would break. She wanted to touch him. That's all she knew. She wanted to feel his skin under her fingers.

The soft cotton of his vest melded with her fingers as inch by inch she traced a path from his abdomen up to his chest. The solid frame of his body was unmoved, apart from the slow and even rise and fall of his breath.

'Honor.'

The gravel in his voice made her raise her head to meet his gaze, her fingers continuing upwards, lingering over every defined muscle they encountered.

She was too scared to reply. If she opened her mouth to speak, if she engaged with the situation she would withdraw. Right now she was caught someplace new, in the middle of a feeling she hadn't experienced for so long. She didn't understand it but she didn't want it to stop.

She brought her hand up to his face, touching her fingers to his lips. Her index finger whispered over his bottom lip before moving to graze the thin layer of stubble of his cheek.

He balled his hands into fists and squeezed his fingertips into his palms. This was torture. He was the smallest fraction away from losing control and disrespecting her. Her touch was burning into him, igniting desire, forcing him to feel. She put a hand on the belt of his jeans, drawing her body towards him. His eyes locked with hers. She was an angel. Beautiful, pure – wounded, yes – but with an inner strength that had seen her through.

He could see in her eyes that she wanted him and here he was, unable to react. His body was flaming with lust but his heart was on lock down and his head was telling him he would do nothing but hurt her. The very last thing he wanted to do was hurt her.

He could feel her breath; see the longing written in her expression. Any other man would have kissed her by now, put their hands in her hair and worked her out of that shirt. Should he? Could he?

Her heart was pacing so fast she could hear it in her head. She was just lost in his eyes, those deep, gray irises that seemed as if they were looking right inside her. He hadn't moved. Not one inch. They were body to body, as close as two people could be and she was almost melting with need. This was Jed Marshall, just a name on a CD up until a week ago and now... now he almost knew her better than anyone ever had.

He raised his hand and she shifted, expectant, wanting to feel his skin on hers.

Her fingers found the edge of his top, wound their way under the fabric until he caught her hand, holding it firm.

'I really should take you home,' he stated.

Chapter Thirteen

The drive was a little over thirty minutes but every second was ticking by so slowly. She was tight to the passenger door of his truck, her head out the window, letting the breeze blow her hair off her face. She was pissed. And he didn't blame her. It had been obvious what she wanted to happen and he'd rejected it, thrown the offer back at her by not reacting. The worst of it was, from what he knew of her, she wasn't the type of girl to put herself out there. She'd shown him that sentiment and he'd panned it. Even though he'd wanted it... real bad.

He pulled down the peak of his cap and shook his head. He was a fucking idiot. He was letting this girl get under his skin when really it should be just business. Why did he want her on tour so badly? Because she was good? Or because the way she looked in tight jeans hollowed him out? Maybe he should just call Buzz and get Raintown signed up. If he left things too long he might end up with Dan Steele. Hell, what an almighty fucking mess that would be.

He was driving way too fast but she didn't care. The wind whipping at her face was what she needed. She'd just made a first-class ass of herself. She'd offered herself on a plate to Jed Marshall, the hot property of Nashville, the platinum artist Mia kept telling her was one of the world's most eligible bachelors if you liked them a little rough and ready. Given a little encouragement, she'd have been up for anything just because he'd been a little nice to her when she'd been a hell of a lot crazy. She'd behaved like a hyped-up, panting cougar and he'd done the decent thing. The only appropriate thing. Because that's what her behavior had been... completely inappropriate. Her only saving grace was she hadn't tried to seduce him in public. At least this way they could hopefully keep it between them and not share it with the local news station.

Why had she done that? Was it because he'd listened when she poured her heart out about her foster homes? She hadn't given him much choice about listening. Full-sugar Coke and Mexican food had loosened her tongue and dropped her guard.

Her street was coming up and she was glad. She just wanted to get home, clap the lights down low, pour a little wine and immerse herself in a scalding hot bath. Larry and whatever other cell-phone messages she had would have to wait a little longer. The fact was, she didn't have an answer to any of the questions they were bound to ask.

He pulled the truck to the curb and she was opening the door before he hit the brakes.

'Thank you for coming to the studio and Target. I'm sorry about the mirror and... I'll see you around.'

She rushed the words out as she climbed down from the cab, flipped her hair over her shoulder and turned toward the path.

'Hey, wait up!'

Why couldn't he just let her leave? She needed to go and rid herself of her idiocy with bubble bath and Chardonnay. She scuffed the pavement with her sneakers, not raising her head.

'So when am I gonna see you again?'

He was coming around the front of the truck towards her and right away her insides were churning up. It wasn't the enchiladas either. It was him. The heat was at her cheeks before she could keep it in check.

'What?' She furrowed her brow.

'We just made a record together this afternoon. I want to do something about that. I want you to sing on it. We should pitch it to Gear.'

What was he talking about? They'd fooled around with something he'd written, something good, warranted, but it was his song – she'd just tightened it up a little. It wasn't a *record*.

'I'm signed to Micro and I don't do duets,' she stated.

'You did one with Vince Gill in 2003.'

She swallowed.

'Micro is old school and you haven't sung a thing for them in years. They're throwin' you off with this "greatest hits" bullshit.'

Damn he hadn't meant to be so blunt. And what was he thinking anyway? He didn't do duets. In fact when Buzz had suggested a duet one time, he'd told him Hell would turn into a Ben & Jerry's parlor before he ever sang with someone else on a record.

'I didn't mean that,' he backtracked. He stepped towards her, onto the verge.

'Yes you did and you're probably right. But it isn't your issue.'

She was looking at him now, her head held up. How could someone so vulnerable be so feisty?

'Listen, what happened back there at my place...' He had to say something. If they were going to work together, which was what he wanted, if he was going to have a chance of getting her on his tour then there couldn't be any awkwardness.

'Nothing happened.' Her reply was instant and he felt it hard.

'Sure. I know.' He didn't know what else to say. He could still sense the imprint of her fingers on his chest.

'I'm going to go and work out what I'm going to do and stuff so... you can go,' she said, nodding towards his truck.

He was a pace away from her and she was taking baby steps back to get further away from him.

'Sure. Well, I have a mirror to hang and everything so, like you,

I'm real busy.' The sentiment came out angrier than he'd really meant it. There was nothing left to say.

He was walking back to the driver's side of his flatbed now, leaving. Was that what she wanted? Forgetting how his presence made her feel, he was offering her a golden ticket back into the game if she wanted it. Perhaps a duet would be a new start. Only half the focus on her, less pressure. It was an opportunity most singers would jump at. Jed Marshall was at the top of his industry, he didn't just sell records, he shifted them by the truckload.

She stood there, kicking up tufts of grass, torn. He got into the truck and waved a hand at her. That was her signal. He was going and she'd made a big mistake. There was only one thing she could do.

Turning away she started off up the path.

There were twelve missed calls on her cell and the red dot told her she had voicemail. The light on the answer phone was flashing like a beacon too. She didn't blame Larry – the messages had to be Larry. He had set this up and had probably taken a lot of time to get Micro interested in collaborating new material onto a hits album. He had her best interests on the top of his agenda, he always had. Yes, maybe for his own financial gain too, but she knew he cared for her in a surrogate father kind of way. He was a staple in her life and perhaps she didn't respect that enough. She'd messed him around today, left him to make excuses for her when the record company representative showed up.

She stretched her arms out over the island in the kitchen and pressed her cheek to the marble, closing her eyes. Staying here in Nashville, she should have known this was going to happen at some point. There was only so much hiding you could do in Music Central.

Her eyes snapped open in response to a loud knocking on the door. Raising herself up she hurried from kitchen and down the hall as the rapping continued. That wasn't Larry's style. He rang the bell and if she didn't answer he waited. Was it Mia? The last time she'd beat on her door she'd been drunk and puked on the carpet.

She put her eye to the security hole. It was Jared. His fist thumping on the wood made her step back, putting a hand to her chest. She'd thought he'd gone.

'Come on, Honor, open up!'

She put her hand to the latch and pulled it open. He didn't wait for an invitation to step over the threshold and into the house. She bowled back as he frisked past, startling her.

'Now I've been sat in the truck for twenty minutes mulling this all over and I just... I just want you to know something.'

She widened her eyes, taking in his furious stance, the tension in his torso, the look on his face. He was mad and wild and she was frozen to the spot.

'Back there at my place...' He took a breath. 'I wanted to rip off that dumb-ass shirt you're wearing.'

She couldn't speak. Her lips had shriveled and the inside of her mouth had turned parched.

'But I wouldn't have stopped there.' He set his eyes on her. 'I wouldn't have been able to stop there.'

His breathing was ragged. His gaze was on her and it almost felt like the dumb-ass shirt was being removed by his eyes alone. On instinct she put a hand to the top button and held it in between her fingers.

'I'm a jerk. There. That's it.'

He gave her a determined nod, then pulled the peak of his cap down lower on his forehead. 'I'll see you.'

He stepped out as quickly as he had entered and closed the door behind him.

Chapter Fourteen

'Ladies and gentlemen, put your hands together for Jed Marshall, wasn't he fantastic?'

He waved a hand in appreciation and swung the guitar up over his neck as he dismounted the small stage. One of his team was there to take the instrument from him and Buzz stepped up, inputting into his iPad.

'Nice work, Jared. That should secure us a good deal more radio station promos before the tour.'

Someone handed him a bottle of Pure Nectar. He looked at the drink with disdain but, noticing the photographers in the crowd, thought better of throwing it to the floor and uncapped the lid.

'And speaking of the tour, Raintown are keeping their schedule free and are just waiting for the final confirmation,' Buzz continued.

'Man,' he cursed, shaking his head.

He'd not heard from Honor since he'd burst into her house and told her what he wanted to do to her. It was probably for the best. The reason he'd told her was for her benefit, not his. She'd been through a hell of a lot of rejection and he didn't want to be party to any more. He didn't want her to think he didn't want her because of anything she'd done.

'Jared, I agree Honor Blackwood was a talent back in the day but I'm just not on board with this whole reincarnation vibe Micro is spinning,' Buzz told him.

'What you talkin' about, Buzz?'

'You've not been on-line today? Not checked out Twitter?'

'Shit, man, spit it out.'

'Here, see for yourself.' Buzz passed him the iPad.

#HonorB was trending. There was a whole timeline of tweets about an apparent personal appearance at Cody's Bar & Grill that evening. What was going on? When he'd last seen her she wasn't in the right place to complete a recording, let alone perform a PA. What had changed in a few days?

'You know what Micro is like. They're labeling it as the Second Coming. If you ask me it's all gonna end in disaster. The girl hasn't sung a note in ten years,' Buzz said.

Jared passed him back the iPad with a thump. 'I've gotta go.'

'What? Well, shall I confirm with Raintown for the tour? They won't hold on forever!'

It was just one song. Just *Goodbye Joe* and that was it. There might not be many people there. After all, there were far more artists than ever before in Nashville, hugely talented artists who weren't quaking with fear like her. The only reason people might come along was to see if she actually made it through the song without freaking out. And who could blame them? She'd be thinking the very same thing.

'Hey, doll, do we have any more of Vince Gill's *When Love Finds You*?' Mia called.

'Is the computer down?'

'No.' Mia raised her eyes indicating the waiting customer and dropped her voice to a whisper. 'Haven't synced the latest order on yet.'

Honor nodded her understanding and smiled at the waiting middle-aged man wearing a black Stetson. 'I'll go check.'

The stock room was in the basement and she was glad of the relief from the front of house. She wasn't on her game today because of the event looming over her. Being busy was a distraction, but she was starting to wonder if it was the right one.

Should she be rehearsing? Shouldn't she be making sure she was lyric and note perfect? Or would that just make the nerves worse and remind her the performance was a reality?

Larry would hate that she was here. He was back on his blood pressure medication after everything that happened last week. He'd reluctantly agreed to meet her at the venue but he hadn't been happy about the idea. If she'd given him his way he'd have strapped her into a baby stroller and wheeled her into position himself.

She hadn't explained herself to anyone about the 'incident' at the studios. When she'd finally got up the nerve and made her decision about the future she'd not let Larry speak until she'd said what she needed to say.

She'd set up a recording session of her own. Three days ago she'd gone into the studio with the minimum amount of people she could get away with and her guitar from home. They'd laid down *Goodbye Joe*, Micro had loved it and now... well now the industry machine was taking over.

But while all this was going on around her, while she took on board exactly what she was getting herself into, the only thing on her mind was Jared Marshall. She knew he was the reason she'd recorded the track. Spending that time in his studio had taught her so much. Musically she *was* country through and through. Hiding away from that fact was only doing two things: making her miserable and letting Simeon Stewart win. As terrified as she was, she had the rest of her life to lead and being the town's resident recluse was doing her no favors.

So why hadn't she called him? Didn't he deserve to know what was happening? He'd coached her, told her to dig deep and if it hadn't been for him then... Well all she knew was she wouldn't be getting ready for her first public appearance in ten years. She'd probably be wandering around Target looking for cheap homeware she didn't need.

She found the latest delivery, the box not even opened. Tearing at the tape she checked the inventory.

What Jared had said to her had made fire run through her veins. The way he'd looked at her, the way his breath had rushed from his mouth, the words penetrating her skin and resting on a part of her that palpitated with need. For a second she had held herself still, waited to see what would happen, looked expectant. And then he'd turned and went and she was left even more confused. What had she really expected from him? Despite her almost wanton behavior in his studio, she wasn't in the market for any sort of relationship. She still didn't understand what had made her behave that way. The inch or two of bare abdomen above denim when his vest rode up was one explanation, but that shouldn't have been enough to make her display desire so readily. And she had. Then he'd turned her down, and later told her he'd wanted to. Did he have someone? Maybe she should Google or ask the Wikipedia of Nashville, Mia. Was she interested in knowing? Didn't she have enough on her plate already?

She retrieved the Vince Gill album from the box and headed back upstairs.

It was his third beer in thirty minutes. He didn't know what he was doing; he just knew he needed something to get him through it. He was angry. He wanted to go to the music store and tell her just how mad he was. The trouble was, he knew he had no reason to be feeling that way. She didn't belong to him. He had helped her a little but so what? She didn't owe him anything. He should be pleased she'd finally recorded again. She was getting back to what she loved, moving on with a new release. Soon she'd be on stage at the Opry and it'd be like they'd never met. And why should it be any other way? Up until a week or so ago he'd never even heard of her.

He got his cell phone out of his jeans and pressed a contact.

'Hey, Byron it's Jed. Listen, are you doin' anything later? I was thinkin' of headin' to Cody's.'

Chapter Fifteen

'ChapStick,' Mia announced.

Honor couldn't believe the record company had sent a stylist over to Cody's. It was going to be one song and some autograph signing, not a sold-out festival gig. She'd looked at the Asian girl with plaits and three types of rollers in her hand and almost freaked out. Mia had taken charge and ushered her away while Honor had headed for the dressing room. It contained a battered table and chair, a warped mirror and a box of Kleenex.

'What?' She was looking at her reflection, squinting her eyes and trying to work out whether she had enough foundation over the scar on her cheek.

'Listen, doll, I know you don't want to hear this but Countrified 103 have been plugging this PA all day. Fans have been calling up requesting your songs and on my last look the place is buzzing out there. We don't want them looking at some over-the-top red gloss on your mouth, we want them focusing on the voice.'

'You're starting to sound like Radley.' Honor traced a finger along her scar, turning to look at the reflection of her side profile.

'Who?'

'Radley Stokes. He's my new contact at the record company. He told me to go on out there and be myself. I can't imagine how much money they're paying him to say stuff like that.'

The two women connected a look and shared a laugh. As Mia passed her the ChapStick, Honor caught her hand.

'Thank you for closing up early and coming here with me.'

'Come on, doll, where else am I gonna be? Besides, there was no way I was missing out on this big news they've been tweeting about.' Mia brushed some loose powder onto Honor's cheeks.

'What news?' She was jittery enough about this event, the last thing she needed was something sprung on her. Would Micro do that? Had they set something up and not told her about it? Her heart paced quicker and she reached for her bottle of water.

'You not seen it? Along with #HonorB they've got #newvoice going out too. People have been asking about it but there's been very tight-lipped responses. But it's probably nothing earth-shattering; you know how they hype things.'

The way she was sucking back the Mountain Dew had changed Mia's tone towards the end of the sentence. The shaking hands had no doubt said all that needed to be said about her opinion on secret news.

'So, five minutes 'til show time.' Mia primped Honor's curls with her fingers and then placed her hands on her friend's shoulders. 'I'm so pleased for you.'

'Are you? Even if it means me maybe dropping a day at the store?'

'Doll, I'm expecting you to quit after you bring the house down tonight.'

'Oh Lord, what have you brought me to?'

Jared hadn't told Byron about Honor's big night. He knew what he'd think, and was sure he'd try and talk him out of it. Jared knew Byron wasn't big on social media so saying nothing had been an easy out.

'Wanna beer?' Jared offered.

'What in the world is this media circus? #HonorB... wait a minute. Honor B? Honor Blackwood?' Byron stated as the pieces began to fall into place en route to the bar.

'I'll get us some beer.' He hailed the bartender.

'Did you know about this? What am I saying? Of course you knew about this. That's why we're here. What's going on?' Byron wanted to know. He removed his Stetson.

'She's recorded a track. She's showcasin' it here.' The answer was blunt because he had nothing else to tell him. He didn't entirely understand his compulsion to be here either.

'Are you still trying to get her on your tour?' Byron asked.

Jared shrugged. He didn't know the answer to that either. If he *did* still want her to support him on the tour was it for the right reasons?

'What's going on, man?'

'Can we get a couple of Coors?' Jared ordered. Right at this moment it was easier to ignore Byron than attempt to explain anything. He looked to the stage where two guitarists and a drummer were coming up onto the platform. A roadie stood to the side, tuning a black acoustic.

'We should try gettin' a seat,' Jared said. He handed over some money for the drinks and headed into the crowded bar room.

'Two minutes, Miss Blackwood.'

The runner, if that's what he was, looked like a high-school student. This was really happening. In two minutes. She flexed her fingers and gripped the water bottle, putting it to her mouth. Empty. *Don't panic.* Her hand went to the scar on her cheek and she checked her reflection in the mirror again.

'You're gonna be great, doll. Those butterflies you're getting are good butterflies. You'd be a freaking robot if you weren't nervous.'

Honor nodded. She couldn't speak. She was more than just nervous. She was exactly how she knew she would be. She just had to get over herself. It wouldn't be forever. If she did this this one time, the next time would be easier. That's how it worked.

She could hear someone on the microphone addressing the crowd. There were cheers and handclapping. The volume was arena level, not bar and grill level. She wanted to be sick.

'Listen, remember that old guy that kept coming into the store? The one that said he was related to Vince Gill. The one that touched my ass and called me "beauty". I used to see his car pull into the lot and make an excuse to hide in the basement so you had to serve him. Until you told me he was never going to learn anything about respecting people if I didn't go out there, stand up in front of him and tell him to take his hands off my butt or take his business elsewhere.' Mia ran her hands through Honor's curls. 'And you were right. And I did. And we never saw him again. This is no different. You've got no reason to be afraid. You might not have been born in Nashville but you were made here, doll. And you need to go out there and reclaim that life you loved. Because you sure as hell deserve it.'

Mia was right. She just needed to remember why she was doing this. Not for Micro, not for Larry, not even for her fans. She was doing it for herself. She just needed to regain her strength and her focus, think back to the confident, music-industry-dominating artist she used to be.

She stood up and grabbed her guitar. 'I'm ready.'

When the music started he felt the beat thud in his chest. She was really going to do this. In front of all these people, this audience of country music fans, the record company representatives, the dozens of press. He hadn't seen Cody's this packed since Luke Bryan had held an impromptu fan-club event. He was worried. He couldn't believe she was ready for this. He'd seen her lose it just a few days ago in front of a much smaller group. He couldn't believe this change had happened so quickly. Or was it more a case of him not wanting it to have happened without him? He bit his lip and started to toy with the chain on his belt.

'Man, this is a launch! I'm expecting smoke machines and dancers any second,' Byron commented as they watched.

'Ladies and gentlemen! Put your hands together and welcome

her back! Here at Cody's Bar and Grill, Micro Records give to you, the one, the only, the former CMA Female Vocalist of the Year, platinum-selling artist, Nashville's own... Honor Blackwood!'

The over-the-top build-up had him sitting forward on his seat and folding his hands behind the back of his neck. He could feel a slick of perspiration at his nape. Half of him wanted to see what was going to happen here, the other half wanted it all to go away.

When she stepped out from the wings his stomach took a dive. There she was, clad in tight jeans, wearing her brown leather cowboy boots and a white gypsy blouse, her raven hair sitting on her shoulders. The sight of her made him swallow down an emotion that had ridden up fast and hard. The roar from the crowd made it obvious how excited they all were to see Honor back and a wave of jealousy pulled at him. She was back to being public property.

She'd put one foot in front of the other and tried to take herself back ten years. How had she felt then? Excited instead of terrified. Hot and alive, ready to give not just her songs but her soul. She could do that again. There was security surrounding the stage. Larry had made sure of it. He'd promised her. But when the lights went up and the bulbs from the cameras started popping and flashing she couldn't see anything. The sound of appreciation from the audience started to rise in one great cacophony and suddenly she felt hemmed in. She tried to smile, focus her eyes on someone out there she knew. Where was Mia? Where was Larry? Was there security? She looked to her guitarist, Milo.

Chapter Sixteen

Despite missing her initial cue she'd not faltered. Jared was on his feet with the rest of room applauding the return of an outstanding singer. Pride swelled in his chest and coated him all over with a sensation of purpose. If him reaching out to her at the music store was in any way responsible for her come-back then he was glad.

'She blew everyone away. Now I'm believing she could support you on your tour,' Byron remarked.

He nodded but he didn't really agree. He wasn't sure she needed the chance to be a supporting artist. The way the media had rolled today she'd be capable of selling out an arena tour alone.

Her joy was evident though. Her smile was vaster than a queue for Vince Gill concert tickets. Her eyes were bright with delight, her movements showing her pleasure and understated gladness at getting through it.

'So, ladies and gentlemen, give it up one more time for Honor Blackwood and her brand-new single, *Goodbye Joe*, available to download right now!'

The crowd needed no encouragement to go wild a second time, some even started to reach for their iPhones or MP3s at the mention of ordering the track. Honor beamed at their response before moving off to the edge of the stage as the announcer continued.

'But that's not all, everybody. Micro has kinda been teasing you a little on Twitter all day but now the moment has come. I'm gonna hand you over to Micro's Radley Stokes who's going to let you in on this huge news for the label.'

Jared turned to Byron. 'D'you know what's going on?'

'Me? I didn't even know *this* was going on.'

People retook their seats.

Radley Stokes was dressed in a business suit that looked like it was making him sweat. His round face was flushed and his bald head slicked with perspiration.

'How y'all doin'?' The forced accent drew sniggers and snorts from the crowd. 'Wasn't Honor fantastic?'

Jared could see that Honor's new-found confidence was waning. The smile was abashed. She was rubbing her palms on her jeans.

'You've just heard a familiar voice re-launched, now it's time to introduce you to a new voice. Please put your hands together and show your appreciation for a rising star. The latest artist signed to Micro Records... Dan Steele!'

When his name was announced it was like someone had cut into her. The pleasure of her performance simply evaporated. Everything muted. She could see the crowd clapping, see their mouths opening in appreciation, but it was as if she was having an out-of-body experience. She looked to the left and saw Dan approach from the wings. Wearing a black Stetson, plaid shirt, jeans and boots, he almost bounded center-stage to embrace Radley and clap him on the back. This couldn't be happening. This had to be some sort of bad joke. She was back on track with her career at Micro and they had gone and signed her ex-boyfriend. She wet her lips with her tongue, took a step backwards and tried to think about something else, anything else than the car crash of her life unraveling before her.

She should leave. She should back her way off the stage and go.

She wanted to think. She needed not to be here. Her foot caught on one of the leads and she stumbled.

'Fuck! What the hell is going on? That asshole!' Jared was out of his seat, anger burning him up from the inside.

'Jed, come on, man,' Byron started, standing up next to him.

'What the hell are they thinkin'? How can they do this to her?'

He was livid. Micro had taken her moment and given it to Dan Steele. The one guy in the business he'd always loathed. He'd wanted to smash his face in before, now he wanted to smash it in and bury him. He'd done this deliberately. He'd signed with Micro because that's where Honor was. Dan either wanted to taunt her or get back with her. Whichever one it was he wasn't going to stand by and let it happen.

On stage someone had passed Dan a guitar. Honor was looking like she wanted the ground to swallow her up. All color had faded from her cheeks and that glow, that light and passion from a job well done had vanished.

'Move,' Jared ordered Byron.

'Jed...'

'Get outta my way.'

Jared pushed past Byron and started striding towards the stage with purpose and a look of determination set on his face. As realization dawned that another Nashville artist was in the audience, the press guests started snapping Jared's approach. He grabbed the guitar from the roadie at the side of the stage and jumped up onto the platform in one leap.

The cameras were the only thing reacting to Jared's stage invasion. The supposed tight security seemed to have no idea what to do. Did a Nashville star pose a threat? Before anyone could work that out, he'd stepped in front of Honor's guitarist and taken the microphone from its stand.

'Hey, everybody. How are y'all doin'?'

The audience responded positively with whoops, cheers and

whistles.

'Say, wasn't Honor Blackwood amazin'?' The crowd cheered in agreement. 'Come join me, Honor.'

He looked to her. Her puzzled expression mixed with the unease he knew she'd be feeling about Micro's announcement was evident. He couldn't and wouldn't let this guy walk in and take her moment from her. His moral core bound him to do right.

She felt giddy. The heat from the excited people, the lights and the music equipment were enveloping her. She didn't feel like a participant anymore. It was as if time was going slowly, revolving around her, spinning out of her reach.

'Honor, come over here.'

Jared's voice seeped into her senses. Instinctively, without stopping to question, she was moving towards him. A spotlight to her left flashed into vision. Black spots floated in her sight and nausea flooded her throat. Her balance was off. Everything was off.

'I don't know what else you were gonna say there, Mr Micro Records, but I'm just gonna step right on in and let everyone hear some of my new material.'

She couldn't really digest what he was saying. Her ears were buzzing, her heart was galloping and she was trying hard to keep her vision in line.

'Well, I...' Radley Stokes started.

Jared hit a loud, well-timed chord on the guitar that silenced him.

'So, Honor and I, we've been workin' on a little somethin' together and I was thinkin' you might like to hear it.'

The noise from the crowd almost took the roof off the bar. The allure of an exclusive and their reaction to it was what he'd been counting on. If the press kept taking photos like they were doing right now, Dan Steele's news would hardly figure. Now all he had to hope was that Honor would come through.

He moved towards her, tried to get her to look at him. She was static now, looking in the direction of Micro's latest signing. This stunt had to work.

'This is *Trapped by Love*.'

He began to play the song he'd worked on with Honor at his studio. The track she'd helped him with but not sung. Apart from punching out Dan Steele again, this was the only other thing he could think of to make this right.

> *We've come so far, left the past behind*
> *But the memories won't let us switch off*
> *We've hurt so long, we've prayed so hard*
> *Now a new start's all we've got*
>
> *With your hand in mine, we'll try to stop time*
> *Just long enough to run away*
> *You're the only one that's ever made me wanna stay anyway*

She loved the song. She'd love the song the second he'd played her the first verse. It combined everything she adored about country music. There was a strong story in the words, a tight verse, written traditionally with a rock kick. It was going to be a huge hit and it deserved to be. She stepped up to the microphone and joined in with the chorus.

> *Trapped by love, not circumstance*
> *Trapped by heart, it's bad romance*
> *Trapped by lust, no coincidence*
> *Baby, I'm trapped by you*
> *And Lord I know you feel it too*

She took up the second verse as if it had always been destined to be their song. She was so into the music everything else was forgotten.

> *Wasting here, just biding time*

Making up for falling down
The times I cried cos you're my guy
I saw the way my momma frowned

But touching you and feeling this close to something so far away
Has me made feel like a lonely star who finally found the Milky Way

She locked eyes with Jared as he joined her in singing towards the bridge and her whole body began to feel the glow from the performance. This was the sensation she'd missed. These moments with the notes and lyrics, completely absorbed in the here and now, totally immersed in the sound – it was as if there was no one else in the bar at all. She was there in body alone, her spirit flying, her essence soaring up as the music built to its crescendo.

So get the keys, unlock the truck
We won't know where we're going
We'll find somewhere that we'll fit in
With everybody knowing...

Hearing her vocals on the track for the first time was sending shots of heat like molten lava through his veins. He gripped the strings of the unfamiliar guitar, desperate to do the song justice... for her. Listening to their voices combining, he was struck with a feeling so strong it physically rocked him. An emotion deep inside rose up and hit him. This could hurt him. *She* could hurt him if he didn't tighten up. He was caught here, torn, stuck between two places he was equally afraid to revisit.

He played the last chord and raising his head his eyes found hers. They were wide open, clear, moist, telling him she'd shared every emotion of every note. There was a second, a brief contact through the space that separated them before he realized the patrons of Cody's had erupted.

The applauding and roaring jolted her as she became fully aware of just how many people had been watching. She put a hand to her chest and swallowed her anxiety. What should she do? The clapping for her solo performance she'd dealt with and had been expecting, but this! She didn't know what to do with this. And she didn't know what to do about Jared.

Then, invading her line of vision was Dan Steele. His hands redundant on the guitar hung low over his neck. He wasn't putting his hands together in appreciation. He looked pissed. And Micro, her record company, had signed him.

'You need to take a bow,' Jared coaxed.

He was next to her, smiling at her, those gray eyes soft and warm. Before she could speak he'd linked her hand with his and raised it high into the air as the audience cheered harder.

'Miss Honor Blackwood!' Jared yelled. 'Let's hear it!'

Chapter Seventeen

'Champagne, ma'am?'

Honor looked at the tray holding half a dozen glass flutes. As much as she craved an alcohol hit, her throat was so dry. She'd been interviewed by every country music magazine, some radio stations, a prime-time Nashville chat show and done a piece for the Micro Records blog. Everyone had been ordered not to mention the attack of 2004, everyone *had* asked about the duet with Jared. Except Larry. Yet. She was still hiding from him.

'Man, I'll have yours,' Mia stated, taking a glass for each hand.

This event at the Sheraton Music City hotel was completely unexpected and if she was truthful, unwanted. What she'd planned to do after the PA, no matter how it had gone, was escape back home and reflect. A long hot bath and a chance to breathe, analyze how it had gone, decide whether it was the right decision. Instead Radley Stokes had ushered her off stage right and the interviews had started.

She remembered the second she'd had to break contact with Jared. His fingers had been interlocked with hers, his thick rings tight against her hand. She'd hung on, pressed stronger, looped a finger over his until the last second, before Radley maneuvered her off.

'Have you had some food, doll? They've gone all out here for you,' Mia said, gulping down the bubbly from the glass in her right hand.

'No, I'm not hungry,' she lied. She hadn't eaten a thing all day because of her nerves for the show, but now all she could focus on was the room full of people. The few hundred people she didn't want to talk to and the one person who wasn't there.

As if reading her thoughts, Mia spoke. 'So, what's the deal with Dan Steele? You didn't know about that?'

'D'you think if I'd known about it I'd have performed today?'

The answer was instant and from her gut. Was that true? Would she have let him ruin her comeback? She guessed she'd never know.

'Not that anyone's gonna be talking about him after your knight in shining armor stole the show. What *was* that track?' Mia teased.

She felt her face light up as Mia nudged her elbow and snorted a laugh. 'Just something we knocked up together last week.'

'And you wanna share what else you did together last week because from where I was standing the air was crackling with hot promise,' Mia carried on.

Heat flooded to her cheeks and she toyed with a curl, pulling it over her scar.

'Is there something going on?' Mia hissed in a whisper.

Honor shook her head vigorously. 'No... it's not like that.' She had no idea what it was, if it was anything at all.

'We need to talk. I've had every gossip magazine leaving me voicemail messages, Jared. *Gossip* magazines, tittley tattley editions that usually talk about Justin Bieber and his monkey. What the hell is going on?'

He took a long swig of his bottle of beer, working out in his mind exactly what he should say. The truth was, he didn't know what to say. Sometimes with Buzz it was better to say nothing, let him blow off some steam before trying to make any explanation.

'What you did was against everything in your contract with Gear. You can't do stuff like that, Jared. How many times do I have to remind you of that?'

The man's cheeks were puffing out and he unfastened the button of his jacket. Jared could tell he was nearly done.

'You took over another record label's gig. You played a hellish loud minor chord over their new media representative...' Buzz continued.

'They got that on You Tube?' Pride licked up all over the sentence and he straightaway regretted it.

'What are you even doing here?' Buzz threw his arms out, highlighting the lobby bar of the Sheraton.

He couldn't answer that question either. He didn't know. He'd not been invited to the party in the Plantation Ballroom but he'd heard it was happening and he'd made Byron drop him at the entrance. Buzz was there because he knew everybody and got invited to everything.

'Is this still about wanting Honor Blackwood on the tour? Because...'

'Because what?' He gritted his teeth, feeling the fierce loyalty bubbling inside of him. 'She blew everyone away at Cody's tonight. Her own song. Our song...'

Our song. That shouldn't have come out. It was but it wasn't. He hadn't got the right to call it that. And Buzz would pick up on it.

'*Our song*? Are you serious? Jared, what's happening here? You have a responsibility to Gear. They're putting everything into this tour. Millions of dollars.'

'I know that,' he snapped. 'What you tryin' to say?'

'I'm saying I think you're letting your pants rule your head.'

He tightened his hold on the bottle then. 'You're talkin' bullshit, Buzz.'

'Am I? I don't know what it is about this girl but since she's come back onto the scene you've lost...'

'Lost what? Tell me, what have I lost? Because the last time I looked my album was back up in the top ten.'

Buzz shook his head and refastened his jacket. 'For whatever reason, Honor Blackwood is a distraction. And she's a distraction we can do without if we want this tour to go off the way Gear wants it to go off.'

'You don't know what you're talkin' about.' The words came out bitter and rough.

'I've seen it happen time and time again. Girl comes along, boy falls...'

'Stop right there. Do not say another word.' Jared pointed a finger threatening, accusing. 'How old d'you think I am, Buzz? This ain't junior high. You've booked Raintown, I know that. They're gonna be great, I know that too. Just get off my back about Honor, OK? Leave it alone.'

He slammed his beer bottle to the bar and whisked passed his advisor, heading for the door of the function room.

'Honor, there you are. How are you darlin'?'

Larry had found her and Mia behind the large urn of orchids at the end of the buffet table. Mia had piled up a plate of food, all expensive bites of prawn and triangle-shaped avocado pieces. She'd eaten one and hidden the rest behind the flowers. Larry put his arms around her, drawing her into his cream suit, one that wouldn't have looked out of place on Vince Gill in the early Eighties.

'Hey, Larry,' Mia greeted, swallowing down some more champagne.

'Mia,' he acknowledged. He turned to Honor. 'So, it was great tonight!'

His voice had gone high at the end of the sentence and she knew he was testing the water. He was seeing how much of a conversation they could have before she mentioned Dan Steele or he mentioned her performance with Jared Marshall.

'Yes, it went great.' She nodded her head up and down, her eyes matching his. It was just a case of who would crack first.

'Cut the niceties. Did you know Micro was signing Dan Steele?'

Mia blurted, tilting her head and fixing Larry with a death stare.

Honor dropped her eyes then, looked into the glass of water she was holding. She still felt sick about the 'Dan Steele Situation' as Mia had been calling it for the past half hour. She'd filled Mia in on their history on the ride to the Sheraton and although she'd started off being a little put out, this wasn't something she knew already. She'd then quickly changed tack, calling Dan Steele every dirty name Honor knew and some she didn't.

Larry obviously knew the history but didn't Micro remember? Had the name change fooled them? Or was it that they just didn't care? Should they care? They wanted talent. If Dan was as talented as everyone seemed to be saying he was, then that would matter more to Micro than an old, broken relationship.

'Honey, believe me, I had no idea. Not one clue. I found out the exact same minute you did. When he was on that stage tonight.'

She knew he was telling the truth. He'd never lied to her before. She trusted him.

'It sucks though, right? Taking Honor back and then signing the ass that dumped her when she was at her lowest point,' Mia jumped in.

Honor lifted her head from her glass and there he was, just a few feet away. Dan Steele chatting animatedly with Radley Stokes. Everything was so perfect in his world. Back in Nashville, a record deal, people fawning all over him, opening the Marlon Festival... no scar on his still-handsome face. A wave of envy washed up from inside. He'd had it so easy and now, just when she was ready to return, he was spoiling it. Right on cue he laughed. That laugh. Something she'd once found cute now raised her hackles. She took a swig of water.

'Hey there! It's Jed Marshall isn't it?'

The tall, slim blonde wearing a figure-molding black mini-dress clutched at his arm. It was a mistake slipping in here. It was crammed full of all the types of people he loathed being with. This was a show. Music industry moguls, press, promoters, Nashville's councilors with their political agendas. He should have made for the outside and the nearest bottle shop instead of busting into the party.

'That's right,' he replied, taking her hand and lifting it off the sleeve of his leather jacket.

She didn't miss a beat. She took the beer bottle out of his hand and put it to her lips. Inhaling the drink, her mouth fixed around the neck of the bottle, she sucked hard. The show of lip dexterity was for him but tonight he didn't want it.

'I saw you at Cody's,' she continued, passing back the drink.

'Yeah?' he smiled. 'Like what you heard?'

'I like what I see,' she responded.

She was so transparent he couldn't help but let out a laugh. He put the beer bottle on the table and took her all in. From her gold strappy high-heels, up the bronzed legs to the hem of the micro-dress and upwards, encountering a large flash of cleavage, her platinum hair sat on bare tan shoulders and that red-lipped smile. Just a few short weeks ago he would have taken the compliment and whisked her off to a hotel. But something had changed, whether he liked it or not.

'What's so funny, cowboy?'

'Nothin'. Nothin' at all, ma'am,' he responded.

'So what's say you and me get out of here? Somewhere a little more... private.' She put a hand on the peak of his cap and made to remove it. It was like he'd been stung. He grabbed at the hat, pulling it firmly down into place, trying to keep his cool.

'I'm sorry. As much as I'd love to, I really can't.' His voice came out a lot calmer than he felt. 'There's someone I gotta see.'

Chapter Eighteen

Honor stifled a yawn. The whole day had worn her down. She was so tired.

'Honor, Honor come over here. The photographer wants to do a quick shoot with you and Dan.'

Radley Stokes' voice cut through the party atmosphere like a loud hailer in church. The words sliced into her and she gripped her water glass and made no acknowledgement. Perhaps if she made out she hadn't heard he'd simply go away or she could quickly sidle out of here. She should have expected it. The scarred singer and the new voice. It was publicity gold.

'Honor!' Radley called again.

Her eyes caught movement in her peripheral vision. Jeans, a chain hanging from the belt loop, a black leather jacket over a gray Lynyrd Skynyrd t-shirt. His leather biker boots trod the plush carpet. Jared Marshall was heading towards her.

Her heart upped its pace as she watched him draw closer. He was here, at the party and suddenly she was a ball of nervous, excited energy.

'Doll, the record company dude is calling for you,' Mia informed, nudging her elbow.

She heard but she didn't move or speak. She was too busy staring at Jared, mentally trying to talk her cheeks out of burning up.

'Holy Moly, it's the freaking knight in leather armor,' Mia stated, her head turning in Jared's direction.

As each step brought him nearer, Honor experienced something inside of her changing, spiraling, altering shape and motion. It was passion. It was heat. It had been over a year since she'd dated and ten since she'd felt anything close to this. Close, but nothing like it. He was raw. He was deep. He was dangerous. But underneath the harsh exterior she had seen something else. Someone loyal, someone soft and true. His appearance might make everyone, including her, a little weak but it wasn't his looks that made her heart sing.

'Hey,' he greeted, reaching her.

'Hi,' she replied. Her hand went immediately to her hair.

'Ho hey,' Mia added. 'I'll just go find that cute waiter and get me a refill.' He saw Mia give Honor an elaborate wink.

His heart was thudding so hard he could feel it in his neck as well as his chest. He was acting entirely on impulse and the beer he'd had. He wasn't drunk, far from it; in fact he felt a clarity he'd not had in a long time.

'I'm not here to apologize,' he stated, his eyes locking on hers.

'Apologize?' She looked confused. He'd convinced himself, despite the fact she'd joined in with the performance, that she'd be angry he'd invaded the stage and forced her into an uncomfortable situation.

'For droppin' in on ya. For *Trapped by Love*,' he elaborated.

She smiled, shook her dark curls. 'I'm not angry. I know why you did it.'

He watched her gaze shift to Radley Stokes and Dan Steele, who were setting up an impromptu photo shoot just yards away. Tables were being moved, urns of flowers turned and replaced at a slightly different angle.

'It was either steal the limelight back for you or punch him again,' Jared said, forming a smile on his lips.

She returned the smile then spoke. 'Take me somewhere.'

The intensity of her expression had his blood pumping. She was nothing like the woman in the barely-there dress who'd just propositioned him. There was no desperation, no full-on flirtation, nothing obvious at all. But right now, he was more turned-on than he'd ever been, just talking to her, just being near to her.

'Where d'you wanna go?' he asked.

'Anywhere,' she whispered.

His breathing quickened as they looked at each other, unmoving, the rest of the room and its occupants fading away.

'Honor! Could you come and join us over here?' Radley Stokes' voice broke the spell.

'Come on,' Jared said, holding his hand out to her.

She looked at his hand, the large metal rings on almost every finger and remembered how it had felt in hers on stage at Cody's. She didn't hesitate, despite the press presence, taking his hand in hers and letting the warmth enclose around her fingers.

He quickly led her away from Radley and Dan. Stationed just outside the exit was a Yallwire reporter with a camera crew. Jared hesitated and Honor felt his grip on her hand tighten protectively. He headed off to the left, pulling her with him. He came to a stop opposite the fire-exit doors. He turned, looking at her.

'You ready?'

She nodded. Jared pushed down hard on the metal bars. Straight away an ear-splitting, high-pitched alarm went off in the function room.

'Run!' he yelled, breaking into a sprint.

Honor screamed as she was jolted forward with the speed of his acceleration.

'Jared! Stop!' She tried to keep up, her fingers losing their grip on his.

He powered on up the street, passing people, lampposts, until he suddenly broke off and hung a left. He continued on up an alleyway. Honor skidded on her boots, the tarmac wet from the afternoon's shower. Rain water splattered her jeans.

He stopped and brought her to an abrupt halt against the damp wall of a grimy-looking building. She was perspiring and her heart was racing as she tried to catch her breath.

'Do you think... do you think security will follow us?' she asked him, putting a hand to her chest.

'No,' he said, laughing. 'Just might be pissed if they can't stop that alarm.' He took a deep breath, his eyes alight, the sound of his laughter making all Honor's senses react. She put pressure on his hand with hers, squeezing his fingers, wanting to let him know they were still connected.

She looked at him, longing for him to know how he made her feel. Wanting him to know that no matter what was going on in their lives; she seemed to need him in hers. It wasn't something she could explain but, right now, she didn't want to, didn't need to.

His face, coated in that thin layer of brown stubble that so suited him, moved nearer to her, until she could feel the heat of his breath. She didn't want this to be a repeat of their moment in his home studio. This time she wanted there to be no question, no doubt, no chance of misunderstanding.

'Honor.' The way he rolled her name around his tongue, coating it with that strong Southern accent made her skin prickle with anticipation.

'I want you to put your hands on me.'

She knew that's what she had to say to make this happen. Somewhere, behind this redneck boy was an old-fashioned guy who wouldn't act inappropriately when it came to matters of the heart.

He closed his eyes the second the words were out of her mouth. She knew. She got him. Just like that. His values, the way he lived, the person he wanted to be. Was he ready for this? There was no doubt if he let go now, with Honor, it wouldn't just be a thing.

It would be everything.

'Jared... I want you to put your hands on me,' she repeated. There was an edge of determination to her voice. Her hair had fallen over her face and she was looking at him, her mouth slightly open, her breathing fast.

In one quick move he turned his cap back to front, then placed his palms on the wall either side of her.

She took in a sharp breath as the edges of his leather jacket touched her body through the thin material of her blouse. She gazed up at him, his gray eyes, no longer shrouded by the cap, were wide and full of heat. She shivered, the moisture of the wall seeping through her clothes. She needed to feel his hands on her skin.

He raised a hand and she closed her eyes on instinct. She waited, expected to feel his fingers in her hair. When he touched her she snapped her eyes open and let out a gasp. His index finger was tracing a slow, tender path from the side of her face and along her scar. No one had touched her scar before except her surgeon. No one had wanted to and why should they? It was horrible. It was ugly. It was a disfigurement.

As if reading her mind, he spoke. 'You're beautiful, Honor.'

Her whole body melted at that moment and she took hold of his jacket with one hand and forcefully tugged him to her. His body fell against hers and she wound her hands around his neck as his hands lowered onto her shoulders, caressing the skin with a heated touch.

She put her hands to his face and held it close to hers, searching with her eyes, looking for the desire she was feeling mirrored in him. She leaned forward, placing a chaste kiss on his lips. It was a start, a test of the waters. His lips were warm, moist, full and smooth, with that stubble over his top lip to roughen things up a little.

She waited, paused, wetting her lips with her tongue, her stomach convulsing and adrenaline pulsing through her veins.

And then he moved. He put one hand in her hair and drew her face towards him. Their mouths met and the longing she felt for him multiplied on contact. It wasn't anything like she had expected. It was so much more. His free hand found hers and lifted it high, planting her knuckles against the wall. His tongue collided with hers but it wasn't rough or frenzied, it was sensual, erotic. It was a kiss like no other and she didn't want it to end.

He pulled away, parting their lips until she reached for him again, pulling him back, moving her mouth back onto his. He lifted her up the wall and she pressed into him, shifting her weight and moving her legs up with the momentum, wrapping them around his body. She drew him closer and could feel how turned-on he was. She took his crucifix necklace in her hand and toyed with the chain.

She smelt like summer air after a fresh rainfall, tasted like the purest water with a dash of a sweet something he couldn't even begin to describe. That's what Honor Blackwood was to him. Indescribable. Her fingers were working their way down his t-shirt and with every centimeter she covered he got another bolt of arousal. This girl was special. She could break his heart and he could hurt her, but right now they needed each other.

'Honor,' he started as her fingers slid up under the fabric and began tracing a pattern upwards and over his abs.

She ignored him, caught his mouth up in another kiss, teasing his tongue with hers. This time she moved her hands downwards, settling on his studded leather belt. As soon as her fingers found the buckle they both stopped. She withdrew her hand, their mouths unlinked. His rapid breath visible in the air he looked at her. Her eyes were glistening, her skin ruddy, her lips swollen and plump. He'd done that to her. There was that shot of lust again. He swallowed, bringing a hand up to her hair and she nestled her head against his hand. The damp darkness of the alleyway suddenly seemed to matter and he took a step back, catching her hand in his.

She straightened her blouse with her free hand, not taking her eyes from him. She didn't know what happened next. She knew what she wanted to happen but was she really ready for that? The belt buckle had a lot to answer for. As soon as her fingers found it, it was like someone had rung the bell for the end of a boxing round.

'Listen, I don't go much on party food and I haven't really eaten so d'you wanna go get something?' he suggested.

Her stomach straightaway reminded her of how little she'd consumed and she found herself nodding.

'I know a great place just down the block from the Sheraton. It's got a jukebox full of Vince Gill.'

Chapter Nineteen

Betty's Diner was like a step back in time. Booths with tables sporting Formica tops, plastic ketchup and mustard bottles, black and white tiles on the floor and a Wurlitzer jukebox playing George Strait and Alan Jackson.

She'd spent the last hour smiling so much her mouth hurt. And her stomach had some kind of vendetta going on too. It was aching from laughing at Jared's jokes and from consuming the loaded burger he'd ordered for her.

'Honor, you're not gonna be wastin' that food are ya?' he remarked, eyeing up her plate.

'Did you see the size of the darn thing? Is that the sort of portion they have in the Deep South, or wherever it is you're from?'

'Alabama,' he informed. 'I'm from Wetumpka, Alabama.'

She smiled. 'You're so proud of that aren't you?'

'Yes, ma'am.' He smiled back.

'It's nice. I wish I had that. Roots. A family, a place I'm attached to, people I'm tied to.'

He reached across the table and took her hand in his.

'I'll take you there. If you want to. But I can't promise you won't be beggin' to come back after an hour with my mom, my little sister and brother. Not to mention my cousins and my boys from the farm.'

'You're making it sound like *The Waltons*.'
'You could be Mary-Ellen.'
'Stop it!'
He smothered another laugh as he picked up his coffee cup. He looked at her over the rim as he drank.
'Jared, I don't know...' she started.
'Don't say anything.' He paused, his eyes on her. 'Because I don't know either.'
She smiled at him. This, despite being unusual, felt like the most natural situation in the world.

He watched her put the straw in her soda to her mouth and suck some up. She was just jaw-dropping beautiful and he couldn't believe she was here with him.
He didn't care what Buzz said. He didn't care what anyone thought. Honor wasn't a distraction, she was an inspiration.
'Whatcha gonna do about Dan Steele?'
He'd tried not to but he couldn't stop his teeth gritting and forming a snarl around the words. His heart was already thudding a rhythm that usually signaled trouble.
He saw her shoulders sag a little and for a second he regretted asking.
'I don't know. I haven't had a chance to process it. I mean in one night so much has happened I...' She pushed her soda cup away.
'But you had no idea, right? And he turned up at your big moment and...'
'I haven't thanked you for rescuing me when I was like a moose caught in the headlights.'
'That wasn't what I was angling for.' He pushed his coffee cup away and sat back against the booth, raising his arms and putting his hands to the back of his head.
'I don't know what to do. Larry touched on it earlier and it hit a nerve. A raw nerve. And it shouldn't be raw. He's in the past, I just...'

'He's a troublemaker,' Jared interrupted gruffly.

'People tell me that about you.' She smiled.

'And they'd be right. But not like him,' he stated.

'I know and him signing with Micro... I don't think for a minute it's about me. He just saw an opportunity and he took it. The same with them. He's a popular new face, so Mia says. It's just circumstance.'

'It's bullshit.'

'Yeah, that too,' she responded, sighing.

'I still want you on my tour.'

He didn't know why he'd said that. He hadn't been thinking about it until the words had come out of his mouth. He had Raintown but why should that matter? Who said you could only have one supporting artist? His tour was four months long and the thought of spending all that time away from Nashville; away from Honor... he didn't like it.

'You never give up, do you?' She laughed a little and prodded her burger with the fork.

'I said I wouldn't.'

'You also said no pressure.'

'Did I? Did I really say that?' He shook his head.

'I'll think about it. I need to talk to Larry. I need to sort out how I feel about the 'Dan Steele situation'. Shit, that's going to have its own hashtag soon.'

'Not before Honor and Jed are trendin'... not that I really know what trendin' is. Apparently it's a good thing.'

She laughed again and settled her eyes on him. When she smiled her eyes brightened and the scar on her face tightened until it all but disappeared. How had this night turned out like this? So right. So perfect. He reached his hands out across the table and turned the palms up, open. She placed her hands on his and he closed them up around hers.

'I want you to know... I've had the best night,' he stated.

'Me too.'

'So... are you comin' on tour with me?'
'Jared!'
'Can't blame a guy for tryin''

Chapter Twenty

When she'd woken up an hour ago she'd had a warm feeling the second she remembered what had happened between her and Jared. Despite having broken back into the music circuit, the thrill of the performance was very much settled down in second place. However, that cozy glow had cooled the second she'd read the text from Larry. Radley wanted a meeting that afternoon at the record company offices. The message was short and to the point. There was no 'darlin'' or smiley face, just the words. It didn't sound like good news.

The doorbell rang and she put her phone down. She wasn't dressed. She tied the knot on her dressing gown a little tighter and smoothed a hand down her hair. If it was Jared she was screwed in the beauty stakes.

Checking the spy-hole she saw it was a delivery-man and in his arms was a bouquet of flowers. Her heart soared and she unchained the door to greet him. This was the romance she'd been missing.

'Miss Blackwood?' he queried.

'Yes.'

'These are for you. Just sign here,' the delivery guy said, passing the bouquet to her then holding out his pen and clipboard.

She signed, then took a long sniff of the scented blooms. The heady smell of tulips, orchids and irises filled her nostrils.

'Thank you, ma'am. Have a nice day.'

She closed the door and took the flowers into the kitchen, where she laid them on the work surface. She searched for the card. They had to be from Jared. She'd had flowers from Micro before and they usually arrived needing two people to deliver them and a third person to erect the plinth and arrange them. This bouquet wasn't their style.

She pulled out the card and read the words.

You looked beautiful out there last night

Her eyebrows creased into a frown. Jared wouldn't have written that. They'd had dinner together after the show, discussed the performance. The words weren't right. 'Beautiful' was intimate though, hinted at an attraction. There was only one person they could be from.

Now she was fired up.

'Now, ladies and gentlemen, here in the studio with me today is none other than country bad boy, singer Jed Marshall.'

'Hey, Patrick, thank y'all for havin' me.' Jared leaned into the microphone and touched his cap in acknowledgement.

'You're very welcome. As a precaution we've hidden all the sharp implements including the staple guns, so we're all good.'

'Whoa there, that's a low shot but I'll give it to you just this once, man.'

He felt calm, a lot calmer than he usually did when he was being interviewed. He knew that was down to last night and more specifically to Honor. Today he was bouncing, high on life, feeling that after such a long time in solitary things were finally fitting into place.

'So, tell me, Jed, I know you're working on new material for an album out in the Fall and you're also about to embark on a countrywide tour. But what I'm sure our listeners want to know is... will *Trapped by Love* be appearing on that new album?'

He knew his face was glowing and he didn't care. He couldn't recall the last time he'd felt this happy.

'Did y'all come down to Cody's yesterday to see Honor Blackwood? Wasn't she amazin'? I mean, just how good is it to have her back?'

'She's got an incredible voice. And the two of you seem to gel so well together. Is this the start of something we all should know about?'

He looked up to the Perspex screen, saw Buzz's hand slicing across this neck like he was about to have a heart attack. His afro hair was bouncing around like Don King's and his eyes were bulging out of his forehead.

'You know what, Patrick? We're just good friends. We've been spendin' some time together, writin' a little and I'm hopin' to persuade her to come along on the Sweet Home Alabama tour with me.' He gave Buzz a wave that sent him tapping furiously of his iPad.

'You heard it here first everybody. Honor Blackwood might just be on the Jed Marshall tour this year.'

'I'm going to have to write you a script. You knew what you had to talk about today. The Marlon Festival, your collaboration with Vince Gill on the commercial and your deal with Pure Nectar!' Buzz screamed.

'I talked about all of those,' Jared insisted. He grabbed up a Diet Coke from the table outside the radio station studio and opened the can.

'Not as much as you talked about Honor Blackwood.'

'Come on, man. He asked me about yesterday. What was I supposed to say?' He downed some of the drink.

'You weren't supposed to say she might be joining you on your tour! Your tour is all set!'

'Buzz, you need to calm yourself down. I got this.'

'I don't want you to have it! That's what I'm trying to tell you!'

'Listen, you've been workin' way too hard for me. Why don'tcha have the rest of the day off?' Jared offered.

'What? No. I don't need the day off. I need you to listen to what I say.' Buzz was blazing, he could sense that. The guy was literally a walking advert for a seizure.

'Go home. Take your wife out somewhere. I'll be good. I'll be seen in ten different Nashville hotspots with 20oz bottles of Pure Nectar. I won't hit anyone or get arrested. I swear it.'

Buzz raised an eyebrow in suspicion.

'Hell, man. What else can I promise? D'you need me electronically tagged?'

'Now I know why I had to come round the back. What's going on?'

Mia had met her at the rear entrance to Instrumadness. The parking lot out front was full to bursting with customers' cars and trucks of press. It seemed the whole town had gone Honor Blackwood crazy.

'Your Micro blog post went live and one of the bullet point slides informed the world where you worked. I don't mind, although some warning might have been nice. I gave Stuart and Rocky a call and they've been helping me, but the press seem to kind of be waiting for you to turn up. Is there some publicity meet I should know about?'

Mia ushered her into the small kitchenette and flicked the switch on the kettle.

'No. I'm really sorry, Mia. I had no idea.' She sat on one of the two wobbly stools.

'I guessed as much. So, are you here to tell me everything about last night?' Mia poked her arm with her finger.

Immediately Honor blushed and mentally recalled the kiss. 'I don't know what you mean.'

'Damn it, doll, the way he was looking at you last night I don't believe that for a minute. And you bailed on me!'

Honor let the smile take over her face. She wanted to share this feeling with someone and why shouldn't she? It had been such a long time coming.

'Hell! You hooked up didn't you? You freaking hooked up with Jed freaking Marshall! Oh my Lord!'

'We didn't do what you would have done. It was just a kiss... and dinner at Betty's Diner. Then we shared a cab.'

'And then?' Mia had clutched the edge of her stool with both hands, her knuckles turning white.

'He kissed me again inside the cab outside my place and then he went home.'

'But you're together. Dating.'

'You're making me sound like a freshman. Yes, I guess so, I mean we didn't quantify it but he invited me down to meet his family sometime.'

And that suggestion still made her heart swell with gladness. Just the thought of his normal family sitting around a table to eat, a happy home, laughter and caring, all the things the state should've given her but hadn't. She swallowed back the lump in her throat.

'Jeez, Honor! Dating Jed Marshall! You know he's been a serial bachelor for about a hundred years!'

'He's only twenty-seven.'

'Whatever! You're going to have made the female population of the US weep into their Confederate flags.'

'Don't tell anyone, Mia. If it gets out then...' Honor started.

'I'm gonna have to start placing you two on the same shelf. It'll be great for an offer weekend. Buy her and get him for free.' Mia snorted a laugh and Honor smiled at her before checking her watch.

'Are you meeting him?'

'No, I've got an appointment at Micro. I'd better go.' She stood up.

'Sorting out the "Dan Steele Situation"?'

'Something like that.'

Chapter Twenty One

Micro Records. The iconic building rose up from the street as tall and awe-inspiring as it had been when she'd first stood outside it at eighteen. It had held all her dreams, everything she'd ever wished for back then. But now? She still didn't know what the future held for her yet, but for the first time she was really hopeful for it.

As she crossed the street to the entrance she saw Larry was waiting for her. He was dressed in a dark suit, matching Stetson on his head. He was pacing. Pacing wasn't good.

'Ah, here you are, honey. I dropped by the house but...'

'Did you think I'd forget? I called you. I said I'd be here.' This constant need to babysit her was getting a touch annoying. She wasn't so emotionally fragile she couldn't make it to a meeting alone.

'I know, honey, I just...' Larry started.

'Do you know what this meeting's about? Because if it's strategy I've got a few suggestions and one of them is to start letting me know when you're going to try and make a fool out of me,' Honor said, pushing the glass door open and striding ahead.

'Honor, I think...'

'Have you told them? Did you speak to Radley last night? Do they now know about Dan Steele? The history we have...' She stopped. 'The history we *had*.'

She smiled at the receptionist. 'Honor Blackwood to see Radley Stokes.'

'I'm afraid it's business, darlin',' Larry responded.

'What?' She turned on Larry, poised, like a wildcat preparing to pounce. 'What did you say?'

Larry took off his hat, tucking it under his arm. 'You remember how much Micro has supported you over the years? They retained you, kept advertising your albums even though...' He stopped talking.

'Even though?' She was willing him to say the wrong thing. Why was that? Why did she want him to give her reason to be mad?

'I spoke to Radley at the party. I told him the history but...'

'Do you know what this meeting's about?' She put a hand on her hip and stared him down.

'I think you should come on in and hear what Micro has to say.'

'You haven't answered the question.' And that fact had her worried.

'They're ready for you. Conference Room Four,' the receptionist addressed Honor.

'*They*?' Honor narrowed her eyes at Larry. 'Just how many people are in on this meeting?

Larry hadn't answered and they'd spent an awkward elevator ride up to the ninth floor watching every number from the ground up. She was holding the note card from the flowers tight in her hand. If he was here. If he dared to be here she was going to throw it at him and tell him exactly what she thought of him. Wait... she wasn't meant to be thinking about it like that. What had happened to her speech about people just jumping at an opportunity? The flowers. The flowers had happened. They had changed everything. She poked the corner of the cardboard into her thumb until it hurt.

'Listen, honey, my advice would be...' Larry began as the elevator doors opened.

'I don't want to hear it.' She cut him dead as she approached the frosted glass doors to the conference room. It was etched with its number and Micro's logo 'Start small, aim high'. She raised her hand to knock, then thinking better of it she just pushed it open.

'Honor, great to see you! Larry! Come take a seat.' Radley Stokes was out of his high-backed leather chair and beckoning them towards the large table. Honor wasn't looking in his direction. Her attention was focused solely on Dan Steele.

Seated in an identical chair, dressed in a red-and-blue plaid shirt, open at the neck, he looked the epitome of casual. He gave her a smile, all perfect white teeth and clean jaw. Nausea bubbled in her stomach. Just what was going on? She couldn't sit. She hovered, one hand on the back of the chair, the other clenching down on the note card.

'Hey, Honor.' He'd spoken at last. Still smiling, still relaxed.

'*Hey, Honor*? Is that all you've got?' she spat. His mouth dropped then and his eyes told her he was surprised by her retort. Perhaps he thought the flowers would make up for what he did.

'It's great to see you,' he offered.

'You shouldn't have sent me flowers!' She threw the notecard on the table and it slid over and stopped a little way in front of him. 'Radley, what's going on here?'

'Well, if you take a seat I'll take you through the plans we have to promote you both,' Radley said. He pointed a tiny remote control at the flat-screen on the wall.

'Honor, I didn't...' Dan started, the card in his hand.

'Don't speak to me!' She gave him a sideways glance. He looked slightly less calm now.

It was the animated bobble heads on the slideshow that pushed her back up out of the seat thirty minutes later.

'I don't understand this. This whole presentation almost pitches us as a duo. We're not a duo! Is this what the flowers were about? A sweetener? Trying to get me on side after yesterday?' She narrowed her eyes at Dan.

'That isn't our aim. Micro just want to make the most of you both joining and rejoining the label at the same time. It's an ideal opportunity for some joint promotion.'

'What flowers?' Dan remarked.

'Why are *you* here?' Honor turned to Larry next to her. 'Where's *his* advisor?'

Larry shifted in his seat. He'd already unfastened his collar at the beginning of the meeting despite the air conditioning running at full pelt.

'Well, honey, this was something I was going to talk to you about a little later,' he began.

It took only a split second for her to realize what he'd said without actually saying anything much at all.

'No.' She couldn't stop the mix of fear, horror and bewilderment coating her tone.

'Honor, darlin', have a seat. It isn't all it seems. I...' Larry started.

'You lied to me. For how long? How long has this been shaping up?' Her voice was trembling and she hated the fact. 'Was this why you were so keen for me to come back? To help launch *his* career?'

'No, darlin', nothing was discussed until yesterday and nothing's been agreed yet.'

She didn't know what to say. What else was there to say? Her advisor, the guy who'd been there with her from the very beginning was planning to start helping her ex-boyfriend launch his attack on the country music charts. How did he expect her to feel? First Micro had wheeled out Dan into her comeback PA without telling her, and now Larry had turned traitor. She felt like the walls of the boardroom were closing in.

Dan got up out of his seat.

'Honor, I didn't mean for any of this to upset you. I thought we could just put the past behind us and create something new here for the label. I've been reading up on mutual support in entertainment circles and there's a lot to be said for it.'

Put the past behind us. He was talking about it as if it was a bad fashion decision he'd made or a wrong call on a business deal. He'd bailed on her the second he'd seen her scar. He'd been weak and shallow and he'd abandoned her, left her with only Larry. And now he was back to take Larry from her too.

She surveyed them all. Her heart ached, yet it was still pushing the adrenaline anger brought with it through her body at the same time. Why had they done this? Why did they think this was OK?

'This meeting is over.' Her voice was robotic but determined. 'I want to terminate my contract. You can communicate with my lawyer. I don't want to be professionally associated with any of you. Pull the record. Pull it today.'

She'd tried to stop the emotion leaking through into her words but it hadn't worked. By the time she'd spoken the last 'pull' there were tears in her eyes and sentiment in her throat.

'Honor, honey, wait.' Larry scrambled to his feet but she was already marching through the door.

She hadn't texted him. She didn't know if he'd even be home. She just knew she wanted to see him. Someone who understood her. Someone who wouldn't lie to her.

When he pulled open the front door she could have wept with relief.

'Honor,' Jared greeted, a smile immediately forming on his lips. 'I was gonna call you.'

There he was. All six foot of him. Wearing a black vest-top over ripped jeans, bare feet.

'I'm sorry... for turning up unannounced. I just... had to see you,' she blurted out. She was still willing herself not to cry but none of her senses seemed to be listening. During all those years in foster care she'd never let out her emotions, but after the attack everything had snowballed. It still seemed like she was catching up on a whole life's worth of tears.

'Hey, what's going on here? Come on, come here and come on in.'

He put an arm around her and drew her over the threshold, closing the door behind her. Once the outside world was shut away she let the tears fall.

'What is it? What the hell's happened?'

He gathered her into his arms and she clung to his solidity with everything she had. She couldn't answer him yet. She just needed to be held, to know someone was here for her. On her side. Supporting her. How could it be that a guy she'd known just a few weeks was the person she trusted most in her world right now?

'Honor?' He wanted an answer, she knew, but she also knew when she told him he was going to be mad as hell. That's just who he was.

She'd made him go into the den before she opened up. Now that she had he wanted to leave her, head over to Micro Records and destroy Radley Stokes. Dan Steele already had it coming and roll on the next time he saw him.

'Speak to me, Jared. Don't keep it all in. I know how you're feeling.'

She raised her beautiful eyes to him and he felt that kick to his stomach. She knew him. Could read him already. Just like that.

'You want me to tell you I want to rip up that record label guy? Take Dan Steele's head off and make sure your advisor never works again?' He kicked out, barefoot, at the coffee table and it shifted half a meter.

Honor blew out a breath. 'It's done now. It's over.'

'They took you back on. They made you promises. Yesterday they put on that show and then they signed him and did this. That's disrespectful, Honor.' He was gritting his teeth, the rage he felt boiling up as he imagined the scenario.

'I know. But perhaps it was a wake-up call. I mean, who was I trying to kid? The country-music scene doesn't need singers like me anymore. Mia introduced me to Taylor Swift's latest album the other day. I'm nothing like that.'

'Praise be!'

There was no way in this world he was going to let this happen. After everything she'd overcome he was damned if he was going to let the new team at Micro give her another crisis of confidence.

'Listen, today they've lost the best darn vocalist Nashville has ever seen. They're disloyal. They're underhand. Not one of them deserves you.' He sat next to her on the couch, took her hands in his. She was trembling and he just wanted to make the three of them pay for kicking her like this.

'I don't know what to do,' she admitted.

She looked so desperate. Yesterday's high was a distant memory. He wasn't going to let this go.

He released his grip on her hands and reached for her face, cupping her jaw with his fingers. Slowly he brought his mouth to hers, placing feather-light wisps of kisses on her lips. Every time they touched he fell a bit deeper, another piece of his soul loosened a little. This girl was getting inside of him and he was powerless to stop her.

'You are not throwin' away your career because of this. You've fought bigger battles. Where I come from we don't just get even, we get on top – whatever it takes. D'you hear?' He held her shoulders, leveled her eye to eye. She nodded.

'I'll make you a deal. I'll help you get a new label if you help me drink half the Pure Nectar in my refrigerator.'

Honor spluttered a laugh at the suggestion.

'Last count there was sixty-four bottles after I sent over three hundred to the homeless shelter. I could really use some assistance.' He grinned, nudging her arm.

'Deal,' she responded.

'Alright. Then I need to go make a couple of calls.'

He'd only been gone a half hour but when he returned to the den Honor was asleep. As he looked down on her, there was that tightening of the chest again and that swell in his gut that washed all over him.

He'd do anything for her. Absolutely anything. That's why he'd come clean on the phone to Buzz about their relationship. He had a plan to fix this. He wanted to make things right for her. She deserved a break.

He picked up the plaid rug from the back of his La-Z-Boy recliner and carefully draped it over her. He touched her cheek, then quietly backed away, settling down into his chair.

Chapter Twenty Two

Her nose wrinkled to the smell of cooking. What was being made she couldn't identify except to the point that it was something oily. As her other senses came to life she caught the sound of violent sizzling. She opened her eyes and with one hand pushed the rug away from her face. Her head was muzzy. She was on a couch. Jared's couch. It was rough on her skin and it smelt funny. He'd said something about it belonging to his grandmother. She sat up.

Looking at her watch she saw it was morning. Her eyes were sore and her mouth was dry. She didn't remember falling asleep... but she did remember what happened at the offices of Micro Records.

She stood up and stretched her arms above her head as a string of curse words filtered in through the door to the kitchen. She headed that way.

'Darn eggs! You don't come from an Alabama chicken that's for sure!'

Her breath caught in her throat as she entered the room. Jared had his back to her as he stood doing something with a frying pan over the hob, wearing nothing but jeans and his baseball cap. She kept silent, watched the contours of his back, the muscles twisting and shifting as he worked the food around. He had a tattoo at the small of his back, a bird. As he moved around the range she caught brief glimpses of his other markings. The tattoos on his obliques, the scar down his abdomen. She felt her insides take a turn, lust sweep up out of nowhere. What this guy did to her was unexplainable.

He noticed her. 'Hey, good mornin'. I'm having a tussle here with the breakfast.' He lifted up the plastic spatula he was using as if in explanation.

'You have a bird on your back,' Honor said, closing the distance between them.

'Have you been checking out my pecker?' He turned full frontal then and leaned against the range, watching her.

'What?' Her cheeks were already heating up just from looking at that washboard stomach, the tight muscular shoulders and upper arms.

'The yellowhammer. It's a woodpecker. National bird of Alabama. What did you think I meant?' His eyes were sparkling with devilment and she loved that. She adored the way he was so comfortable in his own skin.

She touched his chest then and snaked a finger down the scar on his midriff, making her way south.

'You wouldn't be tryin' to make sure I burned breakfast would you? Because I'm no chef. I do eggs and barbecue and that's about all. You might spoil the only meal I'm capable of makin' for ya.'

He was talking because he was scared. When she touched him he felt it more than skin deep. He was already hard and if she got any closer she would know that too. He couldn't go there, he wasn't ready. That sounded crazy but it was true. He couldn't remember how many girls he'd slept with in the last year – since his career skyrocketed – but he hadn't felt anything. Mild sexual satisfaction, a quick high and then nothing but emptiness. But he hadn't wanted to feel. He didn't deserve to. Was that still true?

He swallowed. Her hand was pulling at the studded belt, slipping it from the buckle. He closed his eyes.

His skin felt slightly damp, like he'd showered. Had she slept through that? The thought of him underneath hot running water had her insides folding. It was all imagination; after all, she'd not seen him naked. She wanted to. It was like he'd opened up a side to her she didn't recognize, let alone know. She pulled the belt undone and felt for the first metal button at his fly. She unfastened it and that's when his mouth crashed against hers. Hot breath, the stubble on his face, his firm insistent lips, the moistness of his tongue dancing with hers. She was getting a head rush with the excitement and adrenaline. She pulled at the second button, then the third. Her hand parted the denim and he was right there. No underwear.

A flood of heat soared through her and then he grabbed her hand and took it upwards and away, placing it on his chest as he kissed her again.

She broke away, out of breath and a little confused. She thought they'd cleared things up. She thought after the other night they both knew what they wanted. Was this another rejection? The way he looked at her, the way his body was reacting to her told her otherwise.

Her eyes were damp before she could check herself. She looked away, focused on the wooden tea, coffee and sugar canisters with moose antlers on each lid.

'I've not had...' He paused. 'Someone like you in my life before.'

The way the words came out sounded genuine and heartfelt. But what did it mean?

'I just... want to get things right. *Do* things right.'

He drew her head back, making her look at him. She blinked, tried to understand exactly what he was saying, see the translation behind his expression.

He let out a guttural sigh. 'Truth? I want to get outta these jeans, rip your clothes off and take you right there, right on my kitchen table.'

Her eyes moved to the large, rustic chunk of wood that stood a little way away from them. It looked hand-carved and it wasn't varnished. There would be splinters for sure. That thought gave her that tingling feeling again, shooting up from her soul.

He let out another noise of frustration and buried his head into her shoulder.

'What is it?' she asked, her hands clasping him to her.

'You're so straight down the line and I've made so many mistakes,' he stated. He lifted his head then, his gray eyes heavy with sentiment.

'So you won't let me touch you because you think I'm too much of a good girl?' The look she gave him was meant to challenge.

'No. It's not like that.'

'Then?' She took her hand out of his and felt for his fly, tugging at the final button.

'God, Honor, you're killin' me here.'

His voice was rough with lust as she pulled at the denim.

'I can't... we can't.' His tone was lace with determination but he hadn't backed away.

A phone rang and broke the moment. He started back, knocking the pan of eggs as he shifted away from her.

'Shit! I'm sorry... I have to get that.'

He straightened himself out and headed to the hall.

'I apologize for the eggs.' They were the first words he'd spoken since he'd come back to the kitchen. Now he was eating with abandon as if nothing had passed between them.

The eggs were charred dark brown on the edges and the yolks were hard. Only the waffles were saving the meal. Truth was he didn't know what was going to save the morning. A part of him was glad Buzz's call had interrupted them. A bigger part of him recalled every sensation she'd pulled out of him.

She shrugged in response. That wasn't a good sign. If he kept putting up the barricades she was going to start losing interest. That was the very last thing he wanted. But what could he say to make her realize it was all because of how much he felt for her? He looked up and saw she'd hidden her face in her coffee cup.

'So, that was Buzz on the phone, my go-to guy. I told him about us last night and...' he started.

'You told someone about us!'

She sounded horrified. Her eyes were out of the cup now and they were somewhere between wild and furious, her mouth open.

'Is it a secret?' he queried. 'Do you not want to...'

'I don't know, Jared. I still don't even know what's really going on.'

Her body language told him everything. He watched her put her coffee cup down.

'I mean one minute your body's telling me one thing and the next you're pushing me away.'

She knew that had hurt him. She saw his eyes cloud over.

He nodded then. A slow, resigned nod that made her stomach turn over.

'Jared.' She felt bad now. Like a spoilt child who wasn't getting the candy she screamed for.

'No, you're right. I shouldn't have taken the liberty.' He stood up, crossing the room. He dropped his plate into the sink and it made a loud clatter against the metal. He stood still then, with his back to her, hands rested either side of the draining board. She could tell he was both mad and sad.

She was being ridiculous and childish. She got up and went to him quickly. She enveloped him, putting her arms around his torso and laying her head against his bare back.

'I'm sorry. I'm so sorry. I just... wanted you so much. It was selfish and...' she tumbled out the words.

He didn't reply but she could feel the motion of his breath as she held him. She just wanted to be close to him. Finally she felt his shoulders rise as he spoke.

'When I touch you – if I get the chance to really touch you – I don't want it to be like anything either of us has had before.'

She lifted her head to pay proper attention.

'I want you to be my girl, Honor. I know you don't know what that means to me but let me tell you.' He paused, took another breath. 'I haven't had a girl in years. Because, the last time, the last girl I really cared about... I needed her to believe in me and she couldn't. I needed her trust and her faith and she just broke my heart.'

'Jared.' She pulled at his hips, encouraging him to turn around and face her. She looked up at him; saw the pain in his eyes. She could tell how hard that had been for him to admit.

'Now I don't want you thinkin' I've been livin' like some sort of monk all this time because that couldn't be further from the truth.' He managed a smile, touching her cheek with his fingers. 'But there's been no one special. No one like you.' He toyed with a curl of her hair. 'What can I say? I'm an old-fashioned Alabama boy at heart.'

She looped her arms around his neck and drew him towards her. She wanted him to know it was OK. She wanted to show him how much sharing that with her had meant.

His heart lightened a little as their mouths met and her body formed against his. He'd told her. He'd shared some of his past with her. It was a start and one he wanted to hold on to.

Chapter Twenty Three

'Since when have I been some sort of go-between for other artists?'

'Buzz, come on, man. This is my girl we're talkin' about.'

'Sshh! Last week I saw that reporter from Star Life magazine in here. It wouldn't surprise me if she's put bugs on the ketchup bottles.' Buzz picked one up and turned it upside down.

'I'm just askin' if you'll talk to Gear. She's a great singer, I want her on the tour and she's done with Micro. It all makes sense,' Jared insisted.

'To you maybe. It makes no sense to me and I can almost guarantee Gear will feel the same.' Buzz folded his arms across his chest.

'Why?'

'Why? Because you're their bestselling artist for two reasons. You're a great musician *and* everybody loves you. The guys want to mate you; the women want to mate *with* you. A girlfriend on the scene now, right before your tour, that's not going to gel well.'

'I want you to ask them. If they don't sign her up someone else will. At the end of the day it's business.' Jared took a sip of his coffee. He was serious about this. Honor needed this. Micro had messed her around and stitched her up. That didn't sit well with him.

'At the end of the day it's career suicide. Why would you want to do this? Why would you want to do this *now* when you have the biggest tour of your career coming up? When you've been nominated for Best Male Vocalist at the Marlon Awards.'

'What?' Jared dropped his coffee cup. 'What did you say?'

His head was thumping. Had he heard right?

Buzz's mouth opened in a broad, white-toothed smile. 'I didn't want to tell you on the phone. This is huge, Jared.'

It *was* huge. Although the CMA's were the biggest and most well-known country-music awards, the Marlon Awards were just as prestigious. Last year Vince Gill had been given his place on the Outstanding Contribution Roll.

The awards night took place on the final night of the four-day Marlon Festival, at the former Grand Ole Opry House, now the Ryman Auditorium. That place had a magic about it. Despite his music being as non-traditional country as you could get, that venue did something to him.

'Jeez! I can't believe it. Man, that's the best news.'

'I know. And it needs to be handled carefully.'

Buzz's tone took him back down to earth with a bump.

'Jared, you don't need any distractions from this opportunity. You need to keep your eye firmly on the prize here.'

He could feel the hairs on the back of his neck rising up. He knew exactly what Buzz was trying to say and he didn't like it one bit. This situation had never arisen before because there had never been anyone in his life like this before. He wasn't about to sacrifice his new relationship with Honor just because Buzz thought it might affect his chances of winning an award.

'I'm not gonna stop seein' her, Buzz.'

Buzz took in air through his teeth and shook his head.

'How long have you known me? I've never had anyone before. I like her, Buzz, I really like her and if it loses me a few crazy-ass female fans as a result then we're just gonna have to deal with that.'

Buzz didn't respond. He was tapping his rubber-tipped pen on the screen on his iPad.

'I want her with Gear. Either you call them and set something up or I will.'

'Do you want her with Gear? Or do you just want her away from Dan Steele?'

That comment had him balling his hands into fists and sitting back against the booth. He took a breath then adjusted his cap. His voice was slow and deliberate.

'This has nothin' to do with him.'

It was true, in a way. He couldn't say he was disappointed Honor wouldn't be working out of the same record company as the guy, but unless he stepped out of line again he wouldn't waste his energy on him. This was all about getting Honor to a better place. Someplace that deserved her.

'Does she know about this? Has she asked for your help?' Buzz inquired.

'Hell no! If she knew she'd probably kill me. She's proud, Buzz, she wants to do everything on her own but...' Jared started.

'You want to look out for her.'

'Sshh! If that reporter's bugged the ketchup bottles my reputation's gonna be in shreds.'

She rolled the owl around in her palm. It was still there on the shelf in Target. The one with the slightly wonky eye. The encrusted shells rubbed against her hand and she took a breath, letting the piped instrumental music roll over her. Why was the local discount store the one place she felt at peace? She did need a little calm after the grocery section, though. She'd invited Jared over for dinner and she really couldn't remember the last time she'd cooked for anyone. Whenever Mia came over she ordered in pizza or Hot Mo's Chicken. Last time they'd both gotten drunk and Mia had entertained herself clapping at all her appliances and doing poor Reba McEntire impersonations, even though she knew Honor's house was a country-free zone. Now she had extended the invitation to Jared she didn't know what the hell to cook. She'd spent ten minutes deciding between a rutabaga and a sweet potato, not really knowing what to do with either of them.

'Hey, doll, will you look at this?' Mia held up a turquoise crop top with the words 'Ride 'em Cowgirl' emblazoned across the front in sequins.

Mia had called her for a rundown of the latest events and when Honor had told her about Micro she'd insisted they met over her lunch hour.

'That will only attract attention,' Honor told her, putting the owl back on the shelf.

'That's what I'm counting on. I have a date tonight.' She draped the top over her forearm.

'Please tell me it isn't with one of those creepy guys we met in One-Eyed Walt's.'

'It's not one of those guys we met in Walt's. It's a guy I met at Cody's after your performance the other day.'

Honor brought the cart to a halt beside her friend. 'Well, don't keep me in suspense, who is it? Is it Vince Gill? I heard a rumor he was there you know.'

'It's not Vince Gill. His name's Byron and he is hot!'

'Oh my God, Mia, Byron Starks? I know him. He's a guitarist. He's a friend of Jared's. He was there when it all went south at Walt's with... you know, the "Dan Steele Situation."' Her voice tapered off towards the end of the sentence. The less she thought about him the better. She'd had several messages from Larry since she'd walked out of the meeting and one from Radley Stokes. She hadn't even listened to them once she knew who was calling. Nothing either of them could say would make her change her mind about quitting. She just didn't know what step to take next.

'I know! Freaking weird, right? But we got talking before we got whisked off to the after-party – you know, the one you left me at – and we're meeting for beer and a bucket tonight,' Mia exclaimed excitedly.

'Beer and a bucket? Romance is not dead in Nashville.' Honor laughed and shook her head.

'Well he suggested that freaking chic place that just opened up. You know the one where you have to dress in silk and pay with a platinum card. I don't have silk, apart from panties, and how can you get drunk when one glass of wine will probably set you back the price of a Les Paul?'

'Oh, Mia,' Honor said, still laughing.

'I'm not a three sets of silverware girl. If he's gonna take me out he needs to know what he's letting himself in for from the get-go,' Mia said with a nod.

'Honesty. I like it. And so will he,' Honor answered, smiling at her friend.

'And how about you? I don't even know what that vegetable in the cart is. Is that a vegetable? Why are you buying stuff you don't recognize to feed a guy who's the face of Alabama Hot Sauce and Old Skool Burgers?'

'He's the what?' She knew about Pure Nectar but how many endorsements did Jared have?

'I can't believe you're dating country hot property and you haven't even Googled him yet?' Mia tutted. 'Before you serve him up something a chicken would turn its beak up at, look him up on Wikipedia.'

Honor looked into the cart. Why had she put in turkey mince? Or any of the other food. She was making dinner for someone she'd tried to disrobe that morning and she hardly knew anything about him. Mia was right. The only way to learn enough in time to get this right was to do an internet search.

'You know more about him than I do, don't you?' Honor remarked, moving forward with the cart.

'Definitely. Especially if you tell me what he's like in bed,' Mia said with a snort of laughter.

'So what did you go for in the end? Ooo ribs, that's a good call. Alabama Hot Sauce, I'm liking your style. Corn dogs. Well

I know you have a thing about them. Coors, the choice of beer is approved,' Mia said as Honor started to pack things into bags.

'Good. If he doesn't show up I'll give you a call and drag you away from Byron and your bucket of chicken.'

'Don't you dare. He's the first really hot guy I've dated for at least three months. Since the gorgeous Leroy left me for Mexico.'

'His loss,' Honor replied, placing the beer down into the bag.

'Excuse me, Miss Blackwood. A customer asked me to give this to you.' A sales assistant had approached them and was holding out the ceramic owl with the wonky eye to her.

'What in the hell is that?' Mia said, looking at the ornament in disgust.

'What customer? Who?' Honor asked, looking over the assistant's shoulder at the shop floor in the hope of seeing something.

'A gentleman, ma'am. It's all paid for. He just asked me to come give it to you,' she responded.

'Now that's freaking weird,' Mia stated.

This was Dan Steele. She knew it. First the flowers and now he was following her around Target picking gifts for her? Her blood pressure headed north.

'What did he look like? Six foot? Dark spiky hair? Kind of handsome?' Honor asked.

'I guess. I didn't really pay too much attention. I just took it and… have I done something wrong?' the young girl asked.

'No, doll, we're all good here. Take that ugly thing, Honor and let's go. If Dan Steele's in the parking lot I'll throw it at him.'

Chapter Twenty Four

After she'd spent ten minutes in the parking lot of Target assassinating Dan Steele's personality with Mia – *he's an asshole, he's a dirtbag, he writes every song in the key of B* – she drove the long way home. She was still so mad; if she knew where he was she'd go there. Why was he doing this? What exactly was this all about? Wasn't it enough he'd taken away her contract with Micro? Actually, thinking about it, she'd done that herself. So then, did he want her back? Was that it? Or did he simply want to make amends? Ordering shop assistants to pass on gifts after he'd stalked her around the store wasn't the best way to do that. In fact there was no way to do it. She didn't want him in her life and it was way too late for *sorry*.

She thumped the groceries into the refrigerator and the flashing light on the answer phone on the kitchen wall caught her attention. She moved towards it and pressed the button.

Larry's voice came over the speaker. 'Honor, darlin', I know you're mad with me right now but, honey, just hear me out. It was just an idea, nothing's been contracted. I know how things looked back there but believe me, if I really thought you couldn't do it... Listen, time's gone by and joint ventures, mutual support, they're the watchwords of success today, darlin'. You know I've always hoped you'd go back to music and...'

She switched it off. She couldn't listen to anymore. The fact Larry had even *thought* him working with Dan Steele was OK was enough.

She picked up the six-pack of beer and smiled. At least something good was happening. She put the bottles into the refrigerator as the doorbell rang.

Barefoot, she padded up the hall and checked the spy-hole. She had to look twice. The nerve of the guy! She unchained the latch and swung the door open.

'What the hell are you doing here? How do you even know where I live? Did you follow me out of Target?'

'Honor, I... What? Target?' Dan Steele looked bewildered.

She took a step back, grabbing up something from the hall table. She pushed the bag-wrapped item at him, making sure it connected hard with his chest.

'I don't want anything from you. And I don't want you following me around thinking you're going to be able to make up for the past.' The anger was making her rush out the words.

'Stop talking! Jeez, Honor just let me get a word in here. You did this at Micro. I'm not letting you do it again now.' His tone was serious, verging on mad.

She closed up her mouth and just stared at him. She shouldn't listen to anything. He didn't deserve it.

'I did not send you flowers. I have no idea about anything involving Target. I don't even know what the hell this is.' He looked at the bag containing the owl and put it down on the ground.

She folded her arms across her chest and met his gaze with defiance. He had always been a smooth-talker but if he tried any of that now it would be a dumb move.

'Can I come in?' The brown eyes didn't look quite so mad now.

She shook her head. 'No. I don't have anything to say to you.'

He took off his Stetson and toyed with it in his hands. 'It was never my intention to come back here and end up like this.'

'No? Then why come back?'

He put his hands to his head and set his eyes on her. 'Because music's my life. You know that. Nothing's changed since we were... since back then.'

'Nothing's changed for you maybe, but everything changed for me.'

'I know that.' He gave a nod. 'I can't imagine what you must have been through.'

She stiffened. 'I don't want you to imagine it. It's nothing to do with you. I don't want your sympathy – which is way too late by the way – I want you to stay out of my life and keep your finger-picking hands off my career.' She put her hands on her hips and glared.

He smiled at her and she felt her cheeks flame with rage.

'There's the firecracker I remember,' he stated.

'Get off of my porch.'

'Listen, Honor, I just came here to try and straighten things out. To try and get you to see that we're not all ganging up on you. This mutual arrangement could benefit us both. Micro are talking arena tours if we team up, joint store signings, fan-club gigs together. I think it makes a lot of sense, a lot of *business* sense. I'm willing to workshop it,' he stated.

'Did I not make myself clear at the office yesterday? Because I'm sure I asked Radley for an out from my contract. And I'm pretty positive I contacted my lawyer this morning and asked him to fix this mess.'

'You'd throw away a great deal, the years of relationship you have with that label, just so you don't have to work with me?'

'You *were* listening the other day.'

Dan let out a breath and replaced his hat on his head. 'Listen, I admit, I went away because I freaked out after your accident. I couldn't cope with what that man had done to you. But it wasn't just the scar on your face like you think it was... it was how you changed as a person. You let that guy take your soul.'

She felt the dart shoot through her chest. His words were harsh but it was the truth in them that was doing more damage than the intent.

'I want to move on from that. I want *you* to move on from that. Don't throw something good away just because you're not quite healed.'

He picked up the package from the floor and handed it to her. 'Think about it.'

'I've just heard you all over the radio. You've been nominated for a Marlon award!' Byron slapped Jared on the back.

'Thanks, man. What are you doin' here?'

'Working with Gary Giles on his new album. How about you? You got the band in?' Byron asked, looking through into the studio.

'That was the plan but I'm a man down. Rico's broken his hand. Don't ask, it sounds like he had a fight with a garbage truck. Say, you couldn't...' Jared began.

'Aw, Jed I wish I could but I'm booked with Gary and...'

'I can wait.'

'I don't know,' Byron hesitated.

'What's the problem? You worried we're a bit too rock for ya?'

'I can play anything, you know that.'

'I know that. That's why I'm askin''

Byron shook his head and smiled. 'Give me an hour OK?'

'You got it. We'll be right here.' Byron headed back out into the corridor and Jared sat himself down on the couch.

He was waiting for a call from Buzz. Despite his advisor's reservations about his relationship with Honor he had promised to contact Gear about signing her. It was a competitive market but the vibe around her performance at Cody's Bar and Grill should have been enough to convince Gear they should snap her up before another record company did.

He wanted to be able to tell her something tonight when he went for dinner at her place. The thought of having dinner with her, there, in those plush, hand-clapping surroundings was freaking him out a little. No one except his mom had ever cooked for him before. It was a date, albeit in private, and he knew by the end of it he'd be struggling to keep his libido in check.

His cell phone rang and he answered.

'Hey, Buzz.'

'Hey, listen, I'll cut to the chase. I spoke to Eddie at Gear and right now they're not looking for someone in Honor's category.'

Jared pressed his lips together as what Buzz had said sunk into him. He started to pace.

'Are you still there, Jared?'

'Yeah I'm still here but I don't like what you're tellin' me. What d'you mean they're not lookin' for someone in Honor's *category*? What's that supposed to mean?'

'It means they're not taking on any traditional country singers right now. I tried for you, Jared, like I said I would but...'

'What? Did you show them the You Tube video from Cody's? Did you tell them about us?'

It all went very quiet on the other end of the phone. Jared came to a halt, grinding his teeth together. He wanted to reach down the receiver and take hold of Buzz.

'You didn't tell them did you? Why didn't you tell them?' He knew his voice was raised a volume above what it should be, but right now he didn't care. This was important to him on so many levels.

'We talked about this. The last thing you need right now is a girlfriend. We joked about this a few weeks ago... Taylor Swift and Leann Rimes, remember?'

'Yeah I remember and things have moved on. I want Honor on my tour and I want Gear to sign her up. They'd be crazy not to.' He was biting the inside of his mouth.

'That's not your decision to make.'

Buzz had all the answers. He wouldn't be surprised if he'd rehearsed the whole conversation. That was what he was good at. Fielding questions, preparing answers and winning the argument.

That's why Jared employed him. And that was exactly why he should be doing more to help, because Jared paid his wages.

'Speak to them again.'

'Come on, Jared, you're being unprofessional.'

'No, Buzz, *you* are. For whatever damn reason, you're not workin' your ass off to make this happen for me. How many times do I have to spell it out to you? I want Honor with Gear. Make it work.' He didn't care that his tone was bordering on threatening.

'I'm not some sort of Aladdin's genie you know.'

'Then you'd better work on that.'

Chapter Twenty Five

When the doorbell rang her stomach gave a flip. He was here. He was on time. She was organized in the kitchen and the eight-foot-long table in her garden room was dressed with white table linen and candles. She felt warm, happy, excited and all the things she hadn't felt in forever.

She brushed down the front of the dark blue knee-length dress. It was a favorite. It had white broderie anglaise at the sleeves and the hem. She hadn't worn it in years, but tonight she'd decided she didn't want to be in jeans.

She took a breath and checked the spy-hole before opened the door to Jared.

'Am I late? I called a cab way before I needed to but they were late on their promise. I got you these. I know bringin' your girl a set of guitar strings isn't the most romantic of gifts but you said you needed them.'

She swallowed down the pulse of heat that had raised up the second she clapped eyes on him. He was wearing jeans without any rips or chains, a dark blue vest that showed off his lean torso, over which was a tan short-sleeved shirt. One bead necklace hung from his neck and of course, he was wearing his trademark cap.

'Honor?'

She realized she hadn't responded to his question and she

hurriedly stepped back to let him in and spoke up. 'No, you're not late. And the strings are perfect.' She took them from him. 'Come in.'

He took a step forward and stopped as he met her body. 'You look beautiful in that dress.'

She felt her face pink as she turned to mush like a teenager. The effect he had on her was crazy. She knew she was old enough to know better but that didn't stop it happening.

'Thank you.' He kissed her cheek and she breathed deep, lingering on the scent of his aftershave. Wood and patchouli, mixed with musk and leather.

She reached for his hand, needing the connection. He was still wearing his rings and the contact stilled her for a moment.

'Hey, is everything alright?' His gray eyes leveled with hers, wide and soulful, concerned.

'Yes, I just... Dan came by.' There was no point hiding it even though she knew what his reaction would be. She felt his fingers tense immediately, the tendons in his arms tightening.

'Dan Steele.' He didn't know why he'd asked that. Of course it was him. It wasn't enough to do Honor out of her recording contract, he'd had to come around and rub it in her face.

'I thought he'd sent me flowers and followed me around Target. Someone bought me the owl, a fan I guess; he said it wasn't him but...'

'Slow down a little bit. He sent you flowers?' He was going to kill him the very next time he laid eyes on him.

'No. Yes. Maybe. I thought so. Anyway, he came around and tried to convince me to stay with Micro.' Her cheeks were red and she was toying with a strand of hair. He had to keep himself in check here. He was mad but he didn't want Honor to think he was crazy-ass mad. That he couldn't control his temper. Because he could. If he really wanted to.

'And what did you say?' He exhaled as he waited for her to

answer.

'I told him I meant what I said at the offices. I'm out. There's no going back.' He saw her swallow, knew despite the determination she was concerned about how this would pan out for her.

'I don't much like the fact he came over here.' That was as mild as he could manage to get the point across.

'There's nothing between us.' She looked up at him with wide eyes, her tone changed, concerned.

'I know, it isn't that. I just don't like the guy and I hate what he and Micro did to you.' That was an understatement.

'I'm OK... I'm glad you're here.'

He squeezed her hand then looked at his watch.

'Can't you stay long?' she asked him.

'No, I mean, sure thing. I'm just waiting for a call.'

He'd given up with Buzz. Despite ordering him to do what he wanted he'd had no word. He'd phoned his contact at Gear and left several messages. No response. So, after Byron had taken the place of his regular guitarist at the studio and he'd asked him to join the band for the tour, he'd told him about Honor's situation. Byron had made a suggestion and together they'd devised a plan.

'And then you might have to go?'

'No. Actually *we* might have to go.'

She looked like she didn't understand and how could she? He wanted to just pull her towards him and take everything bad away.

'But I've made ribs with Alabama Hot Sauce and corn dogs.' She was so sweet, his heart was aching.

'Is my face on the bottle? Because that damn cartoon has haunted me,' he joked, smiling.

She smiled back at him, a little tentative. He put an arm around her shoulders and drew her into his embrace, hooking his other arm in around her waist and holding her close. 'Corn dogs are a habit of mine.'

The ribs had been a little overdone but he'd said they were the best he'd had. He sounded so sincere she didn't actually know whether he was just being nice or telling the truth. They'd shared six beers and he'd told her all the plans for his tour. She'd never experienced anything quite that countrywide in her time. It seemed like Jared was going to be covering every corner of the US. And he was still determined she was coming with him.

'I'd understand if you changed your mind. After all, I don't have a label anymore.' She dropped her eyes to her finished plate of food.

'Are you crazy? It took me this long to get you to agree to it. There's no way I'm changin' my mind.'

She saw him check his watch again. 'What are you waiting for?'

He let out a breath and met her eyes. 'I'm waiting on Byron.'

'Byron? He has a date with Mia tonight.'

'I know. They're eatin' chicken out of a bucket at Kelsey Rio's. But he told me Flynn Fisher is there every week checkin' out the new bands and he's gonna be there tonight. You know who Flynn Fisher is don'tcha?'

Honor shook her head. Should she know? Was he another of the recording artists she'd missed out on in all these years?

'He's the head scout at Gear.'

She didn't know where this was headed but she had a sick feeling penetrating her stomach. She shook her head at Jared. 'What has that got to do with anything?'

'You want a record label. I think you'd do well with Gear.' He took a swig of his beer. 'Being polite and asking hasn't gotten me very far so it's time to accelerate things a little.'

'I can send a demo around in a week or so, when I've got used to the idea of moving on.' She swallowed. Even *she* knew it sounded a weak response. She was positive moving away from Micro was the right thing now Dan was on board, but that didn't mean she wanted the momentum of what came next gathering speed before she was ready.

'You went down a storm at Cody's. If you want to attract attention you need to go grab it.'

She shook her head and picked up her beer bottle. '*I don't grab attention like that.*'

'You're gonna let Dan Steele run off with your confidence as well as everything else?'

His tone was cutting and she knew she deserved it for being so meek. 'You want me to pitch up at Kelsey Rio's, and perform to this guy from Gear? Just like that?'

'Kind of.'

'What does that mean?'

'You have to be a never-before-signed artist to perform tonight. But I know what all the legal stuff is like. It could be months before your lawyer gets you released from Micro unless he can find a loophole. Sign with Gear and they'd pay you out.'

She shook her head, giving the jumbled-up thoughts flying round time to compute to her brain.

'Tonight you're Lindy Marshall and I'm your guitarist, Randy Mitchell.' He laughed and his smile cracked as wide as the Grand Canyon.

She still didn't understand.

'Byron's signed you up to perform. He's gonna call when there's three artists before you. We'll call a cab – a more reliable company than I used to get here – we'll get on stage and he'll be drawin' up the contract before the final chord.'

'We can't do that. I mean it's dishonest and that will be a bad start to a business relationship – if he even considers signing me – and... everyone's going to recognize me the second I step on stage, especially if I sing *Goodbye Joe*.'

'You're not singin' *Goodbye Joe*... and I've got disguises.'

Chapter Twenty Six

Byron had phoned, the cab had been late and on the drive to the strip they'd rehearsed the song she was going to sing. It was the classic hymn *How Great Thou Art.* Jared had told her Vince Gill and Carrie Underwood had done it together and their version was famous for getting standing ovations. He was convinced that no act at Kelsey Rio's was going to sing something so gospel. It would be different. It was perfect for her voice. He knew the guitar part. The guy from Gear had a soft spot for Vince Gill. It was perfect.

'You know this is completely crazy right?' She pulled at the blonde wig she had on. At the moment she was concerned it was too big and was probably going to fall off the second she opened her mouth.

'Sometimes you have to go a little crazy to make things work for ya.' He grinned and tugged at the ZZ Top-style beard he had stuck on.

She took a breath. The cab had dropped them a few meters down from the bar. The strip was busy and there was music emanating from every open door. The atmosphere always gave her shivers but tonight everything was heightened ten-fold.

'Relax there, Lindy, no one knows who you are,' Jared whispered in her ear.

The warmth of his breath had her insides lurching. 'This is

insane, Jared.'

'Not insane. Just a little crazy, like you said. If you're gonna be spendin' time with me things are always gonna be a little bit crazy.'

She smiled at him. She should have known that. Wikipedia had told her about a few stunts he'd pulled in the past. Riding his motorbike through a shopping mall, playing a set in the middle of the freeway. There wasn't much he'd done the straight way.

'We're busting in on Mia and Byron's date.'

'Enough of the excuses, Lindy, we've got work to do. Come on.' He held his hand out to her.

'Wait, can we just do one more run through?' She was nervous as hell.

'There's no time.'

'Please, just once more,' she begged, indicating an alleyway off the main street. She saw him check his watch again.

'One run-through of the intro,' he agreed. She passed him her guitar and led the way into the shadowy walkway.

Once they were out of sight of the drinkers and revelers she cleared her throat as Jared began to play. She prepared to come in.

'Fuck! Man, the string just broke.' He took the guitar off his body and looked at the flailing wire.

'I said she needed restringing. You bought me new ones.'

'Don't suppose you have 'em with you?'

She shook her head. They were on the worktop in the kitchen, next to the dirty grill pan she'd cooked the ribs on.

'Jeez! OK, listen, here's what we're gonna do. We're just gonna have to go in and ask to borrow a guitar. The place is full of musicians, it'll be easy.'

'Musicians in competition. Would you lend your guitar to anyone?'

'One of them maybe. There's at least a half dozen I've never got on with.'

'Jared, these unsigned artists don't have fifty guitars at their disposal and they aren't going to lend you the only one they have.'

Her nerves were hammering inside of her more and more as every second ticked by.

'I could buy one, from the store you work at. The chick's right in there.'

'There's no time. I'll just have to sing it a capella.' She had no idea why she had said that. She was scared enough as it was without putting additional pressure on herself. Singing without accompaniment on little practice was just plain stupid but what choice did she have... if she was actually going to go through with it?

'You can do that? Man, you're better than I thought. No wonder I want you on my tour.'

She formed her lips in a smile and took another deep, long breath. 'I don't know why I'm doing this at all.'

'Singin' for Flynn Fisher? Or wearin' a wig?'

She let out a nervous laugh. 'Both.'

Jared's cell phone began to ring from the pocket of his jeans. 'That'll be Byron. We'd better get gone.'

He took hold of her hand and squeezed her fingers. 'Feelin' scared is just the same as feelin' alive.'

'Do you really believe that?' She raised her eyes to meet his.

'You spend too much time thinkin' about stuff. Come on!' He pulled her back towards the street.

'I can't take you seriously looking like Billy Gibbons.'

The bar room at Kelsey Rio's was buzzing. On stage was a three-piece band doing a cover of a Lady Antebellum number. There was something a bit off about the accordion and the double bass player had sweat dripping down his forehead.

'Don't look at them. Look at me.' Jared could see Honor wasn't fully onboard with his idea. He pulled her hands, directing her attention away from the band and back towards him.

'What are we doing? I'm a professional artist. I don't qualify to be here and I shouldn't be here. I should be doing things the right way.' She put her hand to the fringe on her wig.

'The slow, antiquated, borin', snail's pace way?'

'Did you just say *antiquated*?'

'Truth time, Honor. I want you on the tour but I need to sell that to Gear. We need a big name to love you and sign you and get you out of that damn contract with Micro. Who better than Gear themselves? I asked Buzz...'

'What? You asked your advisor to pitch me?' Perhaps he should have kept his mouth shut. The look on her face was telling him he was about to get a tongue-lashing.

'No... not like that.'

'Then what?' Her hands were on her hips now. 'What *did* you do?'

'Say, there's Byron, maybe he's got some strings on him.' He ignored her last question and headed across the room.

'Jared! I mean... Randy... whatever I'm supposed to be calling you!'

Byron stood up as they approached. 'Loving the look, man.'

'I rock it don't I?'

'She's up next.'

'You got any strings with you? Broke a damn string just outside.'

'I don't. Want me to grab you a guitar? There's a guy I know over there.'

'You're crashing my date, doll, you do know that. Have you colored your hair?' Mia smiled and sucked on her bottle of beer, swaying a little.

'...and next we have Lindy Marshall and Randy Mitchell. Let's give them a warm welcome.' The crowd gave a half-hearted applause.

'Where is he?' Honor asked.

'Who?'

'Flynn Fisher.'

'That's him,' Byron pointed out.

Flynn Fisher was sitting at a table near the front of the stage just a little way away, an iPad, a notepad and a bottle of water on the table in front of him. He was gray from head to foot. Gray hair, gray shirt and trousers, steely expression on his face. Jared didn't recognize him from any meetings he'd had at Gear's offices. He had to be new.

'Lindy Marshall and Randy Mitchell? Are you here?' the announcer called, looking out into the audience.

'Listen, if you wanna...' Jared began.

Honor didn't respond. She just turned and made her way up to the stage.

All of a sudden she was surprisingly calm. She didn't know whether it was the wig or the new name or Jared's completely stupid idea for a stunt, but whatever it was she wasn't nervous. Maybe it was because nothing was really riding on it. If it all went south she'd just think again, adjust. She was learning to do that now. She could make changes if she needed to. Altering her ideals wasn't going to be the end of her. She'd survived much worse.

'I'm Lindy Marshall.' She pulled the hair on her wig a little, desperate to cover her scar.

'Great, er... no Randy?' the announcer queried.

'No.'

The announcer looked at Honor and then behind her at the empty stage. 'No guitar? Backing track?'

'No. I'm good.' She gave him a smile and took the microphone out of its stand.

Looking a little bewildered, the announcer backed off stage to the wings and left Honor alone. It was just her, the microphone and a bar full of drinkers that wouldn't be expecting what she was about to do.

She took a breath, closed her eyes and found the note in her head.

Jared sat down next to Byron, his eyes fixed on the stage, on Honor. He watched her open up her eyes, directing her gaze into the middle distance and then she started to sing.

The very second the first line was out of her mouth the hairs all over his body stood to attention. There was just something about her perfect tone, the pure notes and nuances of her vocals that got to him like no voice ever had. It was angelic, there was just no other word for it. It was as if Heaven had descended into the room.

He moved his eyes to focus on Flynn Fisher. The man who had appeared like a gray version of the Grim Reaper was sat forward on his seat, transfixed by what was happening right there in front of him. Jared turned his head to look at the bar room. The bustle of beer-trading and chicken-bucket-eating had silenced and stilled. There wasn't one person in the room not being bewitched by Honor's song.

She hit the first high note. 'Holy Mother of God,' Mia stated, gripping hold of Byron's arm.

She wasn't on the stage. She wasn't even in the room. The deep, moving words were propelling her along with them. It felt like she was being guided by the story in the lyrics, to do justice to this beautiful, inspiring song and nothing more. The moment was everything. Her voice, interacting with the power of the message, was more special, more necessary and important than putting on a show for a record-company scout. This was her, almost how she used to be, living for the love of song, singing for the love of country.

She hit the final note and held it with everything she had. A whole twelve bars went by before she stopped. She dropped her head and the wig fell off and landed on the floor of the stage. The bar room erupted into a pit of cheering and clapping as people rose from their tables, booths and stools to get to their feet.

When she raised her head there were tears streaming down her face. That song had given her back the feeling she'd been missing. She didn't just want to come back because the world thought she should; now she wanted to come back because this really was where she wanted to be. She wanted to feel how she had just felt forever.

'I'm goin' to her,' Jared said, standing up.

'Just wait a second. See what Flynn Fisher does,' Byron suggested, catching Jared's arm.

'Did you not hear what she just did? It's gone way beyond scoring a contract.' Jared ripped off the fake beard and pushed past chairs to get to the stage.

The announcer was on his way to Honor and they met stage right, Jared rushing to get to the microphone before he could.

'Howdy y'all. We apologize for bustin' in and everythin' but I wanna just share somethin' here with y'all.' He looked to Honor who was wiping at the tears on her face with the back of her hand.

'Woo hoo! It's Jed Marshall! We love you Jed!' a member of the audience yelled out.

'Love you too, man.' He laughed. 'Right, well, first off, I wanna introduce you to someone. You've probably all guessed already after that performance, but this isn't an unsigned artist called Lindy Marshall. This is the talented Honor Blackwood.'

There were whoops and cheers from the crowd but a few shaken heads and groans of disapproval from the other artists who'd performed.

Jared continued. 'I know some of you probably saw her bring down the house at Cody's the other night, right? Well, some things have changed and one of those things is... Honor's looking for a new label. And we're really hopin', Mr Fisher, that you're gonna be the guy to change that.'

Jared looked at the man in the suit in the front row, addressing him as directly as he could without grabbing him by the shirt collar. He was hoping for a sign, a nod of the head, anything to make him know that this trick had paid off. He carried on.

'Because, as you know, Gear's my label. I love the guys over there. They've been so good to me and... I know they know talent better than most. Better than most but not better than you guys. So what do y'all think? D'you think Gear should sign Honor?'

There wasn't a second to think about this going wrong. The audience responded the way he'd hoped by giving a resounding roar and banging on tables with hands, feet and silverware.

Flynn Fisher met Jared's gaze at last and nodded his head at him. The overwhelming feeling of joy and relief flooded his gut and he reached for Honor's hand as the crowd continued to clap and cheer.

'Thank y'all so much. Honestly, thank you from the bottom of my heart. It really means so much to have your support.' He paused, took hold of Honor's other hand until she was facing him. 'It means so much because... the other thing I want to tell you right now is... this is my girl right here. She's come into my life and she's hit me hard and I ain't never felt like that before.'

He could hear and feel the crowd going crazy now. People had cell phones in the air recording the scene and taking photos. This was big Nashville news happening right in front of them, and he knew that and no longer cared.

He cupped her face in his hands and drew her towards him, kissing her slowly, deep and long, unconcerned by the presence of hundreds of people. She put her arms around him and he felt her hold on tighter than she ever had.

Chapter Twenty Seven

'What am I doing here and who put the freaking boom box in my head?'

Mia walked into the kitchen dressed in just her t-shirt from the night before and panties.

'You don't really want to know the answer to either of those questions.' Honor pushed a mug towards her and indicated the hot coffee pot simmering on the worktop.

'Oh God, did I ruin the date with the hottest guy I've had since Leroy?' She slid herself up onto a stool.

'You tried your very best, but no. I hung your head out the cab window so you weren't sick and Byron said he'd call you later.'

'*Call me later*? Did it sound sincere? Because I've had all that before. One guy said he'd call me later and he called me *six months* later, after he was married, when he was drunk one night and needed someone to sleep with.'

'It was the *call me later* of the good variety I'm sure. D'you want some breakfast?'

'God, no! Ask me tomorrow!'

Honor took a sip of her coffee and turned on the TV.

'Ouch! Way too loud.' Mia reached for her head.

'...and there's love in the air for country rock artist, Jed Marshall. Footage has started appearing on You Tube of a blistering kiss with returning newcomer, Honor Blackwood. The man himself announced Honor was "his girl" and that he'd been hit hard. Jed is nominated for the Male Vocalist award at this year's Marlon Awards.'

'Oh my God, it's all coming back to me now. You sang like Carrie freaking Underwood and Jed Marshall told the world you're a couple. After that I still have tequila blur.'

Honor turned down the volume on the TV. 'That's about what happened. That and the fact I have a meeting with Gear later to talk about signing a contract with them.'

'You totally deserve that. That song, that Bible song... you took everyone in that room back to the last funeral they attended... but in a good way.'

'It really made a difference. I've not felt this happy about everything in so long.' She took a breath, a warm sensation spreading over her skin. Last night, after the performance, while Byron and Mia had gone to organize the cab, Jared had kissed her again and held on to her so long she thought her heart would burst. What she felt for this man and what she could tell he felt for her was stronger than anything she'd known. It was all-encompassing.

'I still can't get over the fact you're dating Jed freaking Marshall! Have you taken my advice and Googled him?'

'I might have.' She smiled. 'His birthday is November 28th, he's the eldest of three and he has a tattoo of the national bird of Alabama on his back.'

'You didn't learn that from Google.'

'No I didn't,' she admitted.

Mia smiled at her and laid a hand on Honor's arm. 'Just a couple of days and you look like a different person.'

'D'you think?'

'I know it. Man!' Mia slid down from her stool. 'You actually put that thing in your house?' She reached into the window for the owl ornament. Fingering the shells around its wonky eye she held it up to Honor.

'Dan said it wasn't from him.' She gave a nod. 'I like it.' She hadn't thought much about it if she was honest. She hadn't had time.

'It's creepy and it's also creepy that some stranger buys it for you. You don't think...' Mia started then stopped.

'What?'

'Well, don't get all freaked out or anything but you don't think it could be the guy who attacked you, do you?'

A shiver ran over Honor, the mellow, comfortable feeling melting away. Her whole form stiffened and shrank as a vision of Simeon Stewart, a wild, crazy look in his eyes, being marched from the courtroom and off to jail.

'Doll, don't do that. I'm sorry. I don't know what I was thinking saying that. He's locked up, far away from here.'

Honor blew out a breath and tried to bring herself back into the moment. 'He's not.' She took a slow, steady breath. 'He's out. He's been out a couple years.'

'What the hell? Why didn't you say?'

'Because I didn't want to think about it. Because I know one of the conditions of his release is staying away from me. Because I know he lives in Nebraska.'

She got down off the stool and went to the sink, running the tap.

'But if he's out. If he's as screwed up and unstable as he was when he attacked you, maybe...' Mia began.

Honor filled a glass with water and turned back to her friend. 'Simeon Stewart wasn't a stalker. He didn't have photos of me all around his house or an effigy in his bedroom. I could have been anyone. I don't know why he chose me over The Dixie Chicks or... Miley Cyrus. It was a random act of violence, it wasn't personal.'

'You sound like a freaking cop. You should call them. The cops. They could get fingerprints off that thing and then you'd know.'

'He has no reason to be here and why would he send me gifts? It isn't his MO.'

'Whoa! Stop! Far too much CSI. One word about spatter and I'm heading back to the bathroom.'

'I used to get fans sending me gifts back in the day. Toys, flowers, chocolates...' She paused. 'Fried sausages covered in grease.'

Mia clutched at her stomach. 'You brat!'

Together, always together
It's better, sharing whatever
Cos two hearts, joined up forever
Is the strongest thing I ever knew

The knuckle-rapping on the front door had him dropping down the pencil into his lyric book and heading to answer the caller. When he opened it up, Buzz greeted him with a newspaper slapped onto his chest.

'What the hell!'

Buzz stepped into the house without waiting for an invitation and marched towards the den. Jared looked at the front page of the Nashville News. There was a photo of him and Honor locked in an embrace on the stage of Kelsey Rio's. He knew this was coming and now he knew why Buzz was acting pissed.

'Am I still working for you?' Buzz spun around to face Jared, his eyes bulbous.

'Of course. Why would you say somethin' like that?'

'Because you pay me to advise you and then you go and do something like that.' Buzz pointed to the newspaper in Jared's hands.

'I pay you to advise me. I never said I was always gonna take that advice.'

'Don't get cute with me, Jared. I'm *this* close to severing our relationship.' Buzz pinched his thumb and index finger close together.

'I told you I wanted Honor with Gear.'

'I told you I tried. I also told you not to go public with your relationship and this morning you're making whoopee on the front page of my paper!'

'Makin' what?' He stifled a laugh.

'This is not a laughing matter. This is exactly what I didn't want to happen before the awards next week.'

'Why not? Maybe the public need to see another side to me. Because it isn't all leather and grungy guitar solos. You know that's only half the story.'

'I know that's the half of the story that sells millions of downloads.'

Jared shrugged his shoulders. 'Well, it's done now and this afternoon Honor's gonna sign with Gear. They're talkin' to Micro, gettin' her released from her contract and gettin' her into the studio to record a new album.'

'What?' Buzz looked astounded.

'Not heard that news yet?' Jared threw the paper onto the couch and put his hands into the pockets of his jeans. 'She sang at Kelsey Rio's last night. Brought the house down, it's all over Twitter. Flynn Fisher was there and he couldn't get her number quick enough.'

Buzz didn't say a word.

'Listen, I've not spoken to Honor this mornin' but she's in the market for a new advisor...'

Buzz shook his head. 'You're not seriously suggesting I look after her?'

'She's comin' on the tour, Buzz. It would keep things neat.'

'It would cause no end of issues. You're two completely different artists.'

'Are you sayin' you can't handle it? Or you just don't want to? What is it you've got against her, Buzz?'

Buzz shook his head. Jared could see there was something he was holding back. Buzz was the best in the business at what he did and Jared wanted Honor to have the best if there was a chance.

'I've got nothing against her.' Buzz lowered himself onto the couch and took a deep breath. Jared had never seen him like this before. He was quiet, had suddenly become introverted. He watched him take a moment then raise his head to meet his gaze.

'I was there... that night.' Buzz's voice was weak with emotion.

'What?' Jared leant against the wooden mantle over the fireplace.

'I was there, in Illinois, at the concert, at *her* concert when that madman attacked her.'

Jared sucked in a breath, putting his hand to his cap.

'I was meeting with the support act after the show to see about working with them. Honor was the best there was at that time. She had an unrivalled range and the ability to hold the crowd in the palm of her hand. I was in the very front row, about half a dozen seats away from... him... that guy.' He paused to compose himself. 'It was a small gig. Before anyone knew or could do anything about it, he'd got on stage and he'd cut her face.'

His fingers dug into his palms as raw rage manifested itself deep inside and swirled around, fighting to get up and out.

'The band carried on playing at first. She didn't even scream. The look on her face, the blood on her hands, her eyes so wide and innocent, so shocked.' Buzz rubbed his hands over his face and took a breath. 'I had my daughter with me, Jared. Lucille had a case she couldn't pass over; I took Mona to that concert. A ten-year-old girl had to sit and witness something like that.'

Jared couldn't hold it in any longer. He punched the wooden mantle with his fist. The force of the blow, together with the thickness of the wood, split the skin at his knuckles. He didn't feel a thing. Buzz had just described something he'd only read about on the internet. After he'd met Honor, when he'd found out what had happened to her, he'd wanted to know everything, all the detail. But now, hearing it from someone who had seen it, made the true horror hit home.

'Mona had nightmares for weeks. Kept asking me if someone was going to do that to her one day... if she sang, if she did a show at school,' Buzz continued.

'Stop,' Jared ordered. He rested his hands on the mantle, facing the wall, his head hanging.

'I feel for the girl, I really do, Jared. But it's too close to home. I've put it behind me and...'

'What?' Jared raised his head and slowly turned around. 'What did you say? You've put it all behind you?'

Buzz didn't respond.

'You saw what he did. Your daughter saw what he did, and what? That makes you want to wash your hands of her and stay away? What sort of man are you?'

'You're responding emotionally, Jared. You've hooked up with her and you're not thinking straight.' Buzz got to his feet.

'*I'm* the one who's respondin' emotionally? You're tellin' me you won't represent her because you witnessed some guy sticking a knife in her face and it upset your family balance for a few weeks. What about what she's been through, huh? You shouldn't be retreatin', you should be offerin' her everything you've got.'

Buzz looked to the floor.

'I don't understand it, man. I don't understand it at all.' He shook his head and paced out the room towards the kitchen. He really needed a beer right now. He threw open the refrigerator, only to be greeted by scores of bottles of Pure Nectar. He slammed the door shut and let out a grunt of annoyance. How was he going to work this out?

He caught sight of Buzz in his peripheral vision and straightened up, leaning against the worktop and folding his arms across his chest.

'You're really serious about her? This isn't just a couple of nights and over and done like that waitress?'

Jared shook his head, his eyes narrowing, his expression set on mean. 'Damn straight I'm serious. This ain't nothin' close to anything else. And I don't care how that makes anyone else feel.'

Buzz nodded his head and then buttoned up his jacket, shifting his shoulders back. Jared watched and waited. How was this going to play out? Was this going to be some sort of stand-off position where neither of them would give an inch? He didn't want to find himself another advisor. Buzz understood him... most of the time.

'You were right. I was the one thinking with something other than the business side of my brain. And, if I'm honest, that's how I've been thinking since the second you mentioned her name in conversation. That was unprofessional and... that was wrong.'

Jared's gray eyes met Buzz's ebony ones and he nodded.

'Whatever you want to do I'll support you, you know that. It's always been a given and I don't intend changing things... unless you want to,' Buzz said.

Jared shook his head.

'But if we're going to continue working together you need to forewarn and forearm me so we make the most out of everything and avoid me getting calls from Davey Duncan at Countrified at six a.m.'

'He's got one hell of a nerve.'

'Lucille's never listening to him again.' Buzz smiled.

Jared braced himself to ask the next question. 'And Honor?'

He felt Buzz's intake of breath as well as heard it. 'I think it should be her decision. Larry Welt is a great guy. He knows the industry almost as well as I do and they have history. I don't know what's gone on with them but...'

'But if she asks? If she wants you to?'

'If she asks and she wants to, I'll be there.'

Before he had time to say anything else or backtrack, Jared clapped Buzz into a bear hug, slapping his back.

'Alright, don't crease the suit! Have you any idea how much dry-cleaning costs these days?'

Chapter Twenty Eight

Now they had hit clear road, Jared was going way over the limit. All the road signs were flashing by her like blurry shapes, unrecognizable. He accelerated harder and the bike roared on faster, until all she could think about was the rush and all she could feel was the wind whipping around her clothes. Her heart was pounding, her eyes watered despite the helmet and her fingers dug into the leather of his jacket as he took them on a thrill ride.

By the time he'd parked up outside the Gear Records building all she felt was exhilaration. They'd just had total, mind-spinning, uncomplicated fun. She pulled off the helmet and shook her hair loose.

'If the police had caught us you'd have been arrested! Going way too fast and you weren't wearing a helmet!' She couldn't hide the laughter in her voice or the color in her cheeks as she got off the pillion, playfully slapping his arm.

'It would have been worth it.' He grabbed hold of her hand and spun her back to the bike, gathering her into him.

His lips hovered over hers, the fine hairs of his stubble just tickling the skin above her top lip. He was teasing her, because he knew how much she wanted him. She shifted her upper body back just an inch or so. She could play this game. She couldn't help but snicker.

'What?' he questioned, his gray eyes searching hers.

'Nothing.' She swallowed as he continued to look at her. The heat from his body was radiating into hers. She could feel herself straightening up, parts of her glowing, becoming more aware. She pressed herself against him, her torso meeting his, her breasts molding to his chest.

'We're about to go into a serious business meetin' in there.' He didn't take his eyes off her.

'*I'm* about to go into a serious business meeting. You can go get coffee and wait for me,' she replied, putting a hand to his cap.

He flinched slightly. 'Damn, you're not gonna let me come in?' He sat back a little, put his hand to his hat, distancing himself.

He could see she'd noticed. She let him go, folded her arms across her chest in defense. He was a first-grade tool.

'Do you ever take it off? Apart from changing to a bike helmet?'

The question was blunt and to the point. He didn't want to answer. He didn't really know what he should say.

'I mean, you must shower sometimes.'

He tried to keep himself relaxed but the tension had already started to creep into his arms and was travelling a path across his shoulders.

'Jared?' She had a concerned look on her face now and he didn't want that.

'Hey, I shower... it's just my thing, you know?' Now he just sounded plain stupid.

'Your thing?' she queried. 'An image thing?'

'No, nothing dumb like that.' This wasn't going well.

'Then what?'

He shrugged, leaned forward and got off the bike. He leant against it, his fingers tucked into the belt of his jeans, his eyes on the floor. He wasn't stupid enough to think this would never come up. But he couldn't tell her why without telling her what he'd done and he wasn't ready for that. Things needed to be settled. She needed stability in her life, routine, to know where she was headed.

'I like it, OK? Doesn't it make me look a little sexy?' He smiled at her, pulled the peak down over his forehead and fixed her with his best look.

She didn't look convinced. He changed the subject. 'So, you sure about goin' in there on your own?'

'Sure. This is the new Honor Blackwood. More confident, more determined, more...'

'Damn hot,' he interrupted.

A blush hit her cheeks and she straightaway reached for her hair, pulling a section down over her scar. He leaned off the bike and moved toward her. 'Don't do that.'

'What?' She averted her eyes as he reached her.

'You're beautiful. All of you. The whole thing. Even this part. How many times do I need to tell you that?' He put his index finger to her scar and traced the line of it. 'This might have changed you but it also made you.'

She pressed her lips against his and he wound his hand into her curls, coaxing her head forward to deepen the kiss, her mouth opening. The sweet, pure taste of her filled all his senses. He didn't want to let her go, ever.

She put fingers to his jaw and eased him back with a softer kiss. 'I should go in. I don't want to be late.'

'I'll go order some Pure Nectar and get photographed somewhere. Call me when you're done.' He ran a hand down her hair, caught hold of her hand and squeezed it in his. 'Good luck.'

He watched her cross the sidewalk and push open the glass door. Once inside, she turned back to look at him, waving a hand.

She was glowing, from her toes to her teeth and all the parts in between. The meeting with Gear had been nothing like her get-together with Micro. Flynn Fisher had been there singing her praises to the chief-executive and then a You Tube video of her performance at Kelsey Rio's had been played on the plasma TV to the whole team in the room. To begin with she'd let Flynn Fisher do the talking and that reminded her of how much she'd relied on Larry before. Larry had led discussions, he'd known what to ask, what to look for in the detail, what information needed passing on to her lawyer. She was a singer, not a business mogul, but that didn't mean she couldn't learn. And she wanted to. She'd spent so long living on the back foot it was time to stand on her own two feet to prove to herself, more than anyone else, that she could do it.

Gear's legal team had looked over the contract her lawyer had sent them and both were certain there was an easy way to get her out of it. Nothing was standing in her way of a brand-new start with a different record company. Jared's record company.

As she came out the elevator she saw him outside, leant up against the bike, checking his phone. Seeing him there, waiting for her, made that glow increase, warming her insides, heating her heart. She rushed to the door.

'Miss Blackwood,' the receptionist called.

Honor turned.

'A gentleman left this for you.' She held a package out over the desk towards her.

It was a small oblong parcel wrapped up in gold paper. Honor didn't move.

'What did he look like?' she asked.

'Hmm now, I guess about six feet, jeans, plaid shirt. He just looked like a regular guy. Touch of Johnny Cash about him maybe.'

As Honor stared at the package in the receptionist's hand all she could think about was what Mia had said that morning about Simeon Stewart and what she had said in her confident reply. Was she wrong? Was this him? Was he stalking her with gifts to let her know he knew where she was and that he was watching and waiting?

A shiver ran over her body and she looked to Jared outside. She didn't know what to do.

'Are you OK, Miss Blackwood?'

'Yes, yes, I'm fine. I guess I'd better open it, huh?' She moved towards the counter and took the parcel from the girl.

Sliding her fingers under the paper she ripped it open, parting it to reveal a box of Reese's Pieces. They were her favorite candy. Although she didn't think anyone really knew that. Would Dan remember that? Had she told him when they were together? Was this Dan's way of trying to make things up to her? Was it really his style? Or was it something more sinister? A thought struck her.

'The man... the man who delivered these... did he look like this?' Honor called up Google, tapping away to bring up a news report of her attack, a report she knew had a photo of Simeon Stewart attached to it. She found it, zoomed in and turned her phone to the receptionist, her heart pounding. She could put this to bed once and for all when she got a negative.

'No... at least I don't think so. I didn't really look that hard. I just took the package.'

'Could you just look a little harder and try?' She didn't want to sound desperate but if she knew for sure it wasn't the guy who maimed her she could cope with anything else.

The receptionist squinted her eyes and focused on the photo, putting her fingers to Honor's phone as she held it. 'I'm sorry, I don't think it was him but I can't be sure.'

Honor took back her phone and nodded. She picked up the chocolates and headed for the door. All the positives had been stamped on again. What had she done to deserve getting kicked back down every time life threw her something good?

'How did it go?' Jared asked, studying her as she approached.

'Really well. They're going to get me out of Micro's contract and I really liked the team.' Only a flicker of enthusiasm was evident in her tone.

'What's wrong?'

'I think we need to go to the police.'

Chapter Twenty Nine

She'd been gone almost a half hour and he was starting to get antsy. He'd offered to go into the interview room with her but she'd insisted on doing it alone. Half of him was glad. Although sitting in the waiting area was like being an animal at the zoo, being stared at by everyone, it was a step up from being enclosed in a room with a detective and a recording device.

All that was going through his mind was the thought that if he hadn't left her at the Gear offices he would have been in reception when whoever it was dropped off the chocolates. It could be Dan Steele or the shit that attacked her. Whichever one it was, if he'd been there he could have nailed his ass.

He checked his watch again. He had a shoot for his new video later. They were heading off into the woods and an abandoned barn to record night footage. But if she needed him to stay with her he'd rearrange. Her safety came before anything else. He'd promised her that from the first moment he'd met her and feeling the way he did now, there was no way he was backing up on that promise.

'I understand your concern, Miss Blackwood, but I can confirm that Mr Stewart is currently complying with all the terms of his parole.'

Since when had he become Mr Stewart? She had gotten so used

to him being called nothing more than 'the accused' it felt wrong for him to have his name back.

'Why are you trotting out a line from a manual? I've told you about the flowers and the owl and now the chocolates. All I've asked you to do is look into this. I'm not accusing him of anything; I just need you to rule him out.'

The officer tapped his pen to his notepad and leveled his gaze at her. 'Rule him out of what, Miss Blackwood? What crime has been committed? As far as I'm aware, it isn't illegal to send chocolates in the state of Tennessee.'

She saw the smirk on his mouth and she knew this was a waste of time. She felt anger smart at her insides and she drew a slow breath in. 'I want this noted down and reported officially. I want your name and your number. I want you to file whatever paperwork you have to file so that if this lunatic comes back and puts me back in the emergency room I can make sure I know who to sue.'

She got to her feet and headed for the door.

'Miss Blackwood, hold up a second.'

She paused, her hand on the doorknob.

'I'm just trying to keep a level head here and work on my instincts as a police officer who's been investigating crimes like this for over ten years.'

'Well, ten years ago I wasn't given a split second to work on any of my instincts because "Mr Stewart" got up on stage and sliced my face open.' She pushed her bangs back and showed him the scar she hated so much. 'So I know chocolates don't seem threatening to you, but to me it means someone's giving me attention I don't want and if it's him I want to know about it now rather than when it's too late.'

She hoped the boiling rage and disappointment she was feeling was burning into him. She should have known this would be the response she got. It was true that there had been no threat, no reason to suspect anything but an admirer, but until she knew where Simeon Stewart had been for the past two hours she wouldn't feel settled.

She opened the door and stepped out of the interview room. She took a moment, leaning against the wall for support. This would not get to her. This would not change any of her plans. She was back in the industry. It was where she wanted to be. She was going to do all the things she should have been doing for the last ten years and she was going to enjoy every second. She held her breath, felt her breath, let it calm her, let it bring her back down into the moment as she'd been taught in therapy. She looked down into her hands and realized she'd left the chocolates on the table.

He leapt out of the chair when he saw her approach. She was smiling at him but he didn't feel it from her.

'What did they say?'

'Can we get out of here?'

'Are they checkin' it out? They could pull the camera footage from the front desk at Gear.'

'Officer Dunbar thinks I'm psychotic,' she stated.

'What? Did he say that?'

'He didn't need to say it; I could feel it from him. *Did you know it's not a crime to send chocolates in the state of Tennessee, Miss Blackwood*?'

'He said that? I'm goin' up there.' He moved past her, heading for the stairs.

'Jared, no!'

'They need to take this serious, Honor. We shouldn't have to wait for the horse's head before they make this into a case!'

'Please, Jared, I don't want to do this now. He's probably right.'

'Probably ain't nothin' like good enough. All they need to do is check the prints from the box, pull the CCTV and call his parole officer. They can even search his property for whatever reason they like without a warrant.'

'Can they?'

'It's part of his parole conditions, along with stipulations about knives and guns.'

'Well that's reassuring.'

He saw her let out a breath and he stilled, came back closer and put his arms around her.

'Listen, I'm just concerned for you. I don't want this jerk-off thinkin' he can get away with tormentin' you like that.'

'I know. But it mightn't be him. We have to remember that.'

He breathed in the scent of her hair and tightened his hold. 'Are you sure this has nothin' to do with Dan Steele?'

She shook her head. 'I have no idea.'

'Because if I find out he's behind this, I'm gonna have to do what's right.'

'I just want to move on. I don't want my life to be about anyone else. It's my life. Mine. And no one's going to take this second chance away from me.'

She let him go and looked into his eyes, her determination and grit shining through her expression. He took hold of her hands and locked her gaze.

'The second anything else happens I'm gettin' that CCTV pulled and I'll do whatever it takes to find out who's behind it. You hear me?'

She nodded.

'So, how d'you fancy starrin' in my new video tonight?'

Chapter Thirty

'Ladies and gentlemen, are you ready to rock it country-style? We know out there amongst you are country fans from twenty-seven different countries!' The crowd cheered, blew whistles, stamped their feet, waved cups and banners in the air.

'You've gathered here at the LP Field from right across the globe. And over the next four days and nights you're gonna experience the cream of the Nashville scene! We've got country legends, Kenny Rogers... Dolly Parton... and Vince Gill. And the stars of new country... Blake Shelton... Carrie Underwood... Little Big Town... Jed Marshall... and Honor Blackwood! Welcome to the Marlon Festival! And kicking us off... the wonderful... the awesome... ladies, he wants somewhere to hang his hat... Dan Steele!'

The roar from the crowd took Honor aback even though she should have expected it, should have remembered it. She was in the wings, waiting. She was on next. Straight after Dan. It was probably coincidence or a well-planned schedule for the gossip magazines, whichever it was she didn't have the energy to contest it. She wasn't a diva and she had to stop making her life about everyone else. She was in control of her own destiny now and it felt good.

She watched Dan performing for the fifty-thousand strong crowd. On talent he totally deserved his place on the bill. He'd improved a hundred percent as an artist, had obviously taken time to hone his craft while she'd crawled into a corner with hers.

A pair of arms circled her waist, drawing her body against him. She leant backwards; let his strength prop her up from the inside out. Reaching up a hand she dragged her fingers over the stubble on his face until he moved his head lower and she turned to meet his gaze.

'OK?' he asked her.

She responded by assaulting his mouth, pressing her lips to his, wet, warm, opening for more, desire rushing at her. She couldn't get enough of the way he felt melding with her. He gave her a complete body and head rush whenever they connected.

She looped her arms around his neck and turned full-frontal, staring into his eyes, those slate-gray eyes that set her alight with every flicker.

'God damn, Honor.' He traced her jaw line with his thumb.

'What?' She snaked a hand down from the waistband of his jeans, her fingers nibbling up the centimeters of denim as they tracked a path over his fly. He was everything she wanted. Everything and so much more. He understood her completely. He never asked anything of her. He was always there, solid, determined, on her side without question.

'You wanna know how I feel right now?'

The words had come out as a gruff whisper when he ducked his head low and put his mouth close to her ear.

'Yes,' she responded.

Just the beautiful lilt of her voice sent rivers of heat cascading through him and straight down to his groin. He wanted her so badly it left a physical ache inside of him every time he had to let her go. Why was he still letting her go? She wasn't Karen. She was different, pure, true, loyal to the core. He could trust her.

'You're my everything,' he stated. He held her gaze, watched the movement of her pupils, saw how his statement had affected her.

She caught his hand in hers and interlocked their fingers, pressing them tight up to his knuckle joints until he couldn't tell where he ended and she began.

'Five minutes, Miss Blackwood.' The runner's voice snapped him back to reality. They both had work to do. Whatever he needed to let go of would have to wait.

'Shoot! I'm not ready. Jared, it's the Marlon Festival.' She clapped a hand across her mouth as if it had only just dawned on her what she was about to do.

'Relax, it's all good. Over there's your band.' He pointed to where the musicians were standing by. 'Over there's Ollie and Malcolm, my security guys. Them and me ain't gonna take our eyes off of you for a second. And I happen to know the whole front line of dudes doing crowd control out there is the best there is.' He squeezed her hand in his. He'd been waiting for this reaction for a while. He was concerned she'd got anonymous gifts but he was less concerned now he'd almost ruled out Simeon Stewart.

He'd called in a favor from an old friend who knew ways of finding out everything and anything. According to him, Simeon Stewart was living a quiet existence in Nebraska. He had a job at a fish factory and was Mr Routine. Still a loner but a loner who was living by a tight regime, habits he'd abided by the same time every single day for at least the last week since Mack had been trailing him.

'I can do this,' Honor stated, nodding her head.

'*We* can do this,' he replied, again catching her eyes with his.

She kissed his lips, then let his hand go, snatching up her guitar. 'Milo! You ready?'

'Ladies and gentlemen, put your hands together and let's hear it one more time for Dan Steele!'

Honor rubbed her fingers up and down the fret board of her guitar. She just had to wait for her cue and then she was on. A few weeks ago she didn't think she would ever have it in her to perform on a stage again and now here she was at the Marlon Festival. At the Marlon Festival, with a new record company, new material and a man she adored. She glanced behind her, across the stacks of amps and rows of guitars, to Jared. She swallowed as he made an OK sign with his thumb and forefinger and winked. Most of this was down to him. He'd had faith in her. He'd pursued her for his tour and now he was an integral part of her life.

She blew out a breath and turned just as Dan arrived in the wings. Sweating from the lights and his energetic performance, he received claps on the back from his crew and one of them threw him a towel. Before she could take a step to avoid the moment he was right there in front of her.

'That was wild!' He beamed, his joy at such a great reception from the audience written all over his dewy face.

She plucked at the top string, not knowing what to do or say. Milo took a protective step closer to her.

'You're going to blow them away,' Dan stated. He wiped his jaw with the towel and settled his eyes on her. 'You always did.'

Her stomach contracted with nausea. Now her nerves were running rife. She didn't want to think about before. She had to concentrate on now. She jutted out her chin a little, forcing a smile.

'...a former CMA award winner and now she's back. With a new sound, a new label and a whole heap of guts and determination...' The announcer was building to a crescendo.

'Go bring down the stadium,' Dan told her. He put a hand to her face and the touch had her jerking back like he'd branded her with a hot poker.

'Creep. Let's go, Honor,' Milo said, buffeting Honor forward as her name was called and the audience screamed in anticipation.

She straightened her curls over her scar and took another breath. She adjusted the guitar strap on her neck and willed her legs to stop shaking.

'Ladies and gentleman, put your hands together for, Honor Blackwood!'

He was moving but he saw nothing and nobody. Tramping over cables and equipment, a red mist had descended and his pulse was expanding and contracting out of control. He reached his target, swung back and planted his fist on Dan Steele's jaw.

The slightly taller man fell back against a Marshall amp stack, disorientated. Jared didn't wait for any response. What response was there to give? He'd touched Honor again! He piled in on top of Dan, his anger exploding, raining blows on the other musician until roadies, technicians and other artists started trying to break it up.

'Jed, stop!' A roadie pulled him off, grabbing one of his arms. Jared treated him to a leather-sleeved elbow in the face.

Someone was helping Dan up from the floor. His face was cut from Jared's rings, his nose bloodied. He wiped at it with the sleeve of his shirt, narrowing his eyes.

'What the fuck, man? Somebody call the police! I want him arrested.'

'You want *me* arrested? I warned you what would happen if you touched her again! And you've been stalkin' her! Sendin' her stuff she don't want from you!' He made to move forward but two roadies had his arms. He tried to shake them off but nothing was doing.

'You're fucking insane! D'you hear me?' Dan held the bottom of his shirt to his nose as the blood continued to pour.

'Let go of me! This ain't over until he's not talkin'!' He shook his shoulders, trying to release himself and get back to Dan.

'I'm going to get you charged with assault. How's that going to work with your Marlon Award nomination?'

'You think I give a fuck?' Jared snarled.

Dan nodded, wiping at his nose. 'We'll see.'

He saw the dark-blue uniforms approaching from the arena floor but right now he didn't care. Dan Steele needed to be taught a lesson. He wasn't going to stand by and let him disrespect his girl like that.

'Jared, what the hell is going on here?' Buzz exclaimed, arriving on the scene.

'Great, *all* the cavalry are here. Can I have my arms back now?' He shrugged his shoulders hard and the roadies let go.

'What have you gone and done?' Buzz asked, his gaze drifting to the wounded Dan.

Jared shook his head. 'Yeah, it's all me. Because I'd do something like that to someone who don't deserve it.' He pointed a finger at Dan, who was talking to the police officers. 'He was messin' with Honor.'

Buzz shook his head and drew a breath in. 'Right before the awards.'

'Jeez, Buzz, what was I supposed to do? Leave it a few days and then whup his ass?'

'Jed Marshall?' The police officers were standing in front of him and right away he was blown back ten years. A searing headache sliced across his temples and for a second he was unbalanced. He looked over to Dan, who was having his wounds attended to by a medic. If he got to rewind the last ten minutes would he do the same thing? Or would he let it go? He knew the answer.

He turned his back to the officers and folded his wrists behind his back. 'Read 'em to me.'

Chapter Thirty One

The set had been the tightest they'd ever played and she was buzzing from the crowd's reaction. They'd debuted a song she'd written with Jared and it had gone down a storm. Milo put his arm around her as they left the stage.

'That was awesome, Honor. You had them from the first note and they rocked it out there!'

'Great job, Honor,' Sisqo, the drummer joined in.

'Worked it, honey,' Winnie, the backing singer agreed.

'Thank you so much everybody.' She was smiling so much her cheeks were aching. She couldn't wait to see what Jared had thought about it. She was passed a towel and a bottle of water, which she took, but her eyes were all over the backstage area looking for one person only. She headed down the steps toward the trailer dressing room. Jared wasn't on until later that night with Tim McGraw, but he might have had to do an interview or a meet and greet. She couldn't remember, she'd been too nervous about her own performance.

She scanned the people milling about the artists' area.

'Honor.'

Larry's voice jolted her and she looked in the direction it came. There he was, right in front of her, his Stetson in his hands, looking pious. She didn't know what to say. What was there to say? He was working with Dan Steele now. They might have shared the last ten years but time and people move on and that's what she'd done. She had no business with him anymore.

'If you excuse me I have an interview to get to.' She made to move past him but he caught her arm and stopped her.

'Honey, Jed's been taken downtown,' he spoke.

'What? Is he sick?' Her heart thudded, the feel-good sensations evaporating from that one sentence.

'He's been arrested,' Larry filled in.

She shook her head as if she didn't understand the statement. 'What?' She'd been on stage a little over forty minutes. What could have happened in that time?

'Let me take you there,' Larry offered.

'No. Why would you?' She didn't know what to say. She didn't know what to do. What did you do when your boyfriend was in jail? Did you go there? Did you wait and see what happened?

She put her hands to her head and tried not to panic. But she was panicking. Because the situation was so alien. She was at a festival, she'd just performed, and she was going back on stage later with Lennon and Maisy from the TV series, *Nashville*. This wasn't right.

'Come on, I'll take you there,' Larry said, shepherding her away from a band of media who had gathered at the entrance to the backstage area.

'What did he do?' Honor asked, tears forming in her eyes.

'I'll have my car brought around,' Larry responded.

Word from the hospital was Dan Steele had four stitches in a facial wound and a broken nose. She knew before the words came out of Larry's mouth what Jared had done. It was because Dan had touched her before she'd gone on stage. Because she'd reacted to it, winced and pulled away. Perhaps if she'd not let it bother her. No, she knew he would have reacted the same way. She wasn't condoning it. But she understood it. That's who he was, someone who meted out his own justice, hang the consequences.

'He isn't a bad person.'

Larry had stopped the car outside the police station and she didn't know why she'd felt the need to say that. What was she justifying? His actions? They were his, not hers. She didn't need to take ownership of the situation even if she was caught in the middle of it.

'I'm happy things are going so well for you with Gear, darlin'. You know, I didn't want you to leave Micro but perhaps a change is what we all needed.'

She looked out the window, observed the brick building they'd visited only a week ago when she'd reported the anonymous presents. Perhaps Jared was being interviewed by the same lame officer.

'Professional collaborations don't have to become personal ones.'

She turned her head to look at him. 'You're not my advisor anymore.' Her tone was harsh.

'I know, honey, but I've looked after you for ten years, you don't just switch off the care button.'

Honor shook her head and bit her bottom lip. She didn't want to hear any of this. It was all irrelevant. She was the only decision-maker in her life now.

'Someone like Jed Marshall is always going to have trouble following him around. And if you're with him, then trouble's going to find you too,' Larry told her.

'You don't know him like I do. Trouble doesn't follow him. Trouble's a side-effect of who he is. He doesn't bullshit, he doesn't lie or cheat or disrespect people. If he sees something wrong he puts it right, even if that means cost to him. Like today,' Honor stated.

'We're not in an episode of *Sons of Anarchy* here, Honor.'

'You don't need to understand him, Larry, because *I* do and that's enough.'

She opened the car door and got out, slamming it shut behind her.

They'd taken his watch, his jewelry, his belt, his shoes and his cap before they shut him in the cell. It was like being sixteen all over again. But this time he was entirely to blame and he still didn't regret it for a second. He'd do it all over again in a heartbeat. He looked at the bed and that brought back a whole other set of memories. Sleepless nights filled with yelling and pounding on the walls, screams he tried to ignore, pitch dark.

He put his hands to his head and paced the width. He was done in two strides. Closing his eyes he tightened his core and his resolve. Buzz would sort this out. If they formally charged him he'd hold his hands up, take the rap, respect the law, do the punishment. And if the Marlon Awards panel decided he was no longer worthy of his nomination, then so be it. He wasn't backing down or apologizing because he wasn't sorry.

He clenched his grazed knuckles and tried to ignore the shaking in his hands.

'Pardon me, I think my boyfriend is here...Jared Marshall.'

Everyone was on the phone or shuffling paper. No one seemed to want to talk to her. She'd raised her voice when she'd asked this time and now the waiting area of people were all looking her way.

The female police officer looked down at something on her desk as if she needed to check. Just how many Nashville stars got arrested? If he was here, then Honor knew the whole station would know about it.

'Honor, come sit over here.'

She looked up and there was Buzz, sitting a little way down the corridor. She walked over to him but didn't sit. Sitting meant she was cool with this situation and she really wasn't.

'Is he OK?' she blurted out.

'I haven't seen him. He hasn't asked for a lawyer but I've called him and he's on his way.'

'This is all my fault.' She shook her head and put her hands on her hips, kicking a heel at the floor.

'No. This is down to Jared. He knows it. He's going to bear the consequences.'

'How can you be so OK with this?'

'I've advised him a long time, Honor. This isn't the first time he's ended up in a police station.'

She sighed again and made a reluctant slump into the seat beside Buzz. 'So what do we do?'

'We wait.'

'I can't do that. I want to see him.'

'You don't get a cozy little chat in the interview room like on the TV. There's procedure. We wait for the lawyer, he has to be interviewed, then he'll be charged.'

'What happens then?'

'Hopefully we'll get to take him home.'

'Hopefully?'

'It's not a given.'

'This is so stupid.'

'Agreed on that.'

'Why did this have to happen now? In the middle of the festival, right before the awards.' She stood up again and paced across the corridor, leaning her back up to the wall.

'Jared's never been great with timing.'

Honor blew out a breath.

'Listen, you need to think about yourself in all this,' Buzz told her. He waited for her to meet his eyes before continuing. 'You're representing Gear today. The last thing Jared would want is for you to miss a spot because of him.'

'I can't.'

'You need to. One of you has to be thinking straight.'

'I don't have anything for a couple hours.'

'Then get yourself a coffee and come sit down,' Buzz ordered.

Chapter Thirty Two

'Can we get the hell out of here?'
They'd kept him four hours, insisting on going through all the motions, despite him admitting the crime from the get-go. Everything he was wearing smelled of the place. He just wanted to get out, get showered and get changed.

'Honor was here.' Buzz led the way to the exit.

'What?'

'Did you think she wouldn't come?'

He didn't want to think that Honor had been here because of him. Waiting on those plastic seats, watching the clock tick around like his mom had done.

'I sent her back to the festival. You've already messed things up for yourself – I'm not letting you mess them up for her too.'

Jared nodded as he pushed open the door to outside. 'Thanks, Buzz.'

'My car's over there. We need to discuss damage limitation.'

'...and, Honor, rumor has it Jed Marshall's been arrested for assaulting Dan Steele right here at the Marlon Festival. Would you like to comment on that?'

'Sally-Anne, what sort of a ridiculous question is that, darlin'? No, Honor would not like to comment on it and if any of the rest of you had ideas of asking something similar I want you to can them right now.'

Larry had saved her. Her moose-in-the-headlights impression and mumbled answers about her new album had been challenging enough, but she hadn't realized the news would break so quickly. She was still hanging on to that naivety from 2004. She'd had enough.

'Thank you so much everybody.' She stood up quickly and dismissed herself from the press call.

Once out of the marquee she checked her phone. No calls. Buzz had promised to call as soon as Jared was free. She looked at her watch. She had thirty minutes before she was back on stage.

'Are you OK?'

Honor looked up into the face of a stranger, dressed in jeans and a black Festival t-shirt the roadies all wore. A backstage pass was hanging around his neck.

'Yes...I'm fine. Just hanging out, catching some sun and a little peace,' she responded. After the press interrogation she actually felt a bit faint. It was hot. There was little shade on the field and she knew she hadn't drunk enough water. She needed to remedy that before her next performance.

'Here.' He held out a bottle of water.

She accepted it. 'Thanks.'

'My name's Corbin. I'm working with Lindy Mason this weekend but if you need anything...'

She unscrewed the cap on the bottle and slugged down mouthful after mouthful as if she hadn't drunk in a week. She eventually pulled it from her mouth and wiped the residue with the sleeve of her blouse.

'I actually have my own crew, but thanks, I should really get back to them. Thank you for the water, Corbin, it was nice to meet you.'

She smiled at him and headed back towards her trailer.

It was a cover, a song called 'Telescope' from the *Nashville*

TV show soundtrack and Lennon and Maisy were two of the stars. They'd only had one rehearsal together, but three talented performers didn't need all that long to pull something special together. They brought the song to a finish and the crowd broke into wild applause.

'Thank y'all so much! Thank you!' Honor waved at the crowd and took another bow before leaving the stage. A roadie passed her a bottle of water and a towel and she took both, putting them down on an amp so she could slip her phone out of her pocket. Still no calls or messages. Was Jared still at the police station? Why was no one telling her what was going on?

'Honor.'

She recognized the voice and she didn't want to see him. She hastily pressed keys on her phone ignoring him, pretending she hadn't heard. She felt him approach and she shifted slightly, turning her face towards the side curtains.

Dan touched her arm and she whipped it away. 'Stop it! That's how this whole thing started.'

She looked up at him, taking in his swollen, misshapen nose and the stitches across his cheekbone.

'What do you want?' she asked.

'Can't you see what he did to me?'

'Yeah I see it. What d'you want me to say? It isn't as if he hasn't warned you.'

'He's out of control.'

Honor shook her head. 'You want him to be. You want him out of your way because he's twice the musician you are. That's what all this is about. It's not about me like Jared thinks it is. It's about you pushing his buttons and controlling what happens next.'

'I can't believe I'm hearing this. I'm the victim here!' Dan raised his arms in frustration.

'Why are you back here? You're not on again until tomorrow with Vince Gill. Nice work setting that one up. Who did you have to walk all over?'

Dan shook his head and Honor could see he was biting down his jaw, reining in any smart retorts.

'If you're not here to tell me you're dropping this crazy assault charge then I have nothing to say to you,' she said firmly.

'Honor, I care about you. I care about you being involved with someone like that. He's a loose cannon, everybody knows it and today everybody saw it.'

'Because you made it so.'

'How long's it gonna be before he starts taking his frustrations out on you?'

Fire boiled inside her but she held it in, looked at him, wondering whether this was for real. Was that what he really thought? That Jared was that sort of man? Was that the picture he was going to paint for anyone who asked about the situation? Would he start rumors, write stories, try and discredit Jared for his own gain?

She wet her lips with her tongue and leveled a steely look straight at him. 'Jared Marshall isn't only a better musician than you, he's a better man. You drop the case against him or I'm going to start delivering a few home truths of my own... to Davey Duncan at Countrified or maybe to Yallwire or Nashville Sound.'

Dan shook his head. 'I can't do that. Too much has happened between us and it needs to be stopped for good.'

'You drop the charges, Dan, or I'll tell the world what you said after my attack, when I came to in the hospital.' She was breathing hard, her heart pumping full bore, the disgust she felt for him taking over her whole body.

'What? What are you talking about?'

'Don't you remember?' She scoffed and shook her head. 'Well I guess that doesn't really matter, because *I* remember. Because stuff like that bites into you, eats into your memory every time you're feeling low or having a bad day. And I have to say I've had quite a few of those in the time you've been gone.'

'Honor...' Dan started.

'After I was attacked you said to the doctor...' She paused, the memory flooding her with hurt and pain, stirring up emotions he kept evoking whenever he put himself in her path. 'You said, "when you fix her up, see if you can make her prettier."'

She spat out the last word, driving the point home and trying to get over even one ounce of what that had done to her back then. She held her nerve, kept her eyes on him, knowing what the reaction would be, knowing that once she'd reminded him he'd remember. A flippant comment he'd never intended her to hear, one he probably didn't even mean, but one so ill-timed and placed it had almost destroyed her.

He dropped his eyes to the floor and she finally let her breath go in an audible rush. She had nothing left to say to him. Whether he dropped the case against Jared or not, she'd told him how she felt, finally got rid of what she'd been hauling around with her for too long.

'I can't see public reaction being too great for you if that got out. Kicking someone when they're down isn't really a Tennessee kind of thing. Micro'd have a hard time spinning that around the nice-guy image they're building up. People might just understand exactly why Jared floored your ass.'

He still hadn't picked his head up from looking at the floor of the side stage and she was glad. She picked up the towel and water and pushed herself past. She took the steps off stage two at a time, no idea where she was going. She just knew she'd had more than enough for one night. She didn't want to be leapt on by reporters or get dragged into one of the parties, she just wanted home. She wanted Jared.

'Listen, Buzz, this ain't up for debate, I'm goin' in here. I'm gonna find Honor.'

He'd listened to over an hour of Buzz telling him what he was or wasn't allowed to say to the press about the charges. His advisor had already contacted the Marlon Awards committee and they'd arranged a meeting for the morning. He didn't care about anything except her. He had to know how things were between them. He had to know where he stood. He had to know if she was with him or if he'd just fucked up the best thing that had ever happened to him.

'Jed, we hear the police have charged you with assault. Have you anything to say about that?' A reporter was pushing a microphone in his face and a newsman was training a video camera his way.

'Jed has nothing to say right now. Move along there,' Buzz stated, taking hold of Jared's jacket and ushering him forward.

'Where would she be right now?' He was asking himself as much as Buzz. He checked his watch. She would have finished only fifteen minutes or so ago. Would she have hit one of the party tents? Be doing an interview? His phone was dead and he knew Byron was working with Lindy Mason so there was no hope of getting hold of him. He was running out of ideas.

'We'll find her. Pity you don't know her number, I have full signal and eighty-seven percent.'

'Way to go.'

He flashed his backstage pass at the security by the cordon and he and Buzz passed through. His eyes scanned everyone they walked by – crew, guests, artists – he just wanted to see someone he knew well enough to ask if they'd seen Honor.

'Jared,' Buzz said, catching hold of his arm. He pointed with his other hand.

He could see her. She was coming out of one of the trailers; her guitar case slung over one shoulder, her hair hanging down as she maneuvered out the door. Right at that moment he didn't know what to do. There she was looking so damn perfect and here he was, screwing up again, charges hanging over his head, an award nomination probably dragging in the dirt.

'What are you waiting for?' Buzz asked him.

He shook his head. 'I don't know.'

The damn guitar was stuck in the doorway. What was the matter with the trailer companies? If they were providing trailers for musicians the least they ought to do is make sure a guitarist can get in and out the exit with an instrument on their back. She shifted sideways and tucked the guitar into her body. As it released and she was through she looked up. Jared.

All at once every emotion flooded out of her in a split second. She let the guitar slip from her shoulder and hit the ground and then she was running, haring down the steps of the trailer and tearing across the grass toward him. Her heart was bursting, her eyes leaking tears as she rushed to get to him, to be with him, to make sense of the whole mess they seemed to have gotten in.

She jumped at him, knowing he would catch her and he did. His solid mass hit her like masonry, jarring her, halting her speed, bringing her to a stop in his arms. He put her down and she squeezed him closer, breathing in the scent of him, freshly showered, leather, heat. Running her fingers down his face she kissed his lips, relished the feel of his mouth warming hers in response. It was only after this physical fix, after she'd sated the need for him that she thought about talking.

'Are you OK? I came downtown but they wouldn't let me see you and Buzz said...' She noticed Buzz for the first time as he waved a hand in recognition of his mention. 'Buzz said I should come back to the festival and finish up my night.'

'And Buzz was right,' Jared agreed, holding her hand.

'Listen, am I safe to leave you for a few hours? I could really do with seeing Lucille,' Buzz interrupted.

'Go, man, go see her,' Jared ordered.

'I'll see you for our meeting in the morning,' Buzz reminded. 'Goodnight, Honor.'

'Goodnight,' she responded.

Buzz waved a hand and headed away from them towards the exit.

Jared blew out a breath and kissed Honor's knuckles. 'A crazy day, huh?'

'Something like that. But I remember someone telling me if you don't do something crazy once in a while you may as well be dead.'

'What kind of ass would say something as stupid as that?' Jared smiled.

'The kind of ass I'm in love with,' Honor responded.

She'd kept her voice steady. She wanted him to know but she didn't want it to sound like a proclamation she couldn't play down if he didn't feel the same way.

'What?'

'What?' She swallowed. She didn't know if she had the nerve to say it a second time.

He nodded and kissed her knuckles again. 'You got your car around here? There's somewhere I wanna take you.'

Chapter Thirty Three

'Where the hell are we going? I'm sure we don't have to cross the state line to get good ribs. In fact I know we don't,' Honor said as she followed Jared's directions along the freeway.

'It's only another five miles or so, I swear,' he responded.

She glanced across at him. He was rubbing his reddened knuckles, looking out of the passenger window as they passed the country by. What had happened with Dan was the elephant in the car. They'd driven twenty miles already and they'd talked through her entire set list of the Marlon – which songs she felt had gone well, which songs could be dropped out of her next performance, what she could try next time. Neither of them had touched on the hot topic that really needed some sort of conversation, and hopefully closure.

'I don't regret what I did and I'd do it again,' Jared stated. 'I know it's not politically correct to go beatin' up on people but that's OK. I'll face up to whatever's comin'.' He turned to look at her. 'I just want you to know that.'

'I do know that,' she answered. She kept her eyes on the road.

'He's playin' games with you. Hell, he's playin' games with me too, but I only know one way, you know.'

'I know,' she answered.

'Hell, I *don't* know, Honor. I don't want you to be ashamed of who I am. I can't change it. I don't wanna change it. I've been raised this way and it's the right way, I truly believe that.'

'I know. I understand. It's OK.' She meant it. She meant it with all her heart. It might be rough justice but at least he took a stand. At least he had an opinion, morals, strength; there was no sitting on the fence, no gray areas.

'For real? See, I don't wanna go down this road and...' He stopped talking, turned to look at her.

'What is it?' She could see he was thinking hard. He'd pulled his cap low but she could just see his gray eyes, shadowed by thoughts he wasn't giving up yet.

'Take the next left,' he stated.

'What is this place?'

The car was creeping along the wooded track and Honor was ducking and sitting forward in her seat trying to make out where they were headed. In a few hundred meters they'd be reaching his lodge at the Cedars of Lebanon State Park. He loved this place. It reminded him so much of home. That's why he'd bought one of the small cabins soon after he arrived in Nashville. It was his retreat, his escape when life living in the middle of country music central got too much. He'd hang out there, swim, ride, write songs, just enjoy the simple things.

'Just pull up right over there,' he told her, pointing.

'Here? This place?'

'My place,' he responded, a hint of pride in his tone.

Honor pulled to a stop. 'This is your place?'

'Yeah, wanna see it?' He grinned and pulled the handle of the car door. 'We might have to go collect some wood to get the fire goin'.'

The lodge was basic but homey. A little like his place in Nashville, but even more rustic. The front door led straight into a small kitchen diner which housed a table and a couple of chairs, then followed through to a den. There was a large couch covered with plaid rugs and gingham cushions, a small old-fashioned TV in the corner and the biggest fireplace Honor had ever seen, in front of which was a rug that looked like bear skin.

'I'd like to say I caught it but I'm not sure it's real.'

'What?' Honor turned back to him, watched him putting their guitars down.

'The rug.'

She smiled. 'It's great... the place I mean... not really a fan of bears, alive or dead.'

'Not even if they're sitting on the shelf at Target? I saw you look at a cute little doorstop.'

She let out a laugh and smiled at him.

'You hungry?' he asked.

'Don't tell me, bear steaks?'

'Burgers from the freezer and Alabama hot sauce?'

'Perfect.'

They'd collected wood for the fire, dropped in on the ranger who'd provided milk, coffee and a six-pack of beer and the meat Jared had cooked on the grill was treating her mouth to raw succulence, chili and woodsmoke.

'This is so good,' she said, taking a swig from her bottle of beer.

'I told you before, eggs and burgers is all I do.'

'That's fine by me.'

She smiled at him, watched him press a spot of sauce out the corner of his mouth.

'Damn, forgot the napkins. Never had company here before.'

'No?'

'What, you think this is the place I bring all those hoards of sexy fans I have?'

'Isn't it?'

'Hell, no. Having sexy fans is great for my ego but that's all.' He laughed then picked up his drink. 'Anyway, Miss Blackwood, I've been checkin' out some of the people followin' you on social media.'

'Gear say I have to do at least three meaningful tweets a day. I've been thinking about letting Mia loose on it and paying her.'

'Man, she would take you down.'

'I know, I'd be twerking someone before lunch.' She smiled and sat back in her chair.

'She's cool, though, and Byron likes her,' Jared said, pushing his finished plate away.

'She likes him too. He's the first guy she's been really into since Leroy left her for Mexico.'

'What?'

'It doesn't matter.' She leant forward, reaching across the table for his hand and smoothing her thumb over his damaged knuckles. 'What are you going to do about the awards?'

He shrugged and she could see from his body language it wasn't something he really wanted to discuss. But that was too bad because the fallout was going to affect them both.

'Buzz has fixed up some meetin' with the committee tomorrow. It's just a formality. They don't want someone up on charges in the runnin' for an award and I understand that. I don't blame them.'

She squeezed his hand. 'What if the charges were dropped?'

'Hell, you reckon Dan Steele is gonna miss out on a prime opportunity to take me down? He's been hangin' out for this.'

'I spoke to him.'

He took his hand from hers. 'What?'

'Did you think I was going to just let him do this to you? To us? Like you said, he's been hanging out for this. He's been manipulating you and me and I couldn't just stand by without trying to do something.'

'You shouldn't have done that.' He stood up, picking up the plates and carrying them over to the kitchen area.

'Why not?' She watched him. He banged the plates down then opened the fridge, taking out another beer.

'Because it's my fight. You shouldn't get involved. When the wreckin' ball's swingin' I only want it to take *me* down, not you.' He opened the bottle then leant against the countertop, taking a swig.

'I'm involved already. And we're in this together... aren't we?'

Her heart had stepped up a gear now. She knew what she was getting into with him. She thought he realized that she was all in, no matter what. His lack of reply was biting at her. Why wasn't he saying anything? Why was he just stood across the room hiding his eyes from her?

'Jared.'

'It isn't just about that jerk,' He raised his head and leveled a look at her. 'There's somethin' I've gotta tell you. And when you know it, things might change.'

This was tearing at his heart. He had held off telling her for so many reasons, most of them selfish. He didn't want to go through the same kind of pain he'd experienced with Karen. But what was the alternative? Keep on deceiving Honor? The more he fell for her, the closer they got, the worse it would be.

'Whatever it is, I'll understand.'

She was crossing the room now, coming nearer and he put the beer down, folding his arms across his chest. If she touched him he was done for. It would all come pouring out and he might not be able to stop. He needed to stop somewhere. He couldn't let it all go because it wasn't just about him.

'Jared, tell me.' She paused. 'What are you afraid of?'

'How about just about everythin'? Of losin' you, of hatin' myself, of lettin' someone in.'

She reached out to touch his shoulder and he moved away, took a couple of paces toward the other wall. 'Don't.'

'You're scaring me.'

What the hell was he doing? If he didn't start talking soon he would lose her just for acting like an ass. And that wasn't better, not now they'd come this far.

'Jared, please, just talk to me,' she begged.

There were tears in her eyes already and she was hugging her arms to her body, looking every inch the beautiful woman she was. He wanted to grab hold of her, take her in his arms and kiss every inch. But she had to know about this before or if that happened. Because he was marked on the inside, branded forever, whether the world knew or not.

He blew out a breath and put his hand to his cap. 'When I was sixteen somethin' bad happened.' He looked to her. 'I spent two years in juvenile detention.'

He waited a second for the words to sink into her before carrying on. 'Except I didn't get a private room, education or a fancy gymnasium. My arrestin' officer saw to it that the system screwed me over because me and him – him and my family – had history.' He closed his eyes, remembering the smirk on Officer Finlay's face when he'd finally got to read him his rights. 'For the last part of my sentence I got a cell in a state prison with my momma cryin' every weekend because she felt guilty.'

What he'd gone through in there he kept boxed up at the very back of his mind. The filth, the animals housed in those walls – killers, perverts, wife-beaters – he'd been exposed to everything and he'd just worn it, kept his head down and prayed for an out. But it had changed him, it had hammered at his self-worth, worn down his youthful innocence and the worst of it was, he hadn't even deserved it.

'No one knows, the public I mean. It was a youth record, it was sealed, so at least I could start again. The one thing it gave me was determination. I came out knowin' I had to make it with music and nothin' or no one was gonna stop me.' He nodded as the feeling rolled over him. 'But being in there, Honor – being labeled a criminal, being with those men – when I was just a boy not knowing much about anything... it wasn't right. It wasn't just.' He could feel emotion was getting the best of him now. He could remember the smell of the place to this day. Grim, sweat, urine.

'Every day I'm praisin' the Lord for givin' me this second chance but I'm trapped with these stinkin' fuckin' memories. Two years wasted, two years of hurt for my family – shame, dishonor – all because of some asshole cop. You asked me why I never take the cap off.' He put his hand to the peak. 'It was the first thing they took off me the day they brought me in and it was the first thing I put back on when I got out.'

He put his fist to his mouth and closed his eyes as the tears came.

There was not a second of hesitation. She ate up the space between them in three strides and she took him, clapped her arms around him and held on tight as he cried.

'Sshh, don't do that. It's breaking my heart.' The tears were falling from her eyes, just thinking about what he'd been through when he was so young. While she was cutting her first record and enjoying fame and fortune, he'd been in a prison cell.

'I'm sorry, Honor.' His words were muffled as he pressed his face into her shoulder, taking the comfort she was offering.

'No, I'm sorry, for the both of us. Between foster homes and juvenile detention the system screwed us both. Thank God for music, huh?' She smiled. 'But it's not our fault, not any of it.' She flexed her fingers over the leather of his jacket, wanting him to feel the sentiment behind her touch.

He lifted his head, his grey eyes moist from the tears.

'I don't care what you did,' she stated, forcing him to look at her. 'I don't want to know what you did. It was way back then and it's over.' She held his hands. 'I believe in you... I believe in us.'

'The last person I told... she broke my heart.'

'I'm glad.' She touched his face, holding her hand to his cheek. 'Because she sent you to me.'

'I don't deserve you,' he whispered.

'I love you, Jared.'

Chapter Thirty Four

Her words attacked his heart, ordered it to open the gates. She knew what haunted him and still she was there, offering nothing but support, not judging, not condemning. It was almost too much to take, too much to believe in. He'd spent so long holding back, could he really give her everything – put his faith in her, in them?

'Lord, I love you.'

Putting his hand behind her head he drew her towards him; his lips connected with hers in a hot rush he didn't want to stop. It was like being freed all over again, a thrill was building inside, from his soul and outwards, adrenaline, joy, desire were all combining and culminating at once. Before he stopped to think, before he could put the brakes on or wonder whether it was the right thing, he was shrugging off his jacket and his fingers were at the hem of Honor's blouse.

He didn't want to move his mouth from hers. Her soft, sweet tongue rolling with his was a sensation he never became tired of. He backed them over into the living room, his hand working its way underneath her top, desperate to feel her skin under his hands.

'Jared.' It was more of a sigh than a word and his name on her lips in that way sent a shot of need to his groin.

He took his mouth from hers, slowly, his tongue lingering on her bottom lip. 'What?'

She stilled in his arms and brought her hands up to his baseball cap. He swallowed and waited, knowing what she was going to do. He closed his eyes as he felt her grip the peak and slowly pull the hat from his head. He felt her breath on his face and he wanted to open his eyes but he couldn't. The cap was like his armor. When he wore it he was the person he was now, not the boy he'd been before. He was ready to lay himself bare in every way with Honor, but that didn't mean he wasn't as scared as hell.

'Open your eyes.' Her voice was pleading with him but he was fighting tears again. So many emotions were pulsing through his veins; he couldn't keep a hold on any of them. He felt her hands cup his face, her fingers moving upwards and towards the tawny buzz-cut that covered his head.

'Jared, look at me.'

He looked so different without the cap. Younger, more good guy than bad boy. She ran her hands over his cropped haircut, relishing the feel of it under her fingers. She knew what this meant to him, how symbolic it was now and how much of himself he was entrusting to her. She wanted to share the same with him, because in the past weeks he'd given her more than anyone in her entire life.

He opened his eyes and she balked. Without the cap shading them, those grey eyes were like brilliant pebbles, shining for just her, full of love and longing. She ran a finger down one sideburn and brought the tip across his cheek and down to his mouth, making tiny circles on his bottom lip.

She let out a sound as he caught her finger and took it past his lip, into the warmth of his mouth, his tongue smoothing over her nail and flicking down the skin to the first joint. Her stomach rolled and she put a hand on his shoulder to steady herself. He sucked her finger in and she felt her body twist as a pang of want stirred so hard. She didn't want this to stop tonight. She couldn't wait any longer to be with him completely. She removed her finger from his mouth, running it down the front of his t-shirt, pressing just hard enough to feel the definition of his torso. She didn't move her eyes from his. She wanted to see his reaction, see the burn of desire she hoped was there in him as much as it was in her.

When she reached the belt of his jeans she stopped, watching the rise and fall of his chest as his breathing accelerated. She pulled at his t-shirt, inching the material upwards until he had no choice but to help pull it up and over his head. And there was that incredible body in front of her again. She had to take a breath. Her insides were pounded by feelings so intense, they made her quake.

'Honor.' His voice was coated with emotion and she could feel the hard length of him pressing against her thigh. She didn't want to rush. She wanted to savor every second.

As she traced around the letters of 'Truth', tattooed in black italics on his left oblique, he worked his hands under her blouse, his fingers inching up toward the lace of her bra. She smoothed her hand to the scar that ran from his breastbone to his navel and followed the line, while his fingers were skirting the perimeter of her underwire.

She dropped her hand from him and in one quick move, pulled her top off, dropping it to the floor. She had no hesitation about this moment. She'd yearned for him for so long, but now it was everything she felt before and a hundred times more – because she loved him – because he'd shared something so precious with her. His past, his failings, his fears.

He watched her slip the straps of her bra off her shoulders and ease down the lace cups. He swallowed as she twisted the white material around her body to unfasten the hooks. She removed the bra, slowly, keeping her eyes locked on him before dropping it to the floor.

His gut was telling him to lose a little control, to act on the desire that was raging but seeing her bare before him was evoking something much stronger than sexual need.

'Put your hands on me.'

There was a boulder in his throat. His mouth was dry and he couldn't keep his eyes off her. He raised a hand but stopped, held it there, paused.

'Please, Jared.' She was running her hand across her breast now, her mouth slightly open, her chest rising and falling with every rapid breath. God, she was beautiful.

He grabbed her by the hips and lifted her off the floor, pressing her naked torso to his as he backed her over towards the fireplace. She caught up his mouth in a kiss so dirty he thought he'd explode.

He lowered her to the bear skin rug then dropped to his knees in front of her, breathing hard, wanting to take this slowly but not knowing if he could.

'Lay down,' he whispered.

She folded backwards on his command, arching her back as the pelt brushed against her shoulders.

He took her all in. Her dark hair laying out behind her on the wooden floor, her tight, turned-on breasts, her little waist and those tight jeans wrapping up the rest of her. He'd never wanted anyone so much.

He planted one hand down on the floor at her side, holding himself over her, looking into her eyes and wanting to absorb everything emanating from her. She reached up, put a hand to his hair, caressing his head then drawing him down into another kiss.

He left her lips and trailed his tongue down her neck, stopping to press his lips against the pulse at her throat, her collarbone, the top of her breast.

'Jared.' She twisted slightly, raising her breasts.

He didn't need any more of a direct invitation. Her nipples were telling him everything he needed to know. He touched his tongue against the nub and she squirmed a little. Little flicks and a swirl over the center sent her convulsing under him and her hands were at his fly, feeling for the buttons. He took her hand in his while his mouth drew in her breast and he felt her fingers clench as she let out a sound that dragged at him.

He kissed lower, trailing his head down over her rib cage until he met her navel and the waistband of denim.

'I want to feel you,' she told him, reaching down.

'You're not ready,' he stated.

He unfastened a button then slipped the zipper down, watching her for a reaction. He wanted to know how it felt, he wanted to see how it felt to her, to have him touching her.

He slipped his hands underneath her and pulled at the waistband, drawing the denim out and under her ass until her jeans were free, unrestricted and he was able to adjust his hold, pull from the hem of the legs and take them off completely.

'Jared.' She turned a little on the rug. Just a strip of white lace separated him from finding out how she felt on the inside.

'You're so beautiful.' He put a hand to his chest. His heart was hammering so heavy he needed a second.

'I want you, Jared.'

Her pure, sweet voice telling him that sent another shockwave over him like an earthquake off the scale. 'Lord, Honor, you're killin' me.'

'Touch me,' she begged.

He hesitated, watched the pure white heat of need in her eyes. Putting his fingers to her panties he took a breath, then ripped straight across the side seam.

She arched off the rug a little more and he could feel himself edging closer to something he'd have a hard job holding back from.

He looked at her. Perfect, dark curls, a swirl of moisture just visible. He put his thumb into his mouth and locking his gaze with hers he wet his skin. And then he touched her, pressing his thumb on that sweet spot and listening to her cry out.

'Jared, oh God, Jared.'

She writhed as he moved his hand. Deep, hard circles from his thumb were sending flashes of hot sparks all over her body.

She wanted to scream for him to stop. She wanted to scream for him to carry on, faster, harder, further, but all she could do was let her body take over. She felt him push a finger inside her and she clawed at the floor with her hands.

'What does it feel like?'

The sound of his voice had her moving her hips to the rhythm he was creating.

'Hot... it's hot and... wet and I want it so much, Jared. I want it so much.'

'God, Honor, you're destroyin' me.'

The swirling stopped and for a second the heat lessened. 'Oh God... oh God!' Her stomach clenched as she felt the warmth of his mouth inside her, his tongue pushing her lips apart and circling her center, licking, biting, teasing.

There was nothing she had control of now. Her limbs were flailing, numb. She was coming apart and when she did he was going to feel the whole thing. She was leaving her body, here on the bear skin rug, and floating higher, soaring out of the room and up to the stars, reaching and climbing until finally she was there.

'Jared! Oh my God!' She closed her eyes and felt her toes splay, every part of her longer, fuller, more sensitized. She clasped his head as he brought himself back up to look at her, pulling him hard, wanting his mouth on hers.

She kissed him, pressing her lips hard against his, wanting to taste her own scent, share the intimacy. When she drew away she felt like someone different, someone completely liberated. She was someone who'd been living such a restricted life, too scared to let loose. Now she'd broken free.

She sat herself up, went onto her knees as he shifted back, mimicking her position. Running her hands over his broad shoulders, she stopped to trace a finger around the tattoo of the Confederate flag on his upper arm. She couldn't wait any longer to see all of him.

'Stand up,' she ordered.

'What?'

'Stand up,' she repeated.

The authority in her tone had him on his feet. He was defenseless here and he wanted to be. This was his moment, with his girl, the only girl, the one girl who had taken in everything he'd told her and thrown it down because she loved him and believed in him.

He watched her crawl forward on her knees and then she was parting his legs, running a hand up each denim-covered leg, driving him crazy. When she reached the buttons she didn't waste any time, she ripped the fly open and dragged down the jeans until the only option he had was to lose them. He kicked them across the floor and looked down at her, kneeling naked and perfect in front of him.

She inched forward, her dark bangs falling over her face as she took her eyes from his and focused on what was in front of her. He was tight and hot, a ball of heat. He'd never felt so pent up, so desperate, so emotional. He closed his eyes the second he felt her tongue touch the tip of his penis. She was so gentle it was making him crease inside. She took him in and his hands were in her hair, stroking her curls as her mouth danced around him.

'Honor.' He didn't have the strength to say anything else. He was barely holding it together now as waves of a warm, prickly sensation folded over him. Every motion brought something a little more intense, took him a little nearer. He didn't want to lose it yet. When he came, he wanted to be inside her. As that thought struck he took her head in his hands and pulled her away.

'Did I do something wrong?' She got to her feet, a concerned look on her face.

'Yeah you did. You did too much too darn well.' He took a breath, framed her face with his hand then quickly he moved. He lifted her up, pressing her against his length until they connected. She let out a gasp and clung to him, her fingers digging into his back.

'I love you,' she whispered, looking into his eyes.

'With all my heart,' he responded, edging her down a little and earning a sigh.

He carried her to the couch and with every step he lowered her on to him a little further until she thought she couldn't take anymore. He was so solid, yet so gentle and tender in his motion she wanted to cry out for it. Her body slipped down onto the rugs and cushions and finally every inch of him was inside her. She felt him tuck a hand behind her bottom and pull her closer as she cried out.

'D'you feel that?' he asked, moving slowly back then bringing himself into her again.

'Yes.' Her voice was husky in response, new sensations travelling over her.

'Tell me how it feels,' he begged.

She felt him push harder, a little faster and she reached for him, pressing her fingers into his shoulders again, scratching the skin.

'It feels... like... I don't want you to stop. Like I want to feel it forever.'

He thrust his hips, filling her each time, rocking her into a rhythm like no other, each time taking her back to that knife edge between pleasure and pain.

'Don't stop,' she pleaded.

'I can't stop.' He let out a guttural groan as she bucked against him, matching his pace, pushing herself on to him, feeling every motion as he brought her closer to the point of no going back.

'I can't... Jared... I can't.' She was losing to her body again. She was out of control and falling hard and fast.

'Let go,' he begged her. 'Let go with me.'

'Fall with me,' she whispered.

He cried out and she pressed her lips to his as her wave crested at the same time and she dropped, splashing down into the water, rolling up towards the shore, her heart racing and her emotions shot to pieces.

She clung to him, pressed her damp skin to his and held on tightly. His heart was racing and his breath was hot and staggered against her cheek, their bodies still locked together. She tried to come down, but smaller waves were still breaking, little shockwaves of pleasure sneaking up on her as Jared pulsed inside her.

'Did I hurt you?' He raised his head from her embrace to look at her.

'No.' She brushed her hands over his hair. 'No... it was beautiful... just so beautiful.'

'It was everything,' he told her.

'Yes, it was.' She put her hand in his. 'It was everything.'

Chapter Thirty Five

With two steaming coffee cups in her hand she entered the bedroom, smiling when she saw Jared was unmoved. She put the drinks on the dresser and crawled back into bed, snuggling up close to him and drawing the covers over them both. She lay there for a moment, breathing him in and then she pinched an inch of skin and he flinched.

'Hey, what was that?' He shifted in the bed and turned to look at her.

'Good morning,' she greeted, smiling.

'One thing you're gonna have to learn about me is I ain't no mornin' person,' he stated, rubbing at his eyes.

'I've made coffee.'

'I'm awake.' He grinned and wrestled her into him, making her squeal as he tickled her ribs.

'Stop!'

'What is this?' He pulled at the t-shirt she was wearing. 'Are you really wearin' my limited-edition Lynyrd Skynyrd tour t-shirt?'

She pulled it up and over her head, throwing it down on the duvet. 'Not now. What you gonna do about it?'

She watched him wet his bottom lip with his tongue. 'What am I gonna do about it?'

She nodded, sat up a little straighter, pushed her hair back, unashamedly bare.

He studied her, watched as the lack of covering and his scrutiny made her breasts change and harden. He could look at her for always, just look, and before last night that would have been enough. But now he knew how perfect she was in every way, how her body responded to his, he never wanted to be parted from her in any sense.

He sat himself up and reached out for her, his thumb lingering over her nipple until she closed her eyes for him. He cupped her breast and then pulled her in for a kiss.

'How hot is that coffee?' he drawled, nipping at her bottom lip.

'It'll keep,' she responded, pushing herself up against him.

The tune of 'Sweet Home Alabama' erupted from Jared's phone on the dresser. He groaned and let her go.

'It might be Buzz. After yesterday I can't let it go,' he stated, his eyes meeting hers.

'Go, go answer it,' she urged.

He left the bed and moved to pick up the phone. 'Buzz... well I'm not at home right now. What's up?'

She pulled the cover up around her and watched him as he spoke. It was only just past eight. She didn't know much about Buzz's daily agenda for Jared but Larry never used to call her before nine unless there was a problem.

'You what? Are you serious?' He turned around to look at Honor, his eyes wide. 'No, I know, it's good. I just don't understand it is all.'

She tried to listen harder, decipher what was going on by watching his body language. She mouthed the word 'what?'

'Yeah I will. We have a sound check slot at three. Listen, thanks, man, for sorting all this out and for everything. Are you comin' tonight? Then, hell, I'll see you there.'

He ended the call, put down the phone and leapt back onto the bed.

'Hey! That was almost my strumming hand,' she said, scooting back a little as he advanced.

He took hold of her hand and put it to his mouth, kissing the skin. 'That was Buzz. Dan Steele's dropped the charges against me. My lawyer called Buzz and that's it, it's all done.'

She stilled, not knowing how to react. Had Dan really done what she'd asked him? Had what she said really sunk in and had an effect? Or was this just another one of his games just so he could be in control. Did he have some other plan? Perhaps there was something else going on they didn't know about yet.

'Hey, what's up? This is good news. Buzz says he's told the Marlon Awards board and they no longer want a meet, which means I'm still in the runnin'. I'm performin' tonight at the festival and, when that's done and the awards are over, we can head off to Alabama to meet my mom, with no pending trial over my head.' He brushed a hand down her hair then held her chin up with his thumb and forefinger.

'You really want me to meet your mom?' The thought of being invited into a family filled her with mixed emotions. Joy that she was going to be able to interact in that way like she'd never had the chance to do before and fear because she didn't know how that would feel.

'Yes I do. We've only got six weeks before the tour. We start rehearsals next week and it's gonna be full-on. I don't know when we'll get the chance to get to Alabama again. We don't hit there until the Fall.'

Honor nodded her head and forced a smile.

'What? Are you worried about meetin' my mom?'

'No... I guess... maybe a little. I just have no idea what it's going to be like. I never had a mom, remember? I had care workers and I'm hoping that it isn't anything like the same.'

'I don't know, she was damn straight-down-the-line with me and my brother. Anna seemed to do better. She'd put on her cute face and force the tears out.' He laughed.

'How old are they?'

'Jacob's the baby, he's coming up twelve. Anna's fifteen.'

'So you're the eldest.'

'Yes, ma'am but I look well on it don't I?'

Honor smiled and looped her arms around his neck, tugging him towards her for a kiss. She pressed herself against him and shivered as his arm went around her waist, pulling her into him.

'I love you, baby,' he whispered into her ear.

'With all my heart,' she replied.

'So, where's Baby Blue Bonnet really from?'

He was showing her the park. They'd headed off into a trail through the woods and when he asked that question she felt the need to kick a stick.

'I have no idea. I was left in Michigan but you're right, I could be from anywhere. My parents could have been visiting, just passing through, just dropping off their unwanted brat on the Mayor's doorstep.'

'I'm sorry, that was a real dumb-ass question to ask. I just can't imagine havin' no history like that. I can trace my ancestors back as far as... well I think one of my great granddaddies helped Noah with that Ark.'

Honor spat out a laugh and thumped him on the arm.

'Hey, that's my frettin' arm just there and I have a gig tonight.' He put an arm around her shoulders and pulled her close.

'Roots. You need to put down some roots in Alabama with the Marshall family,' Jared told her. 'Just you wait, my mom will have you in her dance dress before you've even met the chickens.'

'Dance dress?'

'It still swamps Anna.'

'I bet she's a great cook too,' Honor said.

'Yeah, and she can sing.'

'Now you're being bad, stop it.'

'She's gonna love you, Honor.' He stopped walking and turned to look at her. 'She's not gonna believe that someone like you is with someone like me but...'

'Don't do that. Don't put yourself down. We're all marked by things that happened in the past.' She moved her hair and touched her scar. He raised his hand and touched hers with his.

'If I ever see the guy that did that...'

'We'll dial 911 and wait for the cops. It took me a long time to realize that people like him just don't have any sense of right or wrong. Even after psychiatric treatment it's doubtful that the inbuilt, screwed vision of life he has can be changed. When he attacked me, he just attacked me. He didn't do it because he thought it was bad, he did it just because he wanted to.'

'Never again, not on my look-out.' He kissed her cheek, then linked their hands and started to walk again. 'So, you gonna watch me later on?'

'Hell yeah. Is that how it goes?'

'You're catchin' on to those Southern ways, baby. C'mon, I need to show you how to get real dirty in these woods over here.'

Chapter Thirty Six

'Are you OK?' Honor had to shout to raise her voice above the noise of the band. Jared's musicians were on stage at the Marlon Festival starting up the opening number while he waited for his cue.

'Sure! This is what I love the most. I'm gonna go out there and have the time of my life... and you're gonna be watchin'!' he called back.

'Thirty seconds, Jed.'

'I'd better go. I'll be in the pit with Mia. I'll be the one screaming harder than anyone else,' Honor told him.

'I love you, girl,' he told her.

'I love you too. Go!' She kissed his lips, holding onto his hands.

'Ten seconds, Jed, let's go.'

She let him go, watched him rush along the backstage area before she hurried down the steps and around the side of the stage to the VIP pit.

'HOW Y'ALL DOIN' TONIGHT?'

Jared's voice reverberated around the arena and the noise rising from the crowd disorientated her. There were fifty thousand people screaming at the tops of their voices for her man. She'd watched a couple of other acts the previous day but the reaction was nothing on this. Southern flags and banners were being held up in the air, drinks were being spilt because of frenzied clapping and rock hands.

'ARE YOU READY FOR THIS OUTLAW?'

She flashed her pass at security on the cordon and looked for Mia. The audience screamed louder, hats were waving, women were sitting on the shoulders of men, flashes from cameras and glows from cell phones were erupting everywhere.

Mia had her mouth wide open in a screech when Honor reached her. She pulled her arm.

'Where've you been? You're missing it! WOO HOO! YEAH!' Mia jumped up and down, waving her arms in the air. 'Did you bring corn dogs?'

'What? No.'

'Look at Byron! God, he's so sexy! BYRON!'

Honor caught an elbow in the ear as Mia jumped again, waving her arms.

'LET'S BREAK ALL THE GOD-DAMN RULES... IT'S TIME FOR SOME DRINKIN' DOWN SOUTH!'

The band kicked into one of Jared's most popular songs and the crowd reacted immediately with more air-punching, photo-taking and joining in with the lyrics. Honor had never experienced anything like it. Ten years away from the music scene and she had no idea it was going to be like this. Everyone around her was worshipping Jared like a god and looking at the stage, seeing him perform, hearing the fantastic band, she could understand why. *She* was almost awestruck. He was charismatic as well as supremely talented and he held every single person watching in the palm of his hand.

Mia elbowed her in the side. 'I totally forgot. You've never seen him live, have you, doll?'

Honor shook her head, aware of what she'd missed. He was a true country rock star, not just a song-writing genius but an energetic performer who know exactly how to have a party on stage and transmit that feeling to the entire room.

'He rocks it, doesn't he?' Mia called to her.

'Yes he does,' she answered.

'I want to thank y'all so much for comin' to hang out with me tonight. I've had such a blast, so thank you for making me feel so welcome.'

The crowd responded with whoops and yells. He couldn't see any of them. They were a black mass of shadows, stretching out in front of him and ending who knew where. But he could feel them. They'd clapped and shouted their appreciation, joined in with all the songs and made the gig one of his best performances of the year. This was why he did what he did. When he found out he could be so admired for just bringing the style of music he loved playing to the stage, it was a dream come true. He loved, lived and breathed what he did and every day he praised the Lord for giving him the chance to do it.

'Now, this last song I'm gonna play is a brand new one. It's gonna be on my new album and I wrote it for my girl.' He whirled his hand in the air and a spotlight moved, falling over the VIP pit, lighting it up.

'She's down there somewhere, Miss Honor Blackwood. Let's hear some appreciation for her y'all, because she's one talented lady.' He saw Mia had grabbed up Honor's arm and was waving it in the air as Honor looked embarrassed from the attention.

The crowd responded straight away, clapping and screaming their acknowledgement as he knew they would.

'So, being in love an' all.' He paused. 'It brings out all these sorts of feelings I barely knew existed.' He stopped and the crowd whistled. 'So, Honor, this one's for you. This is *All For You*.'

Here I am, and God I think I'm fallin'
Can't hold on, you've got me floored
Can't forget, Lord I think I'm drowning
Going down without a care
You didn't even know how much you reached me

You didn't even know that you could teach me

But it's all for you
Everything I do
Cos now you're here with me, baby it's all true
Yes, it's all for you
Every single day
And baby now I've found you, there's no other way

She knew Mia was staring at her but she couldn't stop. The tears were leaking from her eyes as she watched him and his favorite acoustic guitar work magic on a song he'd written for her. It was perfect. *He* was perfect.

'Oh! I might just orgasm. This is *the* best corn dog I've ever had.' Mia was stuffing it into her mouth as they waited in the holding area for Jared and Byron to finish up and join them.

'I thought we were going to eat someplace,' Honor remarked as the rest of the corn dog got pushed down Mia's throat.

'We are. I mean, this is a good corn dog an' all but it's basically just a snack. D'you know how long I've been here? D'you know how much more it costs me to have someone else take care of the store instead of you? I deserve this.'

'I slept with Jared last night,' Honor informed.

'Holy fuck! For real? For a minute I thought you were gonna hang on till the wedding night.'

Honor took a swig from her water bottle.

'Well? You can't just lay that on me and not give me details. What's he like?'

'I'm not giving you details. We've never given each other details.'

'You're kidding me? I've given you a blow by blow account – literally – of all of my conquests.' Mia looked affronted.

'It was special... really special and that's all I'm saying,' Honor stated.

'I saw the two of you on You Tube in his new video and I swear the screen misted over. I'll hedge my bets that he was damn good.'

'And Byron?' Honor asked quickly.

'Oh he's got a body to die for. You have to be fit for all this touring they do. He's the most sought-after guitarist in Nashville you know. Everybody wants him, Lindy Mason, Jared, Vince Gill, you name them, they want him. I call him Deacon Claybourne but he doesn't really get it.'

Honor laughed.

'Miss Blackwood.' The middle-aged roadie she'd seen the day before approached them, something in his hands.

'Hey... it was Corbin wasn't it?' she replied, frowning as she tried to remember.

'Yes, that's right. You remembered.' He smiled.

'I really appreciated the water yesterday.'

'I'm Mia, Byron Starks' girlfriend and Honor here's my very best friend. You are...?'

'Corbin Severs, ma'am, pleased to meet you.' He held out his hand to Mia and she took it.

'We're just about to head off so...' Honor started.

'Sure. I just found these backstage. They're picks,' he stated, handing her a tiny plastic box not more than a couple of inches across.

'Oh,' she took them, her brow furrowing in confusion. She didn't recognize the box at all. 'Are you sure they're mine? I mean, there are so many artists here and...'

'They're personalized.' He took the box back from her hand and opened it up.

There were maybe a dozen guitar picks all with her photo or cover art from her first albums, the logo of her name in gold or pink, one was sequined, with HB engraved into it.

'Wow, they're awesome! I need to get some of those for the store. Would you sign some?' Mia asked, looking past Honor into the box.

'I've not seen these before,' Honor stated, lifting her eyes to look up at Corbin.

'They were just backstage... you know maybe your new record company had them done and they kind of got lost en route?' he suggested.

'Whoa, hang on, maybe it's that stalker guy. Flowers, owls, chocolates and now personalized picks,' Mia blurted out.

'I don't think... well I don't know but... well I was just passing these on. I mean if you don't want them I can unfind them again for you,' Corbin suggested.

'No, it's fine. They're pretty.' She took the box back. 'I expect you're right. They're probably something Gear arranged. Jared has some with skulls and stuff on,' Honor said, smiling at the roadie.

'Right, well, have a good night,' he said, waving a hand and turning away.

'Weird,' Mia said, staring at the glittering picks.

'Yeah but no freaky note and look at this one – neon blue,' Honor said, taking it out the box and holding it up.

'What you got there?'

Jared's voice startled her and she closed the box up. If she showed him or told him where they came from he'd worry. He'd think it was another gift from her anonymous admirer or Dan Steele. He'd been through so much in the last twenty-four hours she didn't want to add to his plate. Things were going so well between them and she didn't want anything getting in the way.

'Someone's made her some real cute picks,' Mia stated, snatching the box and opening it up.

'Probably Gear. They were left backstage,' Honor said hurriedly.

'I want some like that,' Byron said, admiring them.

She could see in Jared's expression that something was coming.

'Any note?' he said, his eyes questioning.

'No note. It's nothing. They're not from... whoever it is,' Honor insisted.

'Maybe we should...'

She silenced him with a kiss, grabbing him by his leather jacket and holding him hard against her.

'Are you seeing this?' Mia said loudly to Byron.

'Damn, stop it, or you'll be all over tomorrow's papers,' Byron remarked.

Chapter Thirty Seven

'Does this one say "sexy" or "slutty"?' Mia held up a black dress with a slit from armpit to waist and another from thigh to floor.

'What do you want it to say?' Honor hadn't even looked up. She was lying on her bed, desperately scratching down lyrics while they were in her head. The last day of the Marlon Festival had been a blast but she'd been struck by inspiration so many times, she needed to write down the songs before they evaporated.

'Argh! You're not even listening, you're doodling! Come on, doll, this is important! This is a huge night for me. This is my first official Nashville engagement as Byron Starks' girlfriend. I have to get the look right. All the press will be there and if I choose the right dress I might make it into Countrywire magazine.'

She was right. It was the Marlon Awards and despite recent events Jared was still up for Best Male Vocalist. All the nominees were performing and she knew he was nervous about it. The Ryman Auditorium was a special place. There was a magical ambience about it. She'd performed there once, when she was invited as a new face. She remembered it like yesterday. It was a reasonably sized venue, but it somehow retained an intimacy that enchanted both the audience and the performer. Tonight she was looking forward to being in the seats, watching her guy do what he did best – rock out and entertain.

She closed up the book, rolled over onto her stomach on her bed and propped her head up with her hands, elbows on a cushion. 'What are the choices?'

'OK, we have "sexy and slutty dress", we have "demure dress".' Mia held up a grey body con dress with a beaded neckline. 'And we have "star-spangled dress".'

Star-spangled dress caught the spotlights in the ceiling with its thousands of sequins and diamantes and Honor put her hands over her eyes. 'Put it down. You can't wear that, Byron will need sunglasses just to look at you.'

Mia pouted. 'This one's my favorite. I thought it was real Dolly Parton.'

'Is that the look you're going for?'

Mia slumped down on the bed and positioned herself prostrate opposite Honor.

'It's alright for you. Gear probably got a dozen dresses from top designers for you to wear tonight.'

They had but she had turned them down. She'd done all that before and she didn't want a replica re-run, she wanted something different. She wanted to be able to make new choices, *her* choices, *her* decisions. Not having an advisor was refreshing. She was in charge for the very first time.

'I'm wearing something I picked up in T J Maxx,' she replied. 'And it was on sale.'

'Why?'

'Why not?' Honor challenged.

'Because I happen to know Byron's booked a room for the two of us at the Vanderbilt. Surely Jed must have plans for the two of you that warrants more than something from T J Maxx.'

'Wow, no wonder you're going all out with star-spangled dress.'

'Soooo?' Mia continued.

'We're heading to Alabama tomorrow. I'm going to meet his family,' Honor informed.

'What? Holy crap, are you serious? Meeting the family already?

I mean I know you talked about it, but jeez!'

'Don't! I'm nervous enough already and now you've given me a "holy crap" and a "jeez". Is it a mistake? Is it really too soon?'

'All I know is the longest relationship I've ever had was nine months and I never went near his folks.'

'His family's really important to him.'

'And so are you by the sound of things.'

'I just don't know what to expect. I mean, I know nothing about family. Are they going to like me? Am I going to feel a bit of an outsider? Am I really going to have to wear the dance dress?'

'The dance dress? What the hell is that?'

Honor let out a sigh and put her hands into her hair, scrunching it into a bunch and turning to look at her reflection in the mirror. Could she wear her hair up tonight? Did she dare show her face that much? She wasn't going to be on stage but there would be cameras there, flashlights keen to snap all the musicians' imperfections.

'Do you want me to do your hair?' Mia offered.

Honor shook her head and grabbed up her brush. 'No. This is your big night, Byron Starks' girlfriend. I'm going to do yours.'

His palms were sweating. He wasn't sure how he was going to play later if his hands stayed damp. Buzz was talking at him, going through the schedule and he couldn't really hear him. There was too much running around in his mind. Tonight was so important for so many reasons. He was performing in one of his favorite venues, he was up for an award and tonight he was going to give Honor his ring.

He put his hand to the collar of his shirt as the thought of her bare body filled his head and rode over his senses. Her beautiful cream skin, the curves he'd caressed, those full lips moving against his, nipping at the skin...

'Jared? Are you listening up?'

'Sorry, man, I was just thinkin' about stuff.' He put his hand to his cap and pulled it lower.

'Are you *nervous*?' Buzz made a big deal about saying the 'n' word. It wasn't usually something he ever had to utter. He never suffered with anxiety before a show, but it wasn't just about the show. In fact the performance and even the award were the least-important things about the night. He'd never given a ring to anyone.

'I don't know that word. What does it mean?' he answered.

'That's what I like to hear.'

Jared nodded and picked up his guitar. 'I'm on second, the award for Best Male Vocalist is halfway through the night and I try not to look too pissed when I lose out to Blake Shelton.'

Buzz looked up from his iPad. 'Is that what you think is going to happen?'

'I know I'm not the favorite and after the arrest and everything, chances are Blake's got it.'

'I wouldn't underestimate the power of your fan base.'

Jared shook his head. 'It don't matter, Buzz. It's never been about the awards for me.' He strummed a chord and tapped his hand on the body of the acoustic.

Buzz moved toward the mantle and Jared watched as he picked up the framed photo of his father. He swallowed, emotion already building up as his advisor studied the picture. He knew his momma couldn't be here tonight but he'd see her tomorrow and introduce her to Honor. But, the reason his daddy wasn't here, still haunted him. Such a waste, such a messed-up, fucked-up scenario he'd never get over. He bit his lip.

'He'd be proud, you know,' Buzz stated.

He didn't need this now. It was going to be a night full of heightened feelings as it was without Buzz adding to it like this. Buzz knew his father was dead but that was all he knew. He couldn't begin to understand how much more it was, nobody could. He carried around the hurt and the guilt and the pain every single day of his life.

'So, how many interviews have I got before I can go in? Did

you line up some for Honor?' He had to change the subject and regroup.

'You know she doesn't need me. You heard her tell me that, right?' Buzz put down the photo and turned to face Jared.

He grinned. 'I heard her. But that's just how she is right now. Right now she thinks she can take on the whole damn world. I kinda like it because it's the exact opposite from how she was when I first met her but...'

'But?'

'She'll need you. She's tired already. We've got a tour comin' up.'

Buzz nodded. 'Well, when she's ready, I'll be there.'

Jared smiled. 'Thanks, Buzz.'

'What the hell? Is that the door?' Mia looked to Honor with one foot dangling over the bed, as Honor painted her toenails with bright-red varnish.

'Yeah. It can't be my car, it's not due for another hour. Would it be Byron?' Honor stood up, putting the lid back on the nail polish and the bottle on the nightstand.

'No, that would be freaking weird.'

'I'll go find out,' Honor said, heading for her bedroom door.

'Don't you open it until you've checked who it is, doll!' Mia called after her.

She hurried down the wooden stairs and dashed towards the front door. Checking the spy hole she saw a uniformed courier holding a package. Her heart dropped down into her boots. She didn't want this, not again. Perhaps the picks hadn't been from Gear. She put her hand on the doorknob and tried to breathe. This was just a fan showing appreciation. This was not connected to Simeon Stewart in any way. She had to believe that. She *did* believe that. She blew out another breath and rubbed the palm of her free hand on her jeans. She opened the door and greeted the delivery guy with a smile.

'Package for ya,' he stated, lifting up a large box.

'Whoa, it's big.' She took it from him and put it down against the wall inside.

'I hear that all the time.'

She looked at the man, slightly taken aback.

'Still too much packaging despite the environmental reforms. Sign here.' He thrust a handheld console toward her and she took it.

'You don't happen to know who sent it do you?' She'd tried to keep her tone light, like it didn't matter.

'I just deliver 'em, ma'am.' He took back the console and turned away.

'Sure, thanks.' She watched him get to his van then closed the front door, eyeing the parcel with suspicion. The size of it said this was a step up from all the other gifts she'd received.

'Are you still alive down there?' Mia's shout made her jolt.

'Yes, I'm coming.' She picked up the box and headed towards the stairs.

'It's a guitar! And it's from my store. I can see the edge of our invoice under the plastic there. Take the invoice out and I can tell you who sold it and then I can find out who purchased it within minutes.'

'You're not heading to the store to check the computer.'

'No, I'll call whoever sold it and interrogate them. If your stalker's been to the store then we're going to find out who it is.'

Honor took a breath. As usual Mia's mind was working ten different angles all at the same time and they hadn't even opened the box yet. She wasn't sure she wanted to but with Mia here she doubted she'd be given a choice.

'I actually want a stalker if he's gonna buy me guitars.'

Honor pulled at the cardboard tab to open the box. 'You own a whole store of them.'

'I own stock. That's nothing like the same.'

She pulled open the lid, parted the paper wrapping and there was her favorite guitar from Instrumadness. The limited-edition

Takamine 2011 with the Japanese fish embossed on the body and the gold details on the neck.

'Someone bought you the freaking Takamine you always play.' Mia stated, standing up and staring over the box next to her friend.

'A stalker,' Honor stated.

'A rich freaking stalker.'

On auto-pilot, she reached into the box and lifted the guitar up and out, her hand strong on the neck. She slipped the strap over her head and moved her fingers up the fret board. She started playing, moving her fingers up and down the strings as the original tone of the guitar rode through her.

'There's a card. Holy crap, your stalker might have signed off on this one.'

Honor stopped playing but before she could react to Mia's words her friend had snatched up the card.

'"Because every note means more than ever. With all my heart – Jared". Oh I'm sorry. Here, pretend I didn't read it.' Mia held out the note.

Honor's whole body reacted immediately, every muscle relieved, every sinew loosened. Jared had bought her the guitar. The guitar she'd been playing the day they first met.

'Wow. I've never seen you look like that.'

'Like what?' She looked up at her friend.

'All mush. Like a whole heap of candy canes. Like a big pink marshmallow of puff.'

'I do not.' She giggled.

'It's official. You have it bad for the bad boy and by the looks of things the feeling's mutual.'

She couldn't help the smile broadening.

'Now all you need is some more quality alone-time without a guitar or a momma between you. Shall I call the Vanderbilt and book you a room?' Mia suggested.

'No! And sit still, your nails aren't dry!'

Chapter Thirty Eight

The doorbell rang and this time she knew exactly who it was. She brushed her hands down the front of her dress, then picked up her purse from the kitchen island. Trying to walk straight in her new too-high shoes was a challenge, but she made it to the door and, with one quick check in the spy hole, she opened it to Jared.

'Oh.' She couldn't help the sound escaping because he looked so different. The cap was still on, but he was wearing a black waistcoat over a white shirt and smart black jeans.

'What? Don'tcha think a Southern boy can scrub up when he puts his mind to it?'

She smiled and reached for his hand. 'I got the guitar. It's the most beautiful thing... but you knew I felt like that about it, didn't you?'

'That day we first met, you never took your hands off it once.'

'That's how I want us to be,' she whispered, squeezing his hand.

He pulled her to him and found her lips with his, placing a feather-light kiss there. He stepped back, looking her up and down.

'Look at you. You're an angel.'

The dress was full-length, in a pale sea-green shade covered in white lace. It smoothed across Honor's curves and reached the floor. A side slit to mid-thigh made it easier to move in.

'And you have your hair up,' Jared remarked. He caressed her cheek with his thumb, then moved down to her neck, making her skin prickle.

'Because I'm not afraid of who I am now.'

She smiled at him. She meant every word. This was her time to come out of hiding. To grab life by the horns and wrestle with it. She had everything she'd ever wanted, her career back, the chance to sing and share her music with the world, and Jared, a man who loved her just as she was.

He took hold of her hand and brought it to his lips. 'Your limo is waitin' right over there.'

'A stretch? Gear got us a stretch? I never had a stretch once with Micro!' she exclaimed as excited as a child.

'D'you wanna do the walk down the line together?' Jared asked en route.

He didn't like all the interviews the award ceremonies entailed but it was part of the job. If he did it with Honor they could take turns to answer questions and hopefully bring it all to a speedier conclusion.

'Is that allowed?'

Jared laughed at her. 'You're talkin' to the lord of rule bendin' right here.'

She giggled and hit him with her sequin purse.

'I just want to get you to myself before the whole circus of the night takes over. I'm second on the bill so I'm not gonna be able to sit with you 'til the break.'

'I know. It's OK. Mia will keep me company, or at least scream in my ear the second she sees Byron.'

'He's gone a little rock star on me. His solos are getting longer and longer. Real soon there'll be no lyrics at all. That's what happens when you're tryin' to impress a girl.'

'Is that right?' Honor smiled then looked out the window as the auditorium come into view.

There it was. The spectacular building that housed so much

country history and outside it was a press pack of mammoth proportions.

'Is somethin' up? D'you wish you were gettin' up on stage tonight?'

'No. I didn't expect to be nominated. That all got voted on months ago before I even came back.'

'Then?'

'I've not been to Alabama before, not even toured there.' She let out a sigh and turned to look at him.

'This is nerves about meetin' my mom?' he guessed.

'I know. Dumb, right?'

'Was it me mentionin' the dance dress? Because she actually hasn't got that out for a little while.'

She allowed herself a small laugh but it wasn't heartfelt. She didn't want to feel like a spare part and that was more to do with her than the way she thought Jared's family would be with her. They could be as welcoming as the woman paid to do it at Target, it didn't guarantee she'd know how to react the right way.

Jared took her hands, laying his grey eyes on hers as the car came to a stop. 'Let's do this walk of fame thing and then we can talk about recipes you're gonna be tested on.'

She hit him with her bag again. 'Stop it!'

'...and here we have country Southern rock sensation, Jed Marshall and the gorgeous, super-talented Honor Blackwood. You're looking beautiful tonight, Honor, who's the designer?' the interviewer quizzed, poking out a microphone, her cameraman at her shoulder.

She had no idea. Why didn't she have any idea? She'd done this before; she should have known what they would ask. She let out a consolation noise as she desperately racked her brain for something. 'I got it...'

'I bought the dress,' Jared answered. 'No idea who made it but I saw it and I knew it was gonna look fantastic.' He squeezed her hand.

'An inspired choice I have to say. So, you're up for Male Vocalist of the Year, Jed. How d'you feel about that?'

'I'm truly honored to be nominated. There's some real tough competition, great country talents all of 'em. And win or lose, we're all gonna have a great time tonight.'

'I'm sure you are. So, Honor, first time back at the Ryman. How does it feel?'

She felt the bubble in her stomach growing fuller and fatter by the second. How did it feel? She chanced a look at the Mother Church of Country Music. It was awe-inspiring. A tingle of sensation ran down her back at the thought of being in there again.

'I remember standing on that stage when I was seventeen knowing how many country legends had walked the same boards. It's a place where musical magic happens and I'm really looking forward to enjoying all the performances tonight.'

'We all are. So, tell me, what's next for the two of you? Going on tour together, buying a home maybe? Anything else we should know?'

'Well, I...' Honor began. She should have expected this line of questioning too.

'We're gonna be headin' down to my hometown in Alabama real soon. Honor's gonna come and meet the Marshall family,' Jared informed.

'Wow, things are getting serious already.'

'As serious as a chicken dinner and a few parties round the bonfire gets, ma'am. Thank you for your time. Honor's new video comes out Monday so make sure y'all You Tube it,' Jared added, pointing at the camera.

She managed a smile before he was pulling her over to the entrance and away from the cameras and reporters.

'Now that's over, come with me,' he said guiding her through the venue and away from the reception committee.

This had to be right. It had to be perfect. He was only going to do this once. He hurried on, skipping past people left and right, acknowledging no one, just trying to make it to the place this needed to happen.

'Jared, where are we going? I can't go too fast in these shoes,' she called as he paced on.

'Just hang on in there.' He stopped just before a set of doors barred by two auditorium employees. Igniting his best smile he approached them, pulling Honor behind him.

'Good evenin' ladies. I was wonderin' if me and my girl could just go in for a second.'

'Doors don't open 'til seven do they, Pearl?' one of the women responded.

'Seven,' Pearl responded, folding her arms across her chest.

'I'm performin' tonight,' Jared told them.

'I know who you are, Mr Marshall. Too loud, too rock and too much hell-raising. And you know as well as I do there's an artists' entrance,' the woman replied.

'I do, ma'am but...' He smiled, let go of Honor's hand and leaned forward, whispering into the woman's ear. He stepped back and waited.

'Open the doors, Pearl. This one's going in,' she informed.

Like Aladdin's cave, the doors were pulled back and Jared touched his cap in acknowledgement as he and Honor passed by into the auditorium.

She followed him through the doors and was hit with that same sensation she'd experienced outside as they walked out onto the balcony. The theatre seats were empty but down on the stage, the stage where everyone who was anyone in country had performed, people were setting up for the show. Light was still flooding in from the arched stained-glass windows, casting a pale glow over the pew-style seats. It was beautiful, almost holy and she felt her heart contract with a feeling of belonging.

He squeezed her hand and drew her towards the steps that led down to the very front of the balcony.

'It's some place, huh?' Jared said as they made their way down to the wooden barrier.

'When I was growing up, I used to watch the stars perform here on the TV. They looked so surreal, like made-up characters with their rhinestone clothes and beautiful voices. The first time I played here... it took my breath away. It was like a dream.'

'If you've got country in your heart this place moves somethin' in you,' Jared agreed, standing next to her.

Down below them were rows of wooden seats that later would be filled with country glitterati. Empty, it was as if the memories of all those occasions gone by were floating through the atmosphere, poignant and laden with emotion.

'Honor,' Jared stated, touching her arm with his hand.

She drew her eyes back to him and watched as he pulled something from his finger. He removed one of his rings.

He held it out with his thumb and forefinger. 'Because of... what happened... I didn't get to graduate.' He could feel his hand was shaking but there was nothing he could do about it. 'So, I didn't get a class ring or anything but... this is...' He paused. 'This was my daddy's ring.'

His momma had taken it off his daddy's hand and put it on his finger that day and this was the very first time he had ever taken it off.

'Through all those bad times I clung to the hope that I was worthy to wear this ring. That I was man enough to do justice to his memory, to be the kind of person he was.' He looked down at the ring, the band with gold flames licking over it and the Confederate flag, a crest in the center. The tears were coming.

'Jared.'

'I want you to have it,' he stated, closing the ring in his hand, then reaching into his pocket and bringing out a gold chain.

'I can't.'

'Hey, I know you probably think I'm crazy because this is all goin' like the speed of a freight train but, the way I feel about you...' He took a breath and gazed at her. 'We're gonna be on tour for a few months and it's gonna be hard work and we're gonna probably get on each other's nerves within the first week.' He smiled. 'But when that happens I want you to be wearin' this, knowin' that I love you. Believin' that I'll always love you.'

She couldn't speak. She didn't have the words. She knew and she could see how much this meant to him. No one had put their heart on the line for her before. No one had cared so much. No one had wanted to share their everything with her. And here he was, this slightly crazy, a little bit flawed, gorgeous, generous-hearted guy wanting to start a future with her.

'My daddy had huge hands so it won't fit but...' He held up the ring on the chain. 'Would you do me that honor, Honor?'

A tear snaked down her cheek and over her scar as she nodded; too scared to say anything or risk turning into mush and completely ruining Mia's hard work on her make-up.

He held up the chain and she quickly turned around, glad her hair was up. She felt the heat from his body as he put the chain around her neck, his hands touching her skin as he tried to fasten the clasp.

'I'm shakin' so much I can't do it up.' He let out a nervous laugh. 'There,' he said, as he finally made the connection.

She turned around and straight away put her hand to the ring at her throat, running the tip of her finger over the engraving. 'I love it.'

'I love you,' he told her.

She let go of the ring and cupped his face with her hand, rubbing her thumb over the stubble on his cheek. She watched him close his eyes and she moved, lightly touching her lips against his, moving gently across his mouth. She waited, knowing he would react and wanting him to.

Finally he gave in, his hand at her waist, pulling her close as his mouth explored hers, fiery and wanting.

Then the whistling started. Honor broke away to see some of the crew on stage, waving and jeering at their show of passion.

'Damn roadies, they ruin everything,' Jared joked, flicking them the rock sign. 'Let's go get a drink.'

Chapter Thirty Nine

'Byron was awesome wasn't he?' Mia flapped her clutch purse around her face like a fan as they waited for the second half of the show to start. Jared and his band had pulled off a flawless performance and half the awards had been given away already.

'Totally awesome,' Honor responded, looking at the audience buzzing back in from the foyer.

'What's that tone for? He was note-perfect.' Mia scowled.

'I know, I said. Almost a two-minute guitar solo in a four and a half minute song,' Honor remarked, laughing.

'What is that gross thing round your neck, doll? I tried to ask you before Vince Gill came on but the banjo player went crazy and you didn't hear me.'

'Don't say that,' Honor said. She touched the ring defensively, holding it in her hand.

'Jeez, is that some sort of gift from Jed? Hasn't he heard of Tiffany's?'

'It was his father's. It's important to him.' She held its weight in her palm. 'And he gave it to me,' Honor stated.

'God, I hope Byron hasn't got anything like that up his sleeve. Antiques should only come in the form of furniture in my opinion.'

Honor saw Jared coming towards them and she stood up. 'I like it, so you'd better get used to seeing it.'

'Hey,' he greeted, kissing Honor's cheek.

'Hey, you OK?' she asked as he moved to sit down in the seat next to her.

'Yeah, just...' he started.

'Nervous I'm betting. Not long now until the Best Male Vocalist award,' Mia piped up.

'Something like that,' Jared replied to Honor. 'I don't think I'm gonna win but when your name's in the hat there's always that chance.'

He felt Honor's hand on his and she linked their fingers, squeezing them tightly.

'Win or lose, it doesn't matter. Sometimes I've felt better after not winning,' Honor admitted with a smile.

'And I've got the greatest prize right here,' he said, bringing her hand to his mouth.

He meant every word. He'd never got into the music industry for the accolades. A Marlon Award nomination was flattering but he knew actually winning would mean more to some of the other artists than it did to him.

'Ladies and gentlemen, welcome back to the 15th Annual Marlon Awards coming to you live from the Ryman Auditorium. And what have we got next, Bucky?'

Jared knew what was coming next. It was his category.

'You doing OK here?' Buzz sat down in the seat next to Jared.

'Hey, Buzz, you made it,' he remarked, turning to his advisor.

'Yeah, I made it. Good luck,' he stated, nodding his head at his client.

'...so, without further ado let's hear the nominations for Best Male Vocalist 2014.'

He felt Honor tighten her grip on his hand as the names were read out. After each name was called, a clip from the artist's recent video was played on the big screen.

'Jed Marshall.'

Honor let out a whoop of appreciation and Mia pumped her

fist in the air and screamed. He looked up at the screen and saw a clip from the video he'd done with Honor. There he was standing on the roof of a building, his guitar slung around his neck and there she was leaning over a pool table. A few wolf-whistles ran through the auditorium at that shot.

He saw Mia nudge Honor in the side and she shook her head and then closed her eyes. She was willing him to win, when he really didn't care either way. He had her and that was all that mattered.

'And the winner is...'

He felt Honor digging her fingers into his skin as they waited for the pause to end. He placed his other hand over hers and held it there.

'Blake Shelton!'

He smiled, knowing the cameras would be on all the nominees to get a reaction to the announcement. He patted Honor's hand.

She was surprised how sad she felt. He deserved something. Blake Shelton, she was learning, was a great artist, but he wasn't Jared. When she'd seen him on stage for the first time at the Marlon Festival he had lit the place up, pumped the arena full of life like no one else she'd ever heard.

She clapped her hands together as the winner took to the stage but it didn't feel right.

'I'm happy for him,' Jared whispered to her. 'He's a good guy and a great performer.'

'So are you,' she replied in hushed tones.

'There's still time for my time... he's way older than me,' he said, smiling as he gave her hand another squeeze.

'Just keep on smiling, Jared, there's cameras everywhere,' Buzz said through gritted teeth.

'I'm doin' it,' he responded.

'Have another drink, doll,' Mia said, pushing a champagne flute into Honor's hand.

They'd left the Ryman Auditorium for the after-party at the Hilton. Sponsorship deals stipulated they had to at least show their faces, but all Honor really wanted to do was go home and have Jared to herself. Despite what he'd said about not caring, she was sure he felt a little disappointment at not winning. She did. He wasn't just an accomplished artist; he deserved recognition for being an outstanding songwriter.

'Where is Jed anyway?' Mia asked, looking around the room.

'Buzz took him off somewhere to do some interviews,' she responded, waving across the room at Reba McEntire.

'You know Reba!' Mia exclaimed in awe.

'We worked together once, a long time ago.' It felt like a whole lifetime ago.

'Jeez! Will you introduce me? I adore her. That song she did with Brooks and Dunn about the cowgirl not crying has me in bits every time.' She put her hand to her throat.

'Come on,' Honor said, linking their arms.

Buzz had called him out of the party and now he was stood in some room with nothing but a chandelier and stacks of chairs for company. Buzz's phone had started ringing, his iPad had erupted, several alerts flashing up, then he'd up and left the room without a word.

Jared wanted to be with Honor. He wanted to get home, get packed up and get on the road early to Alabama. He couldn't wait to see his family, couldn't wait to introduce them to his girl.

He put his hands behind the back of his neck, linking them up as the door opened.

He watched Buzz step through and close it up again, leaning heavily against the frame. His usually dark chocolate-colored skin didn't look quite right – he was pale. His eyes studied Jared and unlike the usual warning glare before a lecture on something, this was different.

'What?' he asked, putting his hands down and looking back

at his advisor.

'We have a situation,' Buzz said, marching forward and heading for the stack of chairs. He pulled one off and set it down, then pulled at another and settled it opposite. Jared noticed he was sweating.

'What? A situation? What situation?' He couldn't think of a single thing he'd done since beating up Dan Steele, but still he was racking the back of his mind. Had he said something in an interview or on the line coming in?

'Sit down.' Buzz indicated one of the chairs. 'And before you say anything else I need you to promise me that whatever comes out of your mouth next is the truth.'

The skin on the back of his neck prickled then went cold. This sounded bad. Had Dan Steele changed his mind about dropping the charges? Had the state decided to prosecute anyway and make an example of him?

He sat down on the chair and watched Buzz take the seat opposite, lowering himself down onto it gingerly, like he was going to have a collapse.

'What's goin' on, Buzz?'

'Just... don't say anything... not yet.' The words came out like a desperate order.

Jared put a finger to his mouth and bit the nail. He'd never seen Buzz look this way and he'd seen every kind of expression on his face in the years they'd been together.

Buzz took a long, slow breath before speaking. 'Have you spent time in jail?'

He felt every ounce of life drain out of him and for a second everything went numb. He opened his mouth to speak, to deny it, to say anything to stop this here and now but what Buzz had said about truth gnawed at him.

'No,' he replied on instinct.

Before he'd finished the word Buzz was out of his seat. He grabbed hold of the chair and launched it across the room. It smashed into the pile of seats and sent half a dozen tumbling to the floor.

'I told you. I warned you. Don't you lie to me, boy!'

He'd never heard Buzz talk like that before. His voice was loud, threatening and shaking with emotion. This was real bad. He knew. It was out.

'I... spent time in juvenile detention.' The words fell from his lips in a rush he didn't have control over. The power of Buzz's order, his body language, the wreck of the chair pile had brought the truth out of his mouth.

A mixture of shame and fierce loyalty waved over him and he hung his head, looking into his lap. What was there to say? He just had to wait to hear if he knew it all.

'Jeez, Jared! I mean…hell!'

He could almost feel the steam coming out of Buzz's ears. He couldn't raise his head yet, not when his advisor was on the verge of a full-blown eruption.

'All these years and not a word? Fuck!'

He'd never heard Buzz use the F-bomb ever, even when he'd pulled all sorts of crazy shit. Was there any point saying anything? Just like before, he was already condemned.

He chanced a look up, watching Buzz pacing the floor, his hands thrust in his pockets, then out and at his afro. He resembled a man who didn't know what to do with himself, not the emotionally controlled character Jared was used to.

He bit his lip, diverted his gaze as Buzz turned to him.

'All these years we've known each other and you neglected to mention you shot and killed your father.'

Chapter Forty

He knew everything. Jared dropped his eyes, unable to keep looking at him. Clenching his fists, he balled them up tightly until his knuckles looked like they could break open the skin. His hands started to shake, his body started to vibrate on the inside as his soul began to react to the news and take on board the implications.

He should've known this would happen. It was always just a matter of time. Sealed records or not, it only took one good investigative reporter with time and the scent of something and the facts were there to find. He couldn't make this right, so why say anything? Whatever he said would do no good. He kept his head low and waited.

'Are you going to say anything?'

His shoulders shrugged of their own accord.

'Jared, you shot and killed your father! This news is all over Nashville already. There are hundreds of reporters outside this hotel hungry for all the gory details.'

'What?' No, this was happening too fast. This wasn't how it usually went. Buzz was always able to find out first. He had contacts at the news agencies, who gave him the heads-up if a story was going to break. It couldn't be out, not nationwide, not yet. Honor.

'This was on Twitter minutes after we got here. Tony called me but it was too late. Despite Carrie Underwood winning two awards, *you're* the only person anyone is talking about right now and not in a good way. I mean, rocking the biker, hell-raising attitude is one thing, perhaps a DUI or even assault, but patricide?'

Jared stood, his heart thumping hard. 'Where's Honor?'

'Aren't you listening to me? I need to know the truth... the whole damn truth so I can start working on sorting this out before you set foot outside of this room!'

'I can't do that. I need to see Honor.' He was pacing for the door now, his heart feeling like it was being squeezed by a vice. He didn't care what the press thought of him, he didn't even care what the world thought of him. The only person that mattered was Honor. He couldn't let her walk into this. He couldn't let her find out what had happened any other way than from words out of his mouth. He should have told her when he'd told her about prison. Why hadn't he? Because he was terrified of losing her. Because he couldn't tell her everything without breaking his moral code. It was all about protecting the people he loved.

'Jared! If you leave this room we're done!' Buzz yelled.

He put his hand on the door and took a breath. If the music industry already knew, then he was done for. But if he caught Honor and tried to explain, there might still be a chance.

He pulled open the door. 'I'm sorry, Buzz.'

'Oh my! I can't believe I met Reba McEntire and she was so awesome!' Mia said, putting a hand to her chest and grinning with joy.

Honor checked her watch. 'I hope Jared isn't too much longer. I'm so tired and we've got a road trip tomorrow.'

'I know, I know. You and the bad boy getting cozy in the country with his family! It'll be all hoe-downs, turkey dinners and photos of Jed in his diapers.'

Honor laughed and picked a glass of champagne from the tray of a passing waiter. 'I bet he looked cute in his diapers.'

'Euww!'

'Honor Blackwood, Jemma Curran from Nashville Newswire. A great night tonight but overshadowed by the news of Jed Marshall's imprisonment for the murder of his father, James. What's your reaction to that?'

The reporter had red hair and was dressed in a full-length black sequined dress. A small dictaphone was in her hand and it was now just a few millimeters from Honor's face. She'd spoken so quickly that Honor couldn't have heard her correctly.

'This is a private party and members of the press only have access to the artists at specific pre-scheduled times. Come on, Honor,' Mia said, linking arms with her and pulling her away.

'It's come as a shock to the Nashville community. Tell me, did you know he'd been in prison? Had he told you about the death of his father? Miss Blackwood, just one comment!'

'Fuck off back to charm school,' Mia snapped. She pulled on Honor's arm, heading toward the door.

Honor's breathing was wild and she couldn't see straight. All the partygoers in front of her were blurring into one mound, a writhing mass of beautifully dressed people, their conversations off-kilter, the background music off-key.

'What did she say?' Honor turned to Mia who was still marching her toward the room's exit.

'I don't know. Some crap-ass story about Jed being in prison. Big deal. He probably took a swing at some guy he didn't like. We all know that's his thing.'

She swallowed and tried to recompose herself but everything was fuzzy. Nothing seemed quite right, her surroundings, the way she was reacting to them...

'I'll tell the security guys we have an infiltrator at the party and we'll go outside and get some fresh air,' Mia directed, pulling Honor's arm closer to her body.

Honor nodded. She hadn't heard the words she thought she'd heard. The story that he'd been in prison was out. She should have felt more than this, but the rest... what she thought she'd heard... it had to be made up. That's what reporters did for sensationalism, didn't they? She shook her head and stopped walking. Something about this was off. She pulled at Mia's arm and held her gaze, making her friend look at her.

'What did you hear that reporter say, Mia?'

Mia let out a nervous laugh and unclasped their arms, taking her purse from under her other arm and holding it tight. 'That woman shouldn't be at the party. She's well known for getting places she ain't invited. I'd bet she's got one of the security on her payroll.'

'Please, Mia. Did she really say Jared had been in prison for murdering his father?' The words felt sour, like they were tainting her mouth, making a foul-tasting palate. Bile was rising up through her and she put a hand to her chest, trying to quell the sensation.

'It can't be true though, can it, doll? I mean, he's here somewhere and he's with you. He's been dating you for weeks now. You would know.'

The tears were already forming and the feeling inside, that mixture of fear, hurt and nausea was threatening to burst past the calm exterior she was trying to hold onto.

'He told me.' The words floated past her lips. 'He told me he'd been in prison... well, not prison exactly, juvenile detention.'

She hadn't realized she was shaking until Mia put a hand on her arm to steady her. Her touch didn't have the soothing effect intended. It felt almost as if she'd been scorched. She fell into a step backwards and nudged against the wall.

'I didn't ask what for.' The tears were tracking down her cheeks. 'I said... I said I didn't want to know. I said I trusted him.'

'Doll, we should find him. We should sort all this out,' Mia suggested.

'No.' The word was forceful. She couldn't move. She couldn't take one step anywhere. She was frozen here, at this moment, in this place, just outside the door of the banqueting hall, where almost all of Nashville was celebrating. Her hand wove its way up from her side to the ring hanging around her neck. His father's ring.

A dead man's ring. A murdered man's ring. He'd said it meant so much. How could he have said that when he was the one?

She fingered the gold band as more tears fell, silently, without sobs, without altered breathing; just quiet trickles of salt water tracing their way down her cheeks.

'Look, this all has to be a misunderstanding or something, doll. Doesn't it?' Mia's voice was wavering and over her shoulder Honor could see groups of press all vying for position and hotel employees desperately trying to erect new security cordons outside the entrance.

'Honor, we need to find Jed and Byron. We need to get outta this party,' Mia said, delving into her purse for her cell phone.

But Honor wasn't listening. She could feel the cold plaster of the wall up against her spine through the thin gauze of the dress and she wanted it to numb her, dull her senses, take away the dread that was hanging over her like a black storm cloud.

'Damn it. Why does he never answer his damn phone?' Mia exclaimed, cancelling the call.

He saw her before she saw him. Backed up against the wall, just below a portrait of Vince Gill, she looked like the life had been drained out of her. She knew. He could tell from her expression, the pale skin, the damp cheeks, the salty tears glistening over the track of her scar. She knew already.

'Jed Marshall, Jemma Curran from Nashville Newswire, any comment to make about the death of your father? We'd love to have an exclusive. Tell us your side of things.'

A red-haired woman was poking a recording device in his face, so close he could practically smell the batteries. He raised his hand, ready to rip it out of hers and throw it to the wall. But right at that moment Honor looked up and those eyes, so full of grief and anxiety, met his. He was floored. The room closed in and nothing, no sound, no sense, nothing could break through. He watched her tighten her lips together, blink her eyelids and stay connected to his gaze. If he could keep her with him, connected like this, then maybe... He walked forward, toward her, slowly yet with purpose. He could make this right. If she would just listen to him then maybe it could all work out. He took a breath in and held it, his eyes not moving from hers. Just a couple more strides and he would be...

She looked away.

'Mia, I want to go.' She turned to her friend, feeling his eyes on her but not wanting to see them.

'Honor.' He'd stepped up and was just inches away. She couldn't stand it. She knew, without asking, she knew just from his expression and his body language that what the reporter had told her was the truth.

'What the hell is going on, Jed? Some reporter just came up to Honor and said...' Mia started.

'Honor, just give me a minute... a second even, to explain it to you,' he begged.

Her heart was shattering. She could feel pieces of their love being stripped away as every moment passed. It was like every beautiful thing he'd said to her, all the precious time they'd spent together was dissolving, slipping out of her hands like sand running through an hourglass.

'Is it true?' The sound of her own voice shocked her. It was rough, strained with tears and hurt.

'What have you been told?' His reply was swift and she turned to look at him then.

'Is that how it's going to be? You're going to answer me like you're talking to a judge?'

He shook his head. 'No, I...' He stopped, wetting his lips. 'Buzz just told me what they're talking about and I didn't stop to hear the whole story I just... I just had to find you.'

He reached for her and she recoiled, bustling into Mia.

'Why don't you two go somewhere quiet? That brat with the

tape machine is hearing every word right now,' Mia suggested.

'No.' Her mouth was tight because she was having trouble keeping in the emotion. If she let herself weaken, loosen or listen, she'd break down.

'Should I leave? 'Cause...' Mia began.

'Honor, just hear me out. It isn't like you're thinkin'. I told you about the cop, the cop that sent me to jail. It was all to do with him and...' Jared started.

'Did you shoot your father?' The question was blunt and that's how it had to be. It was all she needed an answer to. One straight answer, a yes or a no, not dozens of descriptive words that glossed over the facts.

He didn't answer. His lips were still, his eyes fixed on her. It was as if she was looking at someone else. Someone she didn't know. A stranger. Not the man she'd fallen in love with, the man who had walked into her life and turned it into someplace better.

'Did you kill your father?' She had to say it again because there'd been nothing from him. And she wanted an answer. She wanted to hear the 'no.' She wanted to hear that it wasn't true, more than anything she'd ever wanted in her whole life. 'Was that what you went to juvenile detention for?'

She couldn't have made it any plainer. She stared at him, saw the pain in his eyes, saw a haunted look appear on his face. There was so much love there, loss too... but still no answer.

He took a breath that looked like it took every ounce of strength he had. 'It's what I was charged with but...'

A sharp pain, like a nail being driven into her, pummeled her core. A shockwave, a release of adrenaline, a surge of detestation flew up through her. It was true. He'd killed his father. The man he professed to love so much. The man whose memory he coveted, who he looked up to and admired. She gagged.

'Honor, look at me.' He grabbed her arm and she started to weep, unable to hold the emotion in any more. 'It's not cut and dried. Let's go somewhere. Let's get out of here and talk.'

The pain was squeezing her dry of any ability to respond. If she went with him he was going to lie to her, just like he'd held back the truth from her in the first place. The love they'd shared, the trust they'd built up, it had all been torn away, tainted by this ugly, awful truth. He was a murderer. Not just a hot-headed guy with fierce morals and a temper to match, but a killer.

'Honor,' he tried again, his hand on her arm, his eyes searching for hers.

'No... don't touch me.' She met his eyes as another sob came out of her mouth. 'Don't ever put those hands on me again.'

'Honor, please. You have to listen to me.' His voice broke as he dropped his hand and took a step back from her.

'I want to go.' She looked at Mia now, pleading with her expression for an out from this.

'Sure, we can go, of course we can go. We'll go out the back, away from them,' Mia said, indicating the press pack at the front entrance.

'Honor, I'm beggin' you. Just give me five minutes, please.'

She couldn't look at him again. The sight of tears falling from his eyes would weaken her. There was nothing he could say that would change the circumstances. He'd admitted it. What was left to discuss? She'd given her heart to someone who'd killed. She said she could forgive him anything... but murder! That was in a whole different ballpark. Never had she considered he was capable of something like that.

She made for the front door in a rush. She didn't care about the photographers and the reporters. She needed air. She needed to not be here with him. She needed sanctuary, safety, somewhere to breath.

The flashes hit her the second she burst from the doors but she didn't see anything, she just kept walking.

'Miss Blackwood, any comment to make?'

'Honor, would you like to tell us how you found out about this revelation?'

'...incarcerated for two years...like a wild animal...'
'...killed in cold blood...didn't call 911.'
She pulled up her dress and started to run.

Chapter Forty One

She sat on the ground, propped up against the front window, the metal shutters harsh against her skin. She'd known it wouldn't be open but she couldn't go home. Target, open or closed, was where she felt safe.

She'd run two blocks before she'd hailed a cab, stopping only at a liquor store for a bottle before coming here. She'd drunk half the wine already and it wasn't making her feel any better. The tears just wouldn't stop. Still silent tears, still quiet tearing of her insides as the news swirled around, slowly taking hold, fermenting, building up, reaching every part of her.

For a few short weeks she'd had everything again. More than everything. She'd had her career back, her love of music, a joy in her heart, a desperate will to live life again, not hide behind her past. And a man she'd adored. A person she'd instantly felt connected to but had grown to love more deeply than she'd ever loved before. Now she felt hollow, disconnected, angry and sad all at the same time.

She put the bottle of wine to her mouth and took another swig. Drinking to numb the pain. That's what she'd done after her attack. This time she might not be physically injured but she felt it just as much. He'd lied to her. He knew how much she'd trusted him, believed in him and he'd taken that trust and abused it. How could he have done that to her?

She heard the truck and closed her eyes as its headlights swung across her line of sight. She didn't care who it was. She'd been half expecting the cops anyway.

'Byron, get a blanket or something.'

Mia's voice. Her friend Mia had come to rescue her. She would tell her everything was OK and stroke her hair. She would take away the wine and fill her up with coffee. But it wouldn't change anything. She would still be the idiot who had fallen for a murderer.

'Honor, come on, doll, let's get you up. Byron, have you got something? She's cold and the ground's wet!'

She couldn't speak. She didn't have the energy and, after all, what was the point? What could you say? What did she really want to say? It was best to just give in.

She let Mia help her up and she swayed, banging an elbow against the shutters, the wine consumption affecting her movement. Mia wrenched the bottle from her grip and held it out to Byron, who was offering a plaid rug.

'Listen, we're gonna take you home and we're gonna ply you with coffee until it hurts and then in the morning we're gonna get to the bottom of all this,' Mia told her, beginning to pull out the pins in her hair and stroking it out with her fingers.

She looked up at her friend, suddenly reconnecting with the occasion. She swallowed, trying to push the taste of wine to the back of her mouth.

'But... you have a room at the Vanderbilt.'

She watched a lone tear fall from Mia's eye as she smiled and shook her head at her. 'It's cancelled. But, hey, I heard they didn't even have guavas in the fruit basket.'

Byron opened the back door of his truck and Mia shepherded Honor towards the vehicle.

Warmth, leather seats and the blanket around her shoulders. With her head spinning, she climbed up into the truck and shuffled over to the far seat. She pulled the blanket tighter and rested her head against the window.

His knuckles were bleeding and there were five empty beer bottles on the floor next to him. Right now, he'd never hated himself more. He kicked out at the coffee table, upturned and broken and it fell to the left, scattering CDs, music magazines and a coffee mug into the debris around it.

The living room resembled the aftermath of a tornado but it was all him. He was the hurricane, the hazardous material, the person who destroyed everything. He'd broken his family back then and now he'd torn Honor apart just like he knew he would. That was why he never got involved. That was why he never let anyone get close. He hurt everyone in his life. He was bad karma personified.

'Jed! Open up!'

He ignored Byron's voice and put another bottle of beer to his mouth, only to find it empty. He threw it to the wall and watched it smash to pieces.

'Jed! C'mon! Open the damn door!'

He didn't want do-gooders trying to talk things better. That was never going to happen. Not now, not even in this lifetime. He'd fucked up. His past had come out and he'd messed up by holding things back from Honor. He put his hands to his head and brought it down to his knees, curling, hiding, wanting to feel as small as he knew he was.

'Jed, you either let me in or I'm gonna bust the door down and give unrestricted access to the entire press pack sat on your front lawn right now!'

He shook his head. Right now he didn't care what happened. They could ask him every question they could come up with. He wasn't answering. What was the point?

'Jed... I've seen Honor.'

His stomach contracted at the mere mention of her, forcing another shot of pain up to his heart. He lifted his head and took a breath. He wasn't stupid enough to think there would be a second chance. Truth was, he didn't deserve one. His lies were enough to condemn him in anyone's eyes.

'She's not in great shape, man.'

He wiped at his eyes with his fingers and noticed the space where his daddy's ring had been. So much hope for the future, *their* future, so many promises he'd made her and he'd let her down. He stood up, kicking his possessions out the way to get to the front door.

Opening it just an inch triggered a thousand flashes from a few yards away. Byron took control of the door and strode quickly inside, closing it behind him. His first step into the den crushed a couple of CDs.

'Jeez, Jed, what happened here?' Byron surveyed the wrecked room.

'I'd offer you a beer but... I'm all out.' He stuck his hands in the pockets of his jeans and looked to the floor.

Byron indicated the sofa. 'Can I sit?'

Jared shrugged. Byron sat down on the sofa. He watched him put his hands together and look over at him.

'So what's going on?'

Jared shrugged again.

'Come on, Jed. This story is everywhere and your girlfriend is sitting in her kitchen like some sort of zombie. She won't drink coffee, she won't talk... it's like the life's been taken out of her.'

He knew that feeling. He was living it. And he had caused it. She was hurt and he was responsible. It was all his fault, not just because of his actions years ago but because of tonight. Giving her the ring, telling her he meant forever, building their relationship then ripping it away.

'Look, if you won't tell me about it at least talk to Honor, explain it to her,' Byron suggested.

Jared shook his head. 'I asked her to hear me out. I begged her to let me explain.'

'So? She was shocked, like we all are. But if there's a reason - if this is all bullshit – then you need to tell her.'

Jared shook his head again and put his hands behind the back of his head. He couldn't think. He could barely breathe. He didn't know what to do. What was the right thing? Try and explain it away? Could he even tell her the truth now? That was the only way if he was going to talk at all. But perhaps it was better to just not say anything, keep his distance, forget her, move on.

'Look, I'm not going to waste my time telling you what to do when I know you won't listen anyhow.' Byron got to his feet. 'But Honor's a mess, Jed and whether she hears you or not, you owe her something.'

Jared looked at his friend. Seeing the seriousness in his expression, he nodded his head.

'Think there's a storm brewing. All those photographers out there are gonna get soaked when the rain comes.' Mia closed up the blinds and moved back over to the central island. She slipped back onto the stool and pushed Honor's coffee cup nearer to her.

'Please, doll, please drink some.'

Honor shook her head. Her hand was at the ring on the end of the chain around her neck, toying with it, rubbing her thumb over the crest, a thousand thoughts speeding through her mind. What had happened to make Jared kill his father? He loved his father, he looked up to him when he was alive and he hero-worshipped him in death. The photo on the mantle, the stories he'd told her about his childhood. He'd painted a picture of family harmony, rodeos and county fairs. Like some sort of mash-up of *Dallas* and *Little House on the Prairie*. What had changed to cause such animosity? Had there been animosity or had it been some sort of accident? She didn't know. Should she? Surely the basic facts were enough. He had killed his father. What else was there?

Mia's phone made a noise like a cow mooing and she snatched it up to read the text. Honor watched her tap out a reply then replace it on the counter.

'Byron's in the studio tomorrow. He's gone to get some sleep.'

Their romantic night at the Vanderbilt, ruined because of her. No, not because of her, because of Jared. This wasn't her fault. It wasn't her fault she'd fallen in love with another ass who lied to her. It was just how things were. Ever since she was a few days old there'd been someone pushing her away, hurting her, making her feel as though she's not good enough.

'I've heard what they're saying and all, and the stories on the net look damning but... don'tcha think you ought to hear him out?' Mia asked.

She widened her eyes at her friend. Could she hear what she was thinking? It was enough that the thoughts were there without Mia adding to it. She didn't need to hear what he had to say. He hadn't denied it and so many news stories only meant truth, else it would be Law Suit Central for most of Nashville's journalists.

'Doll, I just know, if this were Byron I'd need to hear his side of things. Even if the end result is the same, what have you got to lose by giving him a minute?'

Mia was being the voice of reason. This was something she'd never been before. Usually she was the voice of going out and having a good time and not minding the consequences. Reason, never.

'He had a chance. He didn't say he didn't do it. He answered my questions like a career criminal on the stand.' Her voice was angry and bitter. The hurt lodged inside was making her chest swell.

'Come on, doll, you barely gave him a chance.' Mia picked up the coffee pot and poured herself another cup.

'What?' She was shocked.

'Look, I'm not defending him, of course I'm not and if he did what he did without due cause...'

'Without due cause? What due cause is there for murdering your father?'

'OK, wrong, bad choice of words. All I'm saying is, you know him. You've spent these past weeks getting closer than anyone's ever been to him. Before this story broke you were planning a future together. Unless he's the world's best bullshitter with a diploma in dramatic performance, he's still the guy you fell in love with... whatever he's done.'

Her anger deflated and the sorrow stepped up a gear as Mia's words made a direct attack on her heart. That was sense talking, reality, not the gut reaction or fury she'd hit him with back at the hotel.

She put her head in her hands and let the tears seep out of her eyes. She felt Mia's hand in her hair, stroking it consolingly as if she were an injured animal. She had no idea what she was going to do.

He'd parked down the street and could see the press vans, the reporters on the sidewalk, chatting, waiting, drinking take-out coffee they'd got from God knows where. None of them cared what this story was doing to the people involved with it. To them it was just another day of news, just one more scandal to spread to the world. He rubbed his face with his hands. He shouldn't be driving, he knew, but what did it matter now? He may as well add a DUI conviction to everything else and just top it off.

It was all one big fucking mess. If he braved the press gang and went to see Honor what good would it do? He couldn't give her any of the answers she was looking for without taking a huge risk.

There was a light on in one of the rooms at the top of her house. Was she still awake? Should he try, like Byron had said? If she knew the background perhaps she'd be able to see the position he'd been in. He shook his head. But he still couldn't tell her what she wanted to hear without breaking the pact.

The light went out and his stomach dropped. Decision made. He started up the truck, turned it around in the road and drove away.

Chapter Forty Two

'I know you have a dentist appointment. Why don't you believe that I remembered? Because I don't have it tattooed on my arm? Jeez! I'll be there, OK?' Mia ended the call and dropped her cell phone back on the counter.

Honor carried on buttering a slice of toast she knew she wasn't going to eat. She hadn't slept. Every time she'd closed her eyes she'd seen Jared. The sad, scared face he'd worn last night when she couldn't bear for him to be near her. At four a.m. she'd got out of bed and unpacked the bag she'd had ready for her visit to Alabama.

'I'm gonna have to go into the store later,' Mia remarked.

Honor nodded, cutting the toast in half and resting the knife on the worktop.

'Why don't you come with me?' Mia suggested.

'I don't think...'

'Look, I know if you stay here on your own you're gonna watch all the news reels and cry and listen to Vince Gill's greatest hits and I can't let that happen.'

'I'm not thirteen.' She wasn't sure why she'd said that.

'No, but it's what I would do if I was you.'

'Toast?' Honor picked up the plate and offered it to Mia. Mia shook her head. Honor put the plate down on the central island and leant back against the worktop, folding her arms across her chest.

'So, are you going to call him?' Mia asked. She could feel her friend's gaze on her, penetrating and waiting for a response.

'He hasn't called me.'

'And you're not thirteen? This is crazy! You loved the guy! He gave you that horrible ring like it was some sort of marriage proposal and now you can't even speak to him!'

'He killed his father!' She'd yelled the words like an unhinged person.

'So they say.'

'CNN are broadcasting the photo with his prison number and talking about a gunshot wound to the chest.'

'CNN weren't there when it happened. Jed was.'

'This isn't your call, Mia, it's mine.'

'I know that.' She sighed, her hands on her hips. 'But just hear him out. Just once. Just ten minutes.'

She was shaking her head again. At the moment she was doing that constantly, almost like a reflex action. It was a defense mechanism that was stopping her from thinking rationally. If she didn't engage with the situation it couldn't hurt her anymore. Was that what she was doing? Closing her emotions off? Melding the cracks in her armor for the sake of self-preservation?

The doorbell rang and neither of them moved for a second.

'The security were supposed to stop anyone stepping on your property,' Mia remarked.

She didn't care who it was. She didn't want to see anyone.

'It might be Jed,' Mia suggested. 'Although, realistically, I would have expected him to have been swallowed whole by that bitch from Nashville Newswire last night.'

The humor was lost on her. Nothing was remotely funny when you felt as though the past few weeks had been nothing but a fairytale.

'I'll go see who it is then,' Mia said.

'Should we go up?'

Jared heard the concern in his little brother Jacob's voice.

'He's tired, baby. We'll let him rest and we'll make him somethin' nice for lunch,' his mother, Carol-Ann responded.

He put his hand on the door that led to the kitchen, behind which they all sounded so worried about him. He didn't deserve their pity. He'd turned up just before dawn, scared them half to death ranting and raving and pouring out the whole story. His sister Anna had come downstairs with a sobbing Jacob and he'd had to leave, venting his frustrations on the barn door.

Being back here didn't feel right. It didn't feel like coming home. He should have been with Honor, *here* with Honor like they'd planned. His heart sped up, still motoring on alcohol and desperation. He took a breath and opened the door.

Jacob grinned at once, jumping down from the table to greet him.

'Hey, Jared, I've got a soccer game tonight. Can you come watch?' Jacob took hold of his arm and practically marched him to the long wooden table.

'Jacob, what did I tell ya about givin' your brother some space?' Carol-Ann interrupted.

'It's OK, Mom. Sure I'll come,' Jared said, ruffling his brother's tawny hair with his hand.

'Awesome!'

Jared sat down at the table and looked across at Anna. 'How's Megan?'

'We call her Meg now,' Anna responded, not raising her head from her cereal bowl.

'I apologize. I'd forgotten how awful grown up that pony must be now,' Jared replied. 'Tell me, is she too old for sugar cubes? Do you have to monitor her sugar intake?'

Anna let out a laugh. 'No!'

'Praise the Lord because I was plannin' on headin' on out for a ride on Skipper and I thought you and Megan... sorry, Meg, could come.'

'Yeah! Can I go, Mom?' Anna's face lit up.

'They've got school, Jared,' Carol-Ann reminded.

'Shoot! Of course you have school.'

Anna let out a groan of annoyance and rolled her eyes. 'School sucks!'

'Hey, listen up, school's important. How are you gonna get a job rulin' the world if you don't know how to do math?' Jared asked them both.

'*You* didn't finish school,' Jacob quipped.

Straightaway he was back there, his last year, the trouble at the farm, what had happened to his father, what had happened last night. Honor.

'Jacob, that's enough. Go clean your teeth,' Carol-Ann ordered her younger son.

Jared cleared his throat. 'It's OK, Mom.'

'Jacob, Anna, both of you, time to get ready for school,' Carol-Ann repeated.

Jared caught Anna's gaze. 'We'll go out on the horses after school.'

'But you said you'd come to my soccer game!' Jacob cried.

'I can do both, can't I?'

Anna smiled and she and Jacob left the kitchen to thunder back upstairs to the bathroom.

He put his elbows on the table and his hands behind the back of his head, linking his knuckles and inching down his cap. Eyes down, he realized the table was covered by the same familiar gingham tablecloth from his childhood. He felt his mom come and sit down next to him and he straightened up, tried to act like the grown up he should be, not the shell of a man he felt.

'The newspapers have been callin',' she stated, pouring coffee into a mug.

'I'm sorry, Mom. You shouldn't have to put up with that.'

'Shouldn't I? It's the very least I should have to put up with in my opinion.'

'Don't.'

Carol-Ann pushed the coffee cup towards him and put a hand over his. 'I don't want you to go through this again, Jared.'

'It's too late.'

'It's never too late.'

'It is, Mom, 'cause I lost Honor.'

With those words, the enormity of the loss hit him full force and he became a shaking mass in his mother's arms.

'Corbin's here to see you,' Mia stated.

Honor looked up from toying with her fingers to see her friend and the dark-haired roadie entering the kitchen. Self-conscious, she pulled her robe tighter around her and got down from the stool. What was Mia thinking? She was letting a virtual stranger into her house when she was vulnerable and depressed. Apart from Jenna Curran from Nashville Newswire, or Dan Steele, a random roadie was probably next on the list of people she really didn't want to see.

'I don't want to see anyone, Mia. We discussed this.'

'He's bought you some flowers. Look, aren't they lovely?' Mia took the bouquet from Corbin's hands and marched them over to Honor.

'I... look, this isn't really appropriate... to come to my house and...' She was actually worried. Here was this guy she'd met a couple of times at the festival, turning up at her house with flowers. *Her stalker*. This roadie could be the person who'd been sending her gifts. She dropped the bluebonnets to the central island.

'I'd like you to leave,' she stated firmly.

'I'm sorry for barging in on you and everything but when I heard the news about Jed Marshall I just... I had to come... to make sure you were OK,' Corbin told her.

'OK, now this is getting a little creepy. Mia, I don't know what you were thinking letting this guy in but I want you to take him right back out again!'

'I'm just gonna be in the lounge if you need anything,' Mia said, backing to the door.

'What the hell? Mia, no. What are you doing?' Honor hurried towards her departing friend, scared.

Before she could reach the door Corbin took hold of her arm and turned her gently towards him. 'Honor.'

He took a breath and she could do nothing but look back at him, waiting for whatever was coming next.

'You have your mother's eyes. I've never forgotten those beautiful eyes.' He smiled. 'But your hair color... you get that from me.'

Chapter Forty Three

She wasn't sure how she'd got back up onto the stool. At first Corbin's words had triggered a 'fight' response. She'd called him insane, a lunatic, a psycho. She'd bawled and shouted, cried, and then as he'd cradled her in his arms and apologized over and over, what he'd said slowly began to sink in. He was saying he was her father. Why would someone say that if there wasn't any element of truth to it?

'Shall I get something? A drink? Coffee?' He paused. 'Bourbon?'

She shook her head. Her eyes felt like huge, sore boulders, standing out, reddened from all the hours of crying.

'I know I've gone about this all the wrong way but I didn't know what else to do,' he began. 'Then last night, when I heard the news, when I saw you on TV, running from that hotel party I just knew I had to be here for you.'

Honor shook her head. She couldn't believe this was happening. Was it happening? Did she believe what Corbin was saying? Or was this just some elaborate scam to catch her when she was at her most vulnerable? Where was his proof? She didn't know what to say to him.

As if reading her mind he reached into the top pocket of his plaid shirt and brought out an old worn newspaper cutting. He laid it on the countertop between them and pushed it slightly toward Honor.

'I never knew I had a daughter until last year. I got a letter from a lawyer's office asking me to come to their place. At first I thought about ignoring it. In my world, lawyers usually mean trouble, but I went and that photo and a few sketchy details were waiting for me.'

Honor picked up the photo. It was a black and white picture of a baby, a screwed-up wrinkled face, a fist clenched to its cheek, a bonnet on its head. 'Baby Blue Bonnet abandoned outside Mayor's home' read the headline.

'I went to the state. I went to every foster home you'd ever been in and some you hadn't, looking for information. No one would ever give me much until I met Maisy Ryan.'

Honor swallowed. She'd lived with Maisy Ryan from age thirteen until she left at sixteen with fifty dollars, a rucksack of her possessions, her guitar and a heart full of hope. The Ryan's home was the only place she'd ever felt really cared for, like she mattered. But it was too little too late. She'd been hardened long before then.

Corbin smiled. 'She talked about you as if you were her own. Told me stories. Showed me photos. I knew, when I saw those pictures... there was no doubt in my mind that you were mine.'

She couldn't deal with this. How was she supposed to react to this revelation when so much else was going on in her world? For all her life, she'd wondered about her parents. Where they were, who they were, why they'd left her and now, now she had her alleged father in front of her and she didn't have clue what to say.

'Of course then I had to learn everything about you.' He tried to get her to look at him, dipping his head, trying to raise her out of the reverie she'd locked herself into. 'Your music career, that beautiful voice you have...'

This felt so awkward. This man, the man she'd met as a roadie at the festival, talking in such a soft, caring voice, like she was precious. Her hand went to the ring on the chain around her neck.

'...what that maniac did to you on stage.'

She looked up then, wanted to see his reaction to his own words. How would a father feel to know his daughter had been attacked the way she had? Would he have been there? Would he have supported her through her surgeries or would he have been unable to look at her – like Dan?

She saw tears in his eyes, his lips shifting slightly, his thumb toying with the bottom of the cold coffee pot.

'And then I found out where you lived and... I didn't know what to do.' He rubbed a hand over the side of his face. 'I was terrified, Honor. I knew where my daughter lived and I had no idea how to approach her. I know how that sounds dumb, right? But I knew you'd have an image of who your parents were. I know I would have if I'd been in your shoes and... I didn't want to be a disappointment.'

She swallowed again as his words got to her. She felt a warm sensation of affection drift up through her and nothing was battering it back.

'So, I took the coward's way out. I sent you presents and I followed you. Just knowing it was you, my daughter, being able to see you living your life, working at the music shop, performing... everything. I was grateful just to be able to share in that from a distance,' Corbin told her.

Honor closed her eyes and let out a long, slow breath. 'It was you. The chocolates, the flowers, the owl from Target... the personalized guitar picks.'

'Yeah, I got a bit braver there,' he admitted, a flush appearing on his cheeks.

'You shouldn't have done that.'

'I know. I should have had the guts to walk up to your front door but... I didn't want you to reject me. And I know how selfish that sounds but, Honor, I don't have a wife or another family. I've been a loner all my life and the day I found out about you... it meant the world.'

Her stomach contracted. 'I thought I had a stalker.'

He shook his head. 'I know, the other day at the festival... I felt such an ass.'

Her eyes went to the owl, sat in prime position on her windowsill at the kitchen window. 'I kept it.'

He followed her line of sight and smiled. 'I had to have strong words with another shopper before she let me have it. All of the others had matching eyes.'

Honor nodded, then took a breath. 'I don't know what to say to you. This feels kind of weird.'

'I know, it does for me too. And I know... I mean... I don't expect you to take all this in and start arranging father and daughter McDonalds trips every Friday night or anything. I just... I just wanted you to know that if you need me. If you want me in your life then I'm here. I'll be to you whatever you want me to be, if you give me the opportunity.'

For a second, forgetting everything she was having to process, her heart went out to him. Here he was, a middle-aged man with nobody, who had missed out on half his daughter's life. If he was to be believed, if his story was real, then he'd never known she existed.

She nodded. Maybe it wasn't enough, just a nod, but it was all she could give him.

'I'd like to get to know you, Honor. That's all. Just to get to know you,' Corbin told her.

'I'll make some coffee. This pot's cold.'

The sun was so fierce he'd had to take his t-shirt off after mucking out the horses. Skipper was getting on for eighteen years old now but still in good shape. Rubbing him down and checking him over had whiled away a couple of hours, but now he was back to thinking about Honor as song lyrics threw themselves at him.

Sitting up on the straw bales to the right of the barn had always been a favorite spot for composing songs. He wrote furiously, his pencil moving quickly, stabbing at the paper, desperate to get something down. He checked his watch. Thirty minutes or so had passed since he last checked his phone. He hadn't heard it, but maybe... he got it out of his pocket. Nothing. He'd had ten missed calls from Gear last night. They had no idea how to handle the publicity except to provide the press with a 'no comment.' He knew he'd have to speak to them if he wanted to keep his contract, but what could he say that wasn't already being said? He'd been convicted, he'd done a few years of his sentence, then he'd been released.

'Room for another one?'

Jared looked up to see his mom standing at the bottom of the straw pile with two cans of Coke in her hands.

He shrugged, not sure he was in the mood for company.

'Here, catch,' she said, throwing the drinks to him one after the other.

He watched her climb up the bales with ease and she settled herself down next to him. He smiled at her, shaking his head.

'What? You think just because I have a little arthritis I can't climb up some straw? I was raised in the South don'cha know?'

'Yeah I know,' he responded.

She opened her can and he felt her eyes rest on him. 'So, are you gonna tell me what happened with Honor?'

Just hearing her name hurt. All the memories it conjured up, all the good times, the smell of her skin, her hair in his hands, her lips on his...

'She heard the news like everyone else, right after the awards ceremony. She heard I shot my father.' He delivered it like he was a TV anchor.

'And did you talk to her? Did you tell her about Deputy Finlay?'

He shirked. He didn't like talking about it, not even to his mom. It just brought it all back up again. He tried to forget. He had tried to wipe that day out of his memory bank permanently.

'What's the point?' he responded.

'What's the point? Jared, you know what the point is. You're not a murderer. You didn't kill your father. Why would you let the girl you love think that of you?' Carol-Ann asked, her brow furrowed, the fringe of her blonde hair almost touching the tops of her eyes.

'Because I made a promise and I don't break promises.' His voice was firm and unfaltering.

'Didn't you make promises to Honor? You've never invited a girl back here, Jared, not since Karen. I know you're serious about this girl.'

'I am... I was... but... she didn't want to listen,' he stated.

'And just how hard did you try before you ran away?'

'What?'

He hadn't expected a challenge to his decision. He'd come here for support, because his mom was the only other person who had lived through that difficult time. Anna had only been small and Jacob smaller, a baby, too young to remember much about it.

'How hard did you try to make her listen to you? The Jared Marshall I know fights for what he wants. That's how you got so far in the music business. You knocked on doors, gigged at crappy little shows and back-sticks radio stations, because you wanted it so bad. Or is Honor not worth the effort?' She took a swig of her drink. 'Maybe I was wrong, maybe she isn't so special.'

Jared swallowed as a vivid picture of his girl came to mind. Her smile, the way she held his hand, that pure, sweet voice when she sang and when she whispered in his ear.

'She is special, Mom. She's everything.' The emotion was there again. 'But I don't know what to do.'

'Oh, darlin', you need to talk to her. No matter what the press are sayin', she deserves to know what really happened... all of it,' Carol-Ann told him.

'But I promised,' he stated, feeling the tears welling up.

'Who did you promise, darlin'? Because ten years on I'm ready for whatever comes of it.'

He looked up at his mom. 'I promised Daddy.'

Chapter Forty Four

'...and it's a case of "no comment" in the Jed Marshall prison story. It appears Marshall's gone to ground and both his advisor, Buzz Callahan and Gear Records are remaining tight-lipped. More to come...'

Honor flicked the radio back off again. 'Sorry, thought some background music would be good. I should've realized.'

She picked the empty coffee pot up and transferred it to the sink, going back for Corbin's cup. They'd spent a slightly awkward half hour trading snippets of information about themselves until Mia had come in five minutes earlier to tell them she was leaving for Instrumadness.

'I know it's not any of my business but what's the deal with that?' Corbin asked.

Honor dropped the cups into the bowl in the sink. 'What's the deal with what?'

'Jed and the prison story.'

'I...I don't want to talk about that.'

'Sorry, it's just they're all having a fine time hanging him out to dry before they've even got an interview with him,' Corbin stated.

'What?' She turned to face him.

'You can't condemn someone like that without getting their side of the story, can you?'

She felt sick. She felt sick and stupid all at the same time. Mia had said it over and over last night. Now, a virtual stranger, the father she didn't know, was saying it to her too. The reports were stating facts but there was always more to a Nashville story. She should know, she'd been involved in a lot of them back in the day. *Honor Blackwood blinded by attacker*. *Attacker is ex-boyfriend with a grudge* and her very favorite *Aliens made me do it says Honor Blackwood attacker*. Suddenly a shroud was being lifted and good sense was kicking in.

'I need to see him, don't I? I need to hear what he's got to say.'

She slipped down off the stool and wrung her hands together. She knew it was the right thing to do, but the idea of seeing him again was scaring her to death. She looked to Corbin.

'I'm sorry. I know we have a lot to talk about but...'

'Hey, I'm grateful to have gotten coffee.' He smiled at her and the way his eyes crinkled up, almost creasing his temple, sent a pang of emotion to her chest. This could really be her father. They'd have to formalize it, by getting tests or something, but it could be the beginning of the first step towards any sort of family.

'I can drive you,' Corbin said, standing up.

'Pardon me?'

'I'll drive you to see Jed,' he repeated.

'Oh, no, it's fine. He lives just across town. It's not far.'

'Look at you, you're shaking and high on caffeine. I don't expect you got much sleep last night.'

She either looked a whole lot worse than she thought or he could read her a little already.

'No strings. I'll drive you there and I'll wait... or I'll leave.' He rested his gaze on her. 'We can decide on that when we get there.'

She looked back at him while her mind turned over thoughts about Jared. Could they make this right? Was his explanation going to change things or was she just going to give him a chance to say goodbye?

'Thank you.' She smiled at him. 'I'll go get dressed.

The street Jared lived on was eerily quiet. When she and Corbin had left her house the press had been there in droves, bombarding her with questions, shooting off pictures, wanting a response, whatever its content. Corbin hadn't acknowledged any of it. He'd remained cool and calm, just guiding her through the pack to his truck.

Now they were parked up outside Jared's home and there wasn't a journalist in sight. There also wasn't a car in the driveway.

Honor let out a discontented sigh. 'He's not there.'

'No? How do you know?'

'His truck's not there.' She was annoyed and frustrated. She'd built herself up on the drive over and now he wasn't in.

'Maybe he left it someplace or lent it to someone. You should go knock,' Corbin suggested.

She shook her head.

'You could call him.'

'No, I couldn't do that.' The thought of the ringing line, the waiting, the anxiety, the fear flooding through her. No, this was something that could only be done face to face.

'If you call him you can find out where he is,' Corbin suggested.

She couldn't speak to him on the phone, she just couldn't. It would feel awkward. There would have to be some sort of conversation not just a request for directions. And what if he didn't answer at all or he did and he didn't want her to know where he was? It didn't bear thinking about.

'I could...' Corbin began.

'No... no, I don't want you to.'

She needed to think what to do. She could call Mia and maybe she could call Byron. Byron was the closest friend Jared seemed to have. If anyone knew where he was, then Byron might.

'Just... just give me a minute.' She opened the car door, and a breeze wound around her. Her head ached and she steadied herself, putting a hand on the hood of the car. She was losing focus, her mind full up; unable to cope with everything that was going on.

'Are you OK?' Corbin was out the car too, looking at her with concern.

'Yeah... yeah I'm fine. I just need to call Mia. I'll be fine.' She gave him a hopeful smile and took her phone from her jeans pocket.

Mia had only taken a few minutes to make the call to Byron and come back with the news, but it had felt like forever. She'd paced the sidewalk as Corbin had watched from the truck and then she'd gotten her answer. He was in Alabama. He'd gone home, as planned, without her.

With her legs like jelly and her heart bumping a staccato she made it back to the car. He'd left the state. He wasn't here in Nashville. He was in Wetumpka, his hometown. The trip they'd planned together had meant so much to them both. It had all gone so wrong so quickly.

'Honor,' Corbin said in a soft tone that rapped on her heart.

Of course he was waiting for her to say something. She'd just got into the car and stared out of the windshield.

'He's gone home.' She cleared her throat, turned her head to face him. 'He's gone back to Alabama.'

She felt a lone tear leave her eye and she quickly whisked it away with the sleeve of her top. She saw Corbin nod his head, then he started the engine.

'Could you take me home?'

She just wanted to hide, be by herself, process everything, analyze everything until somehow, someway it all became clearer. If that was ever going to be possible.

'I'm not taking you home. I'm taking you to Alabama. Buckle up,' Corbin stated, looking over at her.

'What?'

'You need to see him, I've got nothing better to do today. Let's go to Alabama and try and sort this out,' Corbin stated.

'But...'

'Besides, four hours in a truck together and it'll feel like we've never been apart.'

'I can't. I...'

'Buckle up, Honor. I'm not taking no for an answer.'

They'd traveled an hour without speaking and now Vince Gill was playing on the radio. Truth was, she didn't know what to talk about. They'd only just met. They'd had a tentative conversation over a pot of coffee and now they were cocooned in a vehicle for half a working day.

'D'you need to stop yet?' Corbin broke the silence.

She shook her head. 'No.'

She'd taken off her boots and had curled her feet up underneath her to hug her knees. There were three hours left and it was like waiting for the storm to hit. You knew it was coming, but you also knew there was nothing you could do to avoid it and the outcome wasn't entirely in your hands.

Corbin took a quick look at her before turning his attention back to the road. 'You haven't asked me many questions. I thought you'd have a lot of questions.'

Honor closed her eyes, trying to dampen down her feelings. 'You don't have to drive me to Alabama. If you let me out at the next truck stop I can...'

'You think I'm gonna let you hitch to the next state?'

'I don't know whether I can stand hearing about the life you had while I was living in care.'

There, it was out. She wasn't in the right mindset to take this on. She wasn't ready for it. She'd spent most of her life believing it would never come and now it was here she didn't know how to handle it. Especially now, when everything was upside down and she didn't know what was going to happen.

'That's why we should talk,' Corbin continued, unfazed.

She sighed. 'I don't really know what to say.' She rubbed one palm against her jean-covered legs. There was nowhere to go here in the car, nowhere to hide.

'You haven't asked about your mom.'

Somehow she'd known the exact words he was going to say. It was as if it had been there at the back of her mind, just resting, being ignored. Was it because she didn't want to know? Because she couldn't understand how a mother could leave her baby on a doorstep? Or was it because she was scared to find out? What could Corbin tell her if he only knew he was a father six months ago?

She shook her head. It was all she could do and even *she* wasn't sure whether it meant 'don't tell me' or 'no, I haven't asked'.

Corbin sucked a breath in through his teeth and screwed up his eyes from the sun that was pouring in the windshield.

'She was real pretty and had the voice of an angel.'

Her stomach tightened as his words resonated. She'd heard them before. It was almost an echo. She closed her eyes.

'We spent a couple nights together, Honor, while we were both performing in Wyoming. She sang solo and I was in a band.' Corbin laughed. 'It wasn't the big time. The places we played were barely places at all. But back then, if you hadn't got a contract, you just did it for the love of the music and money for beer.'

The only picture she could see in her head was a version of herself. Younger maybe, a little taller, her hair a little longer, the bottoms of her jeans a little wider. She had nothing else to imagine.

'Her stage name was Alice Ruskin. That's how I knew her. But her real name, I found out, was Alison Robbins.'

Robbins. Her real last name was Robbins.

'She was like a whisper in the wind. A breeze that came into the room and affected everybody. Like a sweet change to the temperature... something different. When she was on stage no one could take their eyes off her,' Corbin continued.

Suddenly she was filled with anger. Here he was, her father, describing her mother as if she were a saintly, admirable woman who sang and charmed and wafted in, bewitching everyone in her path. But she had had a baby, not told the father of its existence and abandoned it. Abandoned her.

'Why do you feel that way about her?' Honor snapped, turning to look at Corbin. 'You spent two nights together, she got pregnant and didn't even tell you! That doesn't sound like a whisper in the wind to me, it sounds like a selfish, irresponsible bitch!'

The harshness of her words took her back. She knew she shouldn't care, should put on a brave face and a barricade like always but now, with Corbin here romanticizing everything, her blood was boiling. She was hurt and mad and she wanted to know every detail. Who Alice was, why she thought it was OK to leave a baby for the mayor to sort out and where she was now. So she could go tell her to her face.

'Honor, I know how this sounds to you...'

'Do you? Do you really?'

'I can only tell you what I know from that short window of time. I can't tell you what she was really like as a person because...' He paused. 'I didn't really know her.'

Honor shook her head. What else was there to say? He couldn't tell her anything. He couldn't tell her if she regretted giving up her child. He couldn't tell her if she went on to have a family. If she wanted to find this out it would mean making contact herself.

'I know she never had any other children. The lawyer told me that. There was a husband... but no children,' Corbin informed.

Something squeezed her heart as she caught hold of something in his tone. '*Was* a husband? What does that mean? She divorced him? Gave up on him like she left me?' She shook her head. 'Figures.'

'No,' Corbin replied.

His voice was deadpan, his eyes set ahead. He pulled the car off the road and brought it to a halt.

'No, I don't want to stop. I want to get to Alabama and I want to see Jared. I abandoned him last night and maybe that was a big mistake. I'm really hoping so right now, because if I have to even think about carrying on without what we had together.' Her voice was shaking. 'I've never felt that way. I've never felt loved like that.'

'Honor,' Corbin said, reaching for her hand.

'I won't let that woman make me cry because she left me. I'm stronger than that. I've been through worse than that.'

'I know you have, I know. And I'm not making excuses for her because I'm in no position to do that. I didn't keep in touch. I didn't know about you. Starting off, for a minute, I was crazy mad that she let me miss out on you. But then I found out she'd missed out on you too.' He gave her hand a squeeze. 'Then I only felt sorry for you. Ending up with two parents you thought didn't give a damn.'

She was gritting her teeth so hard her jaw hurt. She wouldn't let the tears fall. She would hold them in and try and retain what little strength she had left.

'Honor...' He stalled, locked eyes with her, then dropped them. 'Honor, your mom died.'

She heard what he said but it didn't register. She didn't feel anything. He was holding her hand and when he looked back up again his eyes were moist. But there was still no emotion inside her. She was unable to express anything. She had nothing to give for the loss of the woman who had given birth to her.

'The letter I had from the lawyer's office was because she'd passed. She'd left a will and amongst those papers was a letter asking them to contact me,' Corbin started to explain.

She looked at him; his face was creased with emotion for a woman he'd barely known. Had those two nights they'd spent together meant something? Had her mother not been one in a long line for him? Had he really cared for her? If they'd not kept in contact at all why was he shedding tears? Did you cry for virtual strangers just because they'd died? Everybody dies in the end, people died every day.

She was frowning at him, finding this show of feeling confusing as he carried on.

'It said she'd had a daughter. She was *my* daughter, she was positive of that. And she told me you'd been taken into care.'

She couldn't look at him anymore. She turned to gaze out the window, watched the sun streaking the grassland.

'She left the cutting from the newspaper and... that was all,' Corbin finished.

Honor snapped her head back, her eyes narrowing. 'That was all?'

He nodded, wiping at his eyes with his thumbs.

'That was all the letter said? You have a daughter and she's in care. Here's the headline from when I left her at the mayor's house?'

'I'm certain she was sorry. I mean, she had to be sorry. She never had another child, she'd gotten cancer before she was fifty. It doesn't sound like the perfect life to me.'

'But it was the one she chose wasn't it?' The bitterness filled her mouth up and she had to swallow. 'I'm glad her life wasn't perfect.'

'Honor...'

'And I'm *real* glad she didn't have any more children she could let down.'

Chapter Forty Five

'He plays like you used to, you know.'

The Wetumpka Warriors were bossing the soccer game against their closest rivals in the school league. Jacob had set up one goal and was playing better than Jared had ever seen him play before.

'Nah, I was never that good,' he responded.

His eyes left the game for a second when he heard his sister's distinctive laugh. She was with a couple of girlfriends in the bleachers just behind them, flicking back her hair and chewing gum like her life depended on it.

'Has Anna got a guy?' he asked, turning back to the game.

'Not that I know of. But the name Troy Casey has been appearing on notebooks for a minute.'

'That him?' Jared asked, leaning his head toward a dark-haired youth wearing track pants and a tight, white t-shirt.

'Yup, his dad's the team coach now,' Carol-Ann answered.

'And what's the kid like?' He could feel the prickles of discomfort forming on the back of his neck as he thought about Anna with a boyfriend.

'Jared Marshall. Do you have any idea what you were like at Anna's age?' Carol-Ann looked at him with an open mouth.

'Yes, ma'am I do. And if this Troy is anything like I was at fifteen, I want him to stay the hell away from my sister.'

He gritted his teeth and watched Carol-Ann clap her hands together as Jacob's team narrowly missed a chance on goal. She turned her body towards him and he immediately felt uncomfortable.

'It's gonna have been a shock to her, sweetheart.' Her voice was low so no one else could hear. 'Finding out what happened to you the way she did. So public and on a big night.'

Jared shook his head. He didn't want to talk about this. He wanted to forget about it for a while, concentrate on being back home, on spending some time with his family. It was just the three of them on the land now and he never got back as often as he felt he should. He felt responsible for how they were living, for the hard work his mom insisted on doing because she was too proud to take on extra hands. In truth, he knew the work was what kept her going. It had nothing to do with the money, he made sure she never need worry about that side of things.

'Jared, I want you to know that I will do whatever you want me to do to make this right,' Carol-Ann told him.

'No.' His response was immediate. He couldn't do that to his family. He'd protected them all once and he was going to keep on doing it no matter what the consequences were. Even if it meant him losing the things he held most dear.

'Listen to me. You have no reason to walk around here with your head hung low, son. You are the truest, most honorable man I know. What you did for this family...'

He could hear the tears in his mother's voice and the boulder was up in his throat before he could do anything about it.

'Stop, Momma.'

'No, I won't stop, Jared. I don't want you to throw your future away because of the past. It was wrong then and it's even more wrong now.' Carol-Ann's raised voice caught looks from other spectators. 'You owe it... you owe it to that poor girl to tell her the whole truth and let her make any decisions based on the facts.'

He didn't respond, just focused on his brother and the game

in front of them.

'I know you can hear me. You're just too damn stubborn, like your father.' She sniffed back the emotion. 'And look where that got him.'

'The guy in the store says they live about a mile and a half out of town. He's given me directions.'

Honor ignored the fact Corbin was stood outside the car, grabbed the handle and got back into it, thumping up onto the seat and pretending to look intently at the map in her hand.

After hearing her mother was dead and telling Corbin she was glad, there hadn't been much else to say. They'd driven the rest of the way to Alabama in virtual silence, apart from the occasional comment about opening the window or turning up the radio or pointing out a diner for a toilet and drink break.

Corbin got back into the driver's seat. 'Let me see the map.'

'I can navigate. I'm good with maps,' Honor lied.

'Just let me have a look to get my bearings,' Corbin asked.

Honor shook her head and thrust the map at him. 'I should have driven myself. We would have been there by now.'

'Or in a car wreck on the side of the freeway because you fell asleep at the wheel.'

'Well I wouldn't have wanted you to cry for me. We barely know each other.' She snapped the words out and straightaway regretted it. She couldn't blame Corbin, not really. In the last six months he'd looked for her, longing to find her. He wasn't the one who should be the focus for her anger. But he was the only one here.

'I'm sorry,' she whispered, contrite.

'It's OK,' he answered.

'No it isn't. You've taken the trouble to drive me all the way here and I'm acting like a brat.'

'And here I was thinking I'd missed the teenage years.'

She couldn't help the laugh that blurted out. Her mouth turned upwards and it was then she realized it had been almost a whole twenty-four hours since she'd raised a smile.

As if sensing her feelings, Corbin reached across the cab and patted her thigh. 'Let's get you there.'

'I get an extra piece of chicken because I've burned up more energy than anyone –playing soccer!' Jacob announced.

'What? No way! Mom, that's not fair. I didn't eat all my lunch today and I'm starving!' Anna battled back.

'No one asked you not to eat your lunch. Did you want to suck your stomach in to impress *Troy*?' Jacob teased.

'You're a brat, Jacob! Mom, will you tell him!'

'I've got the chicken bucket! I've got the chicken bucket!'

'Jared! He'll eat it all! Stop him!'

He let out a laugh as his siblings leapt out of the truck and chased each other to the front door. 'And I was thinkin' they'd grown up.'

'It's not like you to keep out of a fight for food,' Carol-Ann remarked.

'I'm not hungry.'

'You have to eat, honey.'

'I'm good, really.'

Carol-Ann reached for his hand and gave it a squeeze. 'There's apple pie for dessert.'

He nodded. 'You go in, I'll just go check the horses.'

They both got out of the truck and Jared watched his mom go into the house. He could still hear Jacob and Anna bickering over who was going to get the lion's share of the takeout. He started to walk across the yard to the stables when he heard a truck.

'D'you think this is it?' Honor asked, squinting through the half-light to see anything that might help establish a connection.

'It's the only place around here,' Corbin said, continuing down the track.

She was holding her breath and feeling terrified. For the past hour she'd been running through in her mind what she was going to say to him. How did you start a conversation? She needed answers but she didn't want to go in all mad and accusing or as frenzied as she felt inside. She had to be calm and measured.

The second she saw him she knew calm and measured wasn't going to be an option. He was yards ahead, in the center of the yard, dressed in jeans, a dark t-shirt and his leather jacket. His cap was on his head and he was holding a hand up to shield his eyes from the headlights of Corbin's truck.

'Dip the lights, Corbin,' Honor instructed. 'And pull up.'

Corbin stopped the car and she didn't know what to do. Could he see it was her now he wasn't blinded by the lights? His hand was down by his side now and he just stood, unmoved, staring at the vehicle.

She blew out a breath and rubbed her palms on her thighs, summoning up some sort of courage to make a decision.

It was Honor. Right here. Right outside his home. In a truck driven by a guy who looked vaguely familiar somehow. She was just a few feet away from him and he couldn't move. He couldn't step closer or back away, he was paralyzed to the spot, not knowing what to do next.

The next sound he heard made his heart thunder. The car door opened and she stepped down onto the clay. Her hair was loose and she was wearing a plaid shirt and jeans. His stomach rolled at the acknowledgment of her and his groin concurred. Here she was, the girl he loved… the girl he'd lost.

He swallowed and watched her walk across the yard towards him. Tentative steps, no expression on her face, those wide blue eyes even larger than he remembered. When she came to a stop they were only inches apart. If he reached out he could touch her. He moved his hand just a fraction and…

She punched him hard, with everything she had. Balled up in

her fist was everything he hadn't told her, all the hurt she felt that he hadn't been honest, rage at Simeon Stewart for giving her a scar she'd have forever and twenty-seven years' worth of despair at being an abandoned child.

He rocked back on his heels, putting a hand to his jaw as she held onto her knuckles, which were already throbbing with pain. She straightened her expression, killed the hurt with attitude. She wasn't going to be walked over.

'I'll give you that,' he growled, nodding.

'You deserve more.'

'I know.'

She blinked, looking at him, taking in the sad gray eyes, his cut lip, the roughness of his face. She felt nothing but the intense, overwhelming desire and love for him.

He grabbed her hair and dragged her towards him, his mouth crashing against hers with the force of a tornado. She reached up, pulled off his cap and threw it to the ground, her fingers smoothing over his hair as she felt his tongue inside her mouth, hot, wild, loving.

This was where she wanted to be right now. She needed him, his comfort, this physical fusion. Because when the talking started neither of them knew how it was going to end.

Chapter Forty Six

'We should have got a bigger chicken bucket.'

Jacob had been scowling ever since Corbin and Honor had been invited to share the food. The whole meal had been awkward. His mom was floating around making sure everyone had food and drinks and he just sat opposite Honor, poking at his fries and watching her do the same.

'So, tell me, how do you two know each other? Are you a musician, Corbin?' Carol-Ann asked.

'I play a little, ma'am, yes. Right now I'm picking up some work as a behind-the-scenes technician,' Corbin replied.

'I love your voice,' Anna piped up, fixing Honor with an awestruck expression.

Honor reached for her glass of water, avoiding looking at Jared. 'Thank you.'

'How was the drive?'

He had no idea why he'd asked that. He didn't know the guy and he wasn't sure he wanted to know him. Perhaps it was the thought of him being in a car with Honor for over four hours that was making him antsy. Even though he looked old enough to be her father.

'It was fine. Traffic was light.' Honor interrupted quickly.

'Who does your hair?' Anna asked, leaning an elbow on the

table and looking at Honor as if she was a work of art.

'I...' she began.

'Does your scar still hurt?' Jacob jumped in.

'Whoa! Jacob, I think that's enough table talk for now. Say, Jared, why don't you take Honor into the den and I'll make some coffee. Corbin, perhaps you could come with me and the kids and we'll make up the spare rooms,' Carol-Ann suggested.

'That's very kind of you, ma'am, but I can stay at a motel or something,' Corbin answered.

'I won't hear of it and that's the subject closed,' Carol-Ann said firmly. 'Jared, take Honor through to the den.'

He looked across at her and their eyes met. She looked away. Scraping back his chair, he stood up.

'I'll bring coffee right on through,' Carol-Ann said, looking to Honor.

He lit a fire while she had watched from the leather couch and nursed her reddened knuckles. Carol-Ann had brought in a pot of coffee but it was untouched, still sitting on the small table.

Jared got up, dusted his hands on his jeans and stood, awkwardly.

'As soon as the sun goes down it gets cold this time of year,' he stated.

She nodded, not knowing what else to do. She watched him choose the chair furthest from her and sink down into it, folding one leg over the other and settling with one hand clasped over his boot.

'So, I guess we should talk,' he began, his tone slightly too upbeat.

'Do you want to talk?' she found herself asking.

'I'm not that struck with it, if I'm real honest.'

'And what would you know about honesty?'

'Ouch.' He looked over to her.

She stood up and paced over to the window, looking out. 'I know some of this is my fault. I know I told you I didn't want to know why you'd been sent to juvenile detention. But I can't help thinking if I'd said I wanted to know, if I'd made you tell me something.' She turned back to face him. 'I think you would have lied.'

He nodded his head. 'Yes, ma'am. I would have.'

'What? You're not going to even deny it?'

'No, 'cause I'd be lyin'.'

Honor threw her hands up. This was insane. All she wanted was for him to tell her what really happened, but now she wasn't sure she could trust anything he said.

'You didn't shoot your father did you?'

She watched his reaction. She saw the flicker of grief ride over his features. It wasn't an act; it was real, true, and deep. The affection he had for his whole family wasn't fabricated. He couldn't do anything to hurt the people he loved. She was sure of that. She should have known when the story broke he could never have done it.

'Jared, if you love me, you should trust me.' She looked across at him, willing him to make eye contact. 'What I feel for you is bigger and better and stronger than anything I've ever known. I believe in that feeling. I believe in you and me... even now. Even after all this.'

He raised his head and met her eyes. She saw him swallow and hoped her words were getting through. She meant them, from the bottom of her soul.

'I should have left my faith with you, instead of running away and believing everything the media was feeding Nashville with. I'm so sorry for that.'

He shook his head. 'You have nothin' to be sorry for.'

'And neither do you. If my gut is right, you went to prison for something you didn't even do, didn't you?'

His expression cracked and he hurriedly hung his head. She went to him then, rushing to his side, kneeling down on the floor and taking his hands in hers.

'Just tell me, Jared, please.'

'I can't,' he sobbed. 'I promised.'

Honor turned her head as the door to the den opened.

'Jared, if you don't tell Honor now, then I will,' Carol-Ann stated, entering the room.

He raised his head. 'No, Momma. There's always that chance they could reopen the case.'

'I don't care about that now! I care about doin' what's right by you and you... you need to do right by Honor.'

Jared shook his head and a look passed between them that Honor couldn't distinguish.

'Honor, I shot Jared's father. I killed my husband,' Carol-Ann said in a matter-of-fact tone. The woman sat down on the couch with a sigh.

'Mom... Honor, she's just trying to make things better between us,' Jared spoke.

'Jared, stop it,' Carol-Ann ordered. She patted the sofa next to her and looked to Honor. 'Come sit down.'

Honor got up from the floor, her body trembling as she tried to take in what she'd heard. On auto-pilot she moved to the couch and sat down a little way away from Carol-Ann.

'This place here, where we live, it's everythin' to us. We're a close community and we look out for each other. It's always been that way, some might think it's old-fashioned and behind the times, but there it is.' She took a breath. 'The nearest town... it had some issues and James, he knew two of the larger families there. We're talkin' granddaddies and great-great-granddaddies doin' business together over the years and helpin' each other out, that sort of thing.' She looked at Honor, as if to check she was keeping up.

'Well, law enforcement decided they wanted James to go get information from these families about their businesses and pass it on to the police to use against them.' Carol paused. 'Now I'm all for abidin' by the laws of the land, but you don't cross friends and family no matter what they do for their business and James took the same stand. He told Officer Finlay there was no way in hell he was gonna turn informant.'

Honor watched Jared. He was sat back in the chair, his face stony, his jaw set, tears in his eyes. He was hurting.

'That's when all the trouble started. First it was cattle going missin', then the fire in the barn and the dog gettin' hurt. It was a warnin'. Unless James did what Finlay wanted he'd hurt us, cripple the farm, ruin our livelihood or worse.'

Jared pulled down his cap and turned away, looking into the fire.

'I thought James would stand his ground. That's the sort of man he was. But he was also the sort of man who protects his family.' Carol-Ann blew out a breath and Honor could see the memories were taking her back there. 'They didn't know I was in the barn. James and Finlay were discussin' how James was gonna gain the families' implicit trust, how he could wear a wire once he was comfortable with the situation, how they would protect him if anythin' went wrong. Well, I just saw red, my husband was as good as doin' a deal with the devil.'

'I can't hear this.' Jared stood up and walked over to the fireplace, resting his hands on the wooden mantle.

'Jared, it's time to get this out. I won't have you takin' the blame for this anymore.'

'What happened?' Honor asked. She needed to know. She needed to understand why Jared had taken this on himself.

'I picked up the shotgun and I held it at Finlay. I told him to get off our property and never come back. I told him if he didn't leave my family alone I'd report him for harassment and arson and criminal damage. And d'you know what he did?'

Honor shook her head. She locked her hands together to stop them from shaking.

'He laughed. He laughed at me like I was nothin'.' She nodded. 'And that's when somethin' snapped inside of me. I told him if he didn't move his ass right there and then I'd shoot him.'

'Momma, that's enough,' Jared stated, turning to face her.

'James knew me so well.' Carol-Ann shook her head as the tears welled up. 'He knew I'd do it.'

Honor looked to Jared as Carol-Ann stopped talking and gave in to grief, the tears falling fast.

Jared sat down next to his mother and put an arm around her shoulders, pulling her into his embrace.

'He stepped in front of Finlay. He sacrificed himself for that worthless piece of shit,' Jared finished.

He watched Honor put her hands to her mouth before any sound could leak out. She blinked the tears back, trying to hold it all in as the story sunk into her.

'Tell her... tell her the rest, Jared. It's done now,' Carol-Anne begged as she tried to compose herself.

'It's alright. You don't have to talk about it anymore for me,' Honor stated quickly. 'I should have known... I did know... I knew it wasn't in Jared's heart.'

Carol-Ann turned her attention to Honor and a smile crossed her face. 'What was in my boy's heart was a desire to protect his family, just like his father.'

Honor nodded and wiped at her eyes with her fingers.

'Go see to the kids, Mom. I don't want them hearin' any of this.'

They'd agreed to never tell the younger children any of what happened and he was determined to keep it that way as long as they could. Hopefully until they were both old enough to understand the reasons why it had happened.

Carol-Ann stood up and held on to his hand. 'Tell her, Jared.'

It was a plea. He knew why she was doing this. She wanted Honor to know what he'd given up for them, but even now he didn't feel the pride in what he'd done, he still felt the shame of the circumstance, the guilt that he hadn't been able to save his father.

He waited for his mom to leave and the door to close before he spoke.

'So I heard the shot and I ran into the barn and there was my daddy, layin' on the floor and my mom holdin' the gun.' He shook his head, trying to get rid of the mental pictures. He could still recall them so vividly, in high definition, the blood, the smell of a recently fired weapon in the air. It was acrid, the air was humid, his heart was bursting and he didn't know what to do as panic set in.

'He was still alive, just. I went over and knelt down next to him and the look in his eyes told me I was doing the wrong thing. I wanted to help him but he was just lookin' that way at me and mouthin' what I thought sounded like "Go."' He stood up and began to pace. 'I looked to my mom and she was stuck on the spot, the gun still smokin', her mouth hangin' open, in complete shock. It was then I realized what I had to do.'

He took a breath and looked out the window at the Marshall land. 'I grabbed the gun from her and I aimed it at Officer Finlay. I told him he was takin' me in, for the murder of my father. I told him, bein' as I was the main delinquent in the town, he'd probably earn himself a nice promotion. I told him the feud with our family was over and if he didn't take me in instead of my mom, or if he ever told anyone the truth, I'd kill him.' Jared looked to Honor. 'I meant every word and he knew it.'

He watched Honor dissolve into tears in front of him. She put her head into her hands and leant over into her lap, letting everything flood out of her. He wanted to go to her, to caress her hair, to take her in his arms and hold her tight. But he couldn't. He had to finish it.

'Anna wasn't even in kindergarten and Jacob was just a baby. They needed their mom much more than their goofy older brother. Finlay may have been a bastard but he kept his end of the bargain. Luckily for me he got killed in the line of duty two years later.' He put his hands to his hat. 'That's when mom launched the appeal and I was released after the forensic evidence was re-examined and they couldn't rule out contamination.'

Honor was sobbing so hard now he wasn't sure she'd heard everything he'd said. This wasn't just breaking his heart, it was tearing at his soul.

'Listen, I'm thinkin' that the coffee might be cold right now so I'm gonna...' he started.

Honor raised her head and shook it hard. 'No, don't go.'

Her eyes were red raw and her cheeks were stained with tears. The need to hold her was consuming him but he didn't dare to move. There might have been an honorable reason why he'd done what he did but he'd told lies, perverted the course of justice, kept this secret from her when he'd made her promises for the future.

'Listen, I know what I've done, Honor. I'm not gonna make any excuses for it. I just... don't want you to say anythin' to me right now. You know all there is but it's not gonna hit home right away.'

Those blue eyes were so full of tears it was killing him. He wanted to be taking her pain away not making it worse. His chest was tight and his head was fit to burst.

'I'm gonna go out for a while, OK? I just want to give you some space and some time.' The end of the sentence came out in a whisper.

'Jared...' she began. He moved quickly, turning his back on her and heading for the door.

Chapter Forty Seven

When he'd got to the gravestone he'd fallen down onto the clay and cried hard. He'd shed tears before, for the loss of his father, but at the back of everything there was always that part of him holding back because of the secret he kept. Honor was the only other person apart from him and his mom who knew the real story. But, if Carol-Ann had her way, the whole world would know the truth by the end of the week. She wanted to come clean, for him. Just like he had taken the fall to keep her at home with his brother and sister ten years ago, she was ready to take the consequences now to free him from the scandal, to save his career.

He rubbed his palms into the dirt, as if delving down deeper would bring him closer to James. His father, the man who had taught him so much in the sixteen years they'd had together. He was strong because of him and the sacrifices he'd made.

'I met my father today.'

Honor's voice startled him and he sat up quickly, wiping his eyes with the sleeve of his leather jacket before standing.

'You shouldn't be here,' he replied, his back to her.

'I found out that my mother's dead but my father... he's very much here and wants to get to know me,' she continued.

He turned quickly to face her. 'Honor, I don't know what to say. I'm sorry.'

She shrugged. 'Least I know I don't have a stalker. Just a father.'
'He was the one sendin' you stuff?'
'Yeah.' She took a breath. 'It's Corbin.'
He balked. 'What?'
'Yeah, I know. Crazy, right?' He watched half a smile reach her mouth. 'Leave Nashville for a day and it all goes off.'

She looked at the gravestone in front of them. It was a bronze-colored epitaph with an engraving of the Confederate flag and the usual name and dates chiseled in beneath.

'I know you want to honor his memory and Jared, you do.' She watched him, wanting to reach him with her words. 'If he's looking down right now he would be proud of the way you held the family together, protected your mom, Anna and Jacob.'

He shook his head, unmoved.

'Why do you still think you've let him down?' she asked.

'Because I should have saved him... I could've put a stop to what was goin' on before it all got way out of hand.'

'No.' She shook her head. 'You were still a kid. It wasn't your fault.'

'If I hadn't got into so much fuckin' trouble the cops wouldn't have been interested in our family. They wouldn't have known we even fuckin' existed,' he yelled.

'You can't think like that! You mustn't think like that. Is that what you spent time in jail for? Is that why you protected your mom all these years? So you could come out and still feel you're to blame? Even after everything you did to try and put things right?'

'I don't know what you want me to say, Honor?'

'I want you to stop wallowing in self pity for a start!'

'Oh, is that right?'

'Yes, that's right. I can't pretend to understand everything you've been through because I haven't lived it but, from where I'm standing, you've got to stop taking the rap.'

He folded his arms across his chest and shot her a steely look.

'Your mom is in the house composing a statement right now. I called Buzz and the four of us are going to the police station tomorrow to sort this out. Buzz spoke to your lawyer and he thinks it won't be in the public interest for the cops to reopen the case.' She watched his reaction, saw him taking the implications on board and swallowing it down. 'But people need to know you didn't kill your father.'

He let out a heavy sigh that moved his whole body. He was so tired. So weary of feeling trapped, having a colossal weight on his shoulders, a cloud hanging over him. He didn't know how to let that go.

'And if I'm going to be part of this family we need to set a few ground rules. The first is no more secrets. Not one, d'you hear me?'

His heart lifted at her words. Was she really saying she still wanted to be together? He could hardly dare believe it.

'If you've got a problem, Jared, no matter what it is, I want to hear about it. I might not like it, but that doesn't mean I don't want to know about it.'

He blinked back the tears that were forming in his eyes and managed to nod at her. He didn't trust himself to speak without turning into a wreck.

'The second one is, if you're gonna move into my place that shabby couch has really got to go.'

'Honor...' he began, overwhelmed.

'I mean it. I'm sure there are things living in it.'

He couldn't wait another second. He stepped to her and lifted her off her feet, swinging her into the air and making her scream.

When he put her down her head was spinning a little and she had to grab his arms to rebalance. He moved to wrap his arms around her and held her against him.

'The press are gonna eat us alive, you know that, right?'

'When did you start caring about them? You're the reason DJ Davey Duncan needs counseling.'

He smiled, then moved his hand to touch his father's ring still hanging from the chain around her neck. She touched his cheek with her hand and turned his head to lock his gaze.

'I never took it off,' she whispered. 'Not once.'

He let her bring his face to hers until their mouths met and she felt that soft tingle of his stubble against her lips she so loved. Warm in his arms again, it was like coming home. Reunited in Alabama but definitely made in Nashville.

Epilogue

'Alabama, are you ready?'

The frenzied cheering filled the packed-out arena.

'I said... are you ready?'

Corbin put Honor's guitar strap over her body and made sure her sound pack was in place. She took a swig from the bottle of water Mia offered her.

'Thanks.' She handed it back.

'D'you know you look more nervous now on gig number thirty-three than you were on gig number one?' Mia remarked.

'That's because this one's different. It's Jared's home state, it's the first time he's performed since... well, you know... it means a lot to him.'

It had been three months since Jared had been all over the news. The first few weeks had been completely crazy. Carol-Ann and Jared had spoken to the police and the press and, after that, there had been a week or so of nail-biting as the real story hit and the authorities decided what they were going to do about it.

Eventually, after much deliberation and input from what seemed like everybody, it had been decided it wasn't in the public interest to take any further action. A personal visit from the police chief ended in the conclusion that the Marshall family had suffered enough.

'Plus Carol-Ann, Anna and Jacob are on the front row,' Honor reminded.

'You still rocking that coconut lip gloss she gave you?' Mia asked, grinning.

'If I stop wearing it she's going to start wearing a Kacey Musgraves t-shirt instead of one of mine. She told me.'

'Hey, baby,' Byron said, kissing Mia on the cheek as he passed her by. 'We're heading on. Honor, two minutes.'

She waved her hand and took another deep breath.

'Where's Jed?' Mia asked, looking about the backstage area.

'He... er... he got caught up with some guy from *Maverick* magazine,' Corbin filled in.

She saw a look pass between her father and her best friend. Had he winked? Or was he still having trouble with his contact lenses?

'Ladies and gentlemen, put your hands together and make some noise for... Miss Honor Blackwood!' the announcer roared.

'Shit! That wasn't two minutes! I'm not ready!' Her eyes bulged and she fanned her hands at her face.

'Sure you are, go on,' Corbin encouraged.

She had no choice. There were thousands of fans out there waiting for a show and when the audience was waiting you didn't let it down. She hurried out of the wings and onto the stage as the arena went wild. She walked towards her mark but stopped short as something caught her eye. There on her spot, in the center of the stage was Jared.

All at once the band stopped playing, the lights went down and only a spotlight remained, focusing its glow on them both.

'Hi, Jared, what are you doing here? This is kind of my spot for the next forty minutes,' she spoke into the microphone theatrically for the benefit of the crowd.

'I know that, Miss Blackwood, but right now I'm not plannin' on singin.'

He watched her brow crease as she frowned at him, completely bemused. She really had no idea what was about to happen.

'Well, what are you doing here hijacking my spot?' She turned to the audience, giving them an elaborate shrug.

'D'you think we should tell her?' he asked the waiting fans. They roared their approval.

'You're all in on this?' She laughed and shook her head.

'Are you ready?' he asked the crowd. 'After three. One... two... three.'

Forty thousand people chanted in unison. 'Will you marry me?'

The noise and the question sent pinpricks to every centimeter of skin on her body. She was stunned, shocked into standing dumb, not knowing how to react.

Jared grabbed her hand and brought her back into the moment, his gray eyes soft and full of adoration.

'Honor Blackwood, would you do me an honor? Would you be my wife?' he spoke into the microphone.

As he held her hand, his fingers trembled as though he wasn't completely sure of what her answer would be. But, despite the surprise of the situation there was no doubt in her mind about the reply.

She smiled at him, cleared her throat and looked into the crowd, all waiting. Summoning up all the power she had she leant back, took a breath in and hit the top C with every fiber of her being.

'Yes!'

Awestruck, he waited until she ran out of breath and the audience had erupted before he threw his arms around her and gathered her against his body.

'I love you,' he whispered so only she could hear.

'With all my heart,' she answered.

Printed by RR Donnelley at Glasgow, UK